Biker's Enemy

BWWM Dark Motorcycle Club Romance

Rebel Barbarians Motorcycle Club

Book Four

Jamila Jasper

ISBN: 9798333385529

Thank you to my Patreon subscribers for your support with this book. I could not have done it without you. www.patreon.com/jamilajasper

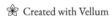 Created with Vellum

Rebel Barbarians Motorcycle Club

DESCRIPTION

HE LIKES HIS WOMEN DARK-SKINNED, VERY
PLUS-SIZED AND UNABLE TO RUN AWAY
FROM HIM.

Juliette's best friend Quin suffered a tragedy that forced her to
stay confined to her house for years...

When Quin emerges with her dark secret and 130 lbs of weight
gain, she turns to her bestie in Santa Fe for help.

The last thing she expects to switch things up is a 6'6" red-headed
multi-millionaire biker who harbors a dark obsession with plus-
sized black women.

What Quin expects to be a one-time-event ends up a permanent
contract with a dark, domineering and controlling biker from a
wealthy family, with a club of monstrous gang members willing
to get his property back if she ever tries to escape...

A dark motorcycle club romance with triggers and a truly plus-sized female lead. This spicy bwwm romance is a heated enemies-to-lovers adventure and third in a series of interconnected standalone small town organized crime stories set in the Midwestern US with a black female lead and a smokin' white alpha. Extremely spicy romance not for the faint hearted.

*You are not too damaged for real love. For the readers who have been through hurtful or traumatic pasts – **you are not too fucked up to find love.***
If he won't do it, another man will — willingly, lovingly &
passionately.

*Here's to manifesting your **happily ever after...***

The female lead in this book is named after my lovely patron, Tamiya. A supporting character, Katrina, is named after another Patron.

Click here to subscribe:
www.patreon.com/jamilajasper

Hollingsworth

Tanner "Cash" Hollingsworth
Rank: Co-President
Patched In: September 2014

Book IV

Rebel Barbarians Motorcycle Club Alpha Chapter Charter

Edition II

The democratic organization of the Rebel Barbarians Motorcycle Club permits club operations within 100 miles as the crow flies from the old Route 66 highway on the traditional Rebel Barbarians bike route.

Club headquarters decided by committee are located in the basement of Hollingsworth's Chicken Basket, run by Deb Hollingsworth-Shaw.

Section I Purpose

Our club monitors and protects the safety and purity of families and associates of the Rebel Barbarians. Members share a passion for patriotism, respect for authority, a desire to protect tradition, and maintain the sanctity of the American race across the Midwest.

Section II Membership

Eligibility: *Eligible members must be over 18 years old, white American males, & receive three references from active members. A preference for: No women. No homosexuals. No niggers. No spics. No immigrants.*

Eligibility will be assessed on a case by case basis determined by connection to active club members.

Once recruited into the Rebel Barbarian's organization, initiates receive their first brand or tattoo prior to a year long initiation.

After the year-long initiation, recruits may become permanent active members, requiring them to pay 15% of their legitimate earnings to the club and 30% of illegitimate earnings. New recruits participate in an 18 month initiation ritual into the organization and during that time, they must follow a strict code of conduct, show respect towards the organization, and demonstrate loyalty to the motorcycle club.

Club members must have several years of riding experience assessed by the club officers and their membership must have the support of active due-paying members. Junior club members have 5-10 years of membership, senior members have 10+ years of membership.

Recruitment: *Recruitment period begins every year in Pontiac, IL club headquarters with the annual July 4th summer barbecue followed by the charity ride for veterans with leukemia and local food banks. The recruitment period ends on Labor Day when all potential recruits must put in an official bid with the club officers.*

Potential recruits must meet the requirements for eligibility and dress in club colors during the recruitment period to signal loyalty to the organization. Once becoming a "recruit", said recruits must spend 18 months in service of the club before becoming full members.

Code of Conduct: *If you're gonna start a fight, make sure you finish it. Never let another man speak ill of your club or brothers. Never touch another rider's old lady. Never cheat a club member. Never touch another man's bike. Never sit on another man's bike.Get drunk. Fuck. Fix bikes. Have fun.*

Section III Club Structure

Officers: *The current officers of the Rebel Barbarians are as follows.*

Co-Presidents - Southpaw, Hawk, Reaper, Cash

Enforcer - to be determined.

Treasurer - to be determined.

Meetings: *Quarterly meetings are held at NEW South West outpost in Tucumcari, Texas, and they are presided over by the club president. Attendance is mandatory unless you are serving a prison sentence, the military, or an equivalent commitment.*

Rank:

Recruits - Fresh recruits are the newest members of the club. Barring special circumstances, recruitment lasts 18 months before graduation to "newbies"

Newbies - Recruits who survive their 18 month trial period with the club participate in the initiation ritual to become newbies. The newbie period lasts five years.

Juniors - 5-10 years of club membership.

Senior members - 10+ years of club membership

Officers - Elected club officers hold the club leadership positions

Junior Officer - Officers appoint one family member to apprentice under them for their position in the club however, the final decision on officers relies on a club election.

⅔ quorum must be reached for all club elections pertaining to membership & officers.

Section IV Rules & Regulations

Riding Rules: Fuck pigs. Stay armed. Shoot if you must. Never ride alone. Never ride without club colors.

Club Colors: All riders must wear a Rebel Barbarian's MC patch dependent on their rank and position within the organization. All club tattoos must be prominently and proudly displayed.

Club Dues: All active members pay club dues of $250/month to maintain club membership. If dues are unpaid for over 90 days, they fall into collections.

Section V Amendments

All amendments must be decided by a 75% member vote and there must be a quorum - over ⅔ of all membership present for any voting to take place about matters pertaining to the club.

Section VI Dissolution

In the event of the tragic end to the Rebel Barbarians, all club assets should be liquidated and proceeds split up amongst the four founding families. S. H. R. C.

ONE
QUIN NASH

My best friend has no idea how bad things have been since she left Kansas. I'm a different person than the one Juliette left behind. I weighed myself the day she left, and now I'm so much heavier than that – 200 lbs – pretty heavy for a woman my height. It doesn't *feel* like I gained an extra fifty in the time she left, but I have objective proof that I did.

It's not like I can help it. Well, I could. But it's the only pleasure available to me in captivity. So I eat. I gain weight. And I text my best friend who is off on her wild adventure like everything is just fine...

Because it has to be. Because that's what I have to pretend for me to survive under these conditions. I *tried* escaping. But you don't understand what it's like to live with not one but two people who feed off each others' darkness, watch them feed off of each other to destroy another person, and then leave that person behind to destroy you. My life started off crazy with the fact that two white Christians adopted me and then later, my older brother. But they had me first, technically.

My adoptive parents, Marie and Klaus Nash met on a mission trip to New Orleans after the big hurricane in 2004. They were older – much older – and when they died last year, they left me in the custody of my older brother. They adopted Eugene after they adopted me, but he's still three years older and he's always been... *strange*.

You would have to understand my parents to understand why they chose *him* of all people. I can hear him from my bedroom as I lie in bed, one hand lazily moving blue Takis from the bag to my mouth. I don't dare let him know I'm awake yet. I can hear Eugene's heavy grunting as he does his "workout" downstairs.

For the first three months after he came home when they passed, I thought he was serious about going back into the Army until I found the dishonorable discharge documents that mean he's out on his ass with no healthcare or benefits, just the money our racist, German parents left us in their will.

Shit. Silence follows the heavy grunting as Eugene shuts the television off. I don't know how he knows I'm awake. Maybe he just senses it, maybe it's because he just knows me too well.

"QUIN! GET DOWN HERE!"

I'm nineteen, right? I shouldn't have to listen to him. I don't have to listen to anyone. I know I locked my bedroom door, so against my better judgment, I defy Eugene's command and throw my blankets over my head. I would *much* rather scroll on Instagram than have another fight.

I *should* just leave. Except Eugene has a shotgun leaned up against the outside of my door and a rifle in his bedroom. Guns cover every last inch of this house and he has made good on his threats to use them. There are still two holes in the front door from where he "warned me" with a .22.

"QUIN GET YOUR FAT ASS UP," he yells. I squeeze my eyes shut and hope he gets bored instead of coming upstairs. I have been Eugene's punching bag since I was ten years old and he was thirteen. I never asked for a brother and I definitely never asked for one like *him*.

When I hear his footsteps coming up the stairs, I can't help but hop out of bed and rush to the door. I've gained so much weight the past few months that it takes everything in me to get to the door.

He won't let me leave the house. He hasn't let me since they died.

When I call the cops, who do you think they believe?

He mutters angrily to himself as he walks upstairs. I think he's hearing voices. I think something happened in the Army that started them, but I don't know what it is. I'm not a damn psychologist. All I know is that I'm stuck with this man until I convince him to set me free or find another way out.

My palms sweat as he approaches the door and the bubbles in my stomach flutter around until they clog my throat. He knocks on the door.

"I can see your feet under the door."

"I'm unwinding, Eugene."

"From what?"

I can see his feet under the door too and judging by the gentle rattling, he's trying the handle and he doesn't want me to know.

"Just leave me alone."

"I want to see you, Quin."

No.

"We hung out yesterday, Eugene. I'm tired. Maybe if I could get some sunlight–"

He interrupts my request by slamming his hand against the door. Hard.

"Goddamn it, you bitch!"

I can't help myself. I flinch and back away from the door. He scares me, but he has limits. Somewhere beneath the demon that took over my adoptive brother's mind, I imagine there are limits. There have to be.

"Relax, Eugene," I respond. "I'm just saying–"

He normally calms down after breakfast. After he gets a few things done. After he works out his demons for a few hours.

"You weren't just fucking saying," he says, rattling the door handle more intentionally this time. "You know I'm keeping your ass safe."

He rattles the door more aggressively. The sweaty palms and tight throat turn into full blown panic symptoms. I already tried using everything in my bedroom that could be a weapon. But have you ever tried fighting off a 6'5", 260 lb American soldier? He wins. Every time. It doesn't matter what weapons I have.

I lick the blue Taki dust off my fingers, but the remnants of salt and cheesy flavor do nothing to bring me the immediate calm I have come to count on.

"You don't understand how bad it is out there–"

Here we go again.

He blames the government for killing our parents. He thinks they "unleashed the virus" and that our parents' unfortunate death from the disease that swept across the globe is a government conspiracy by "pedophile elites". Shortly after they entered the ICU together after their Florida cruise went wrong, Eugene got his discharge.

Their deaths turned him into... *this.* And I am utterly at his mercy.

Or I was.

. . .

Today, I'm tired of being alone. I'm tired of being trapped. I'm tired of the way my body feels from all of this weight gained, lying here in my bedroom staring at a screen while life passes me by just because Eugene is completely fucked up.

"Get away from the door, Eugene."

He stops rattling the door handle, but I'm not foolish to think that means he's giving up. We've been here before. Too many times.

"Why won't you let me in, Quin?" he asks as the tone of his voice transforms. He sounds eerily calm and even more terrifying — insincere.

"Just go away, Eugene," I say, sounding frustrated. "You just need... breakfast."

You never know the right thing to say when you're dealing with someone who doesn't think rationally. I don't quite understand how he connects the dots in his head.

"You're right," he says. "Can you make something for me? My head hurts."

He complains about these headaches on most days and they seem to affect how he functions with various degrees of severity. I approach the door and *almost* unlock it. Our last fight ended with me getting cuts all over the backs of my calves, so I'm hesitant to open the door and subject myself to another brutal beating for some perceived slight.

"Promise you won't do anything crazy?"

. . .

The length of time he pauses should give me cause for concern, but I'm too busy managing the stress wrapping all my muscles in tight, impossible knots.

"I promise."

For all his faults, he has never broken a promise before. I hide the tension I feel with a calm smile on my face. He is too unpredictable for me to show any emotion beyond... *this*.

"Are you sure?" I ask as my hand hovers over the handle.

"I promise, little sister."

It has never sounded right for a pale, 6'5" white man to call me his 'little sister'. Eugene was originally from Ukraine. I remember Klaus saying, "We wanted a white baby in the first place", when they got the opportunity to adopt. He didn't care that I was right there.

Neither of them cared about stuff like that. They acted one way in private and completely differently in public. Living like that was hell. It took a lot of time alone to even figure it out. But they were total hypocrites.

"We teach our kids to see beyond race," my mother said to a group of parents once. "All the stuff is in the past. We don't need black and white. We just need Jesus."

And we had a lot of Jesus. Maybe a little too much Jesus judging by some of the deranged prayers I've heard coming out of Eugene's mouth when he should be sleeping. But he's not talking to himself now and he seems a little more calm, so I remind myself that my body just responds like this out of habit.

He hasn't killed me yet. I can get through this interaction...

So I open my bedroom door.

And scream.

Eugene lunges forward holding a large butcher knife in his hand. I slam my door immediately, squeezing his hand in the frame, but not hard enough for him to drop the knife. He grunts and forces the door open. I take a couple of quick steps backwards before losing my balance.

It hurts like hell when I fall. The pain sears through my hips and back and I nearly black out for a second.

Eugene lunges forward wielding the knife with every intention of hurting me. I can see it in his eyes even if I have no explanation for it...

He wants me dead.

Two

CASH HOLLINGSWORTH

I bought a new place in Sedona two weeks before dad died. $2.7 million adobe style house in the most spiritual part of Arizona, but still close to the highway so I can get to the clubhouse and run the Western branch of our family businesses.

He was so fucking happy about the house.

"It's about time you give me grandkids," he said when I told him about the house, as if houses come built in with kids and a family.

"I'm not seeing anybody," I remind him. "No kids. No need for them."

That was our last conversation on the matter, which I don't think ended on a sour note, just not on a good one. Dad will never get to meet his grandkids if I ever have them.

. . .

After the funeral, I head back out to the house, but I have a bad feeling the second I get out there that I won't be there long. It's just the taste of trouble in the air. I try to put the worry out of my mind but then... shit just keeps happening.

We handled the situation with the cops, we built our new clubhouse, we should be on our way out of trouble and it's the perfect time to settle down. I suppose I shouldn't be surprised that it doesn't matter how much shit settles down, trouble keeps following the club.

Our latest problem has been related to the Shaws... I just hope I'm not the only one the boss sends all the way across the country chasing some runaway.

Southpaw calls.

"I sent Jairus and Jotham to track down Oske," he says without much of a formal greeting. "But I need you to head to Sante Fe"

"Why?"

"Because. The club needs money. I need you, Hunter and Gideon to work out a deal," Southpaw says. I love Wyatt and he's always been a brother to me, but that man has absolutely no understanding of finance.

"What type of deal?"

He sounds immediately frustrated with me.

"You're the businessman, Tanner. Something that can get us $750,000."

"Shit," I mutter. "Okay... I'll have to give it some thought."

. . .

I pace my bedroom a few times when I hear my loud, long, sing-song doorbell polluting the house with noise from downstairs.

"Visitors?" Southpaw asks. "At this hour?"

I was thinking the same thing. I'm not expecting anyone, either.

"Dunno who it is."

I put on my slippers and walk across the cold stone downstairs. No lights on outside. Strange. I have motion sensors out there.

"Right," Southpaw grunts. "How fast can you get the money?"

"Clean? It's going to take at least three months to clean that much money. As for getting it in the first place... I'll need to make some calls."

I get to my front door and it's eerily quiet except for Southpaw's breathing on the other end of the line. He sounds like a thirsty dog, but I keep that thought to myself.

"Anna doesn't want me involved in anything that could carry federal charges."

Here we go. Women. This is what happens whenever you get a woman involved in your life. They start controlling things and making suggestions and next thing you know, she's wearing your balls around her neck.

"Does Anna have $750,000?"

I can't see anyone outside through the peephole. *Oh what the hell.* I don't bother grabbing a gun. I'm 6'6" and played football in high school and at Arizona State for a year before I dropped

out of college to join one of our legitimate family businesses –
managing one of a chain of gas stations out in Missouri with all
its affiliated problems.

"No," he says. "She doesn't. But after the Little League incident, I'm trying not to piss her off."

"An illegal business deal is definitely the way to go about
that."

"Thanks, Tanner."

I open the front door and nearly drop the fucking phone. Shit. I
nearly swear. I try not to have any reaction as I stare at what sits
there on my doorstep.

"Tanner?" Southpaw grunts.

"Wyatt? I'm going to have to call you back."

What the fuck?

The baby looks about eight or nine months old. I'm no expert,
but she can't walk, doesn't appear to have the capacity to talk...
She's pale. With red hair. And there's a letter fastened around her
neck with a loosely tied green ribbon. She stares up at me in utter
confusion. I don't bother bending down to pick up either the
baby or the letter.

Someone left this kid here.

"HELLO?!"

I step outside and activate the motion sensors. Light spreads
across what passes for a lawn out in the middle of Arizona. I have

pretty good landscaping, so you can see lizards and beetles scuttling quickly across the earth once the light sweeps over them.

But there are no signs of human life. Not even footsteps.

My body tenses up and I suppress my initial worry. I've been in enough tough situations to keep my cool, but this address is brand new and well protected. Nobody should know I'm here except Southpaw, Reaper... maybe Hawk and Steel. Most of my family still thinks I'm out at my condo in Springfield, IL.

I don't like feeling vulnerable.

I step forward and suddenly wish I had on more than my goddamn boxers and Nike socks. Scanning around, I see no signs of people or vehicles. *What the fuck?*

My external calm covers up the fact that I am internally freaking the hell out. What am I supposed to do with this toddler? Bring it to the fire station? Give it to someone who wants a kid? Because I sure as fuck don't.

The baby makes a gurgling sound and a mixture of panic and shame surge through me. I can't explain the shame. It's just a feeling. Like I'm not ready for this. Like somehow, I screwed up. I crouch down next to the carrier and try to avoid eye contact, as if this infant could somehow accuse me of something.

She raises out her arms and scrunches up her eyebrows and round face as she looks at me.

No. I glare at her, which immediately makes me feel guilty because she's... a fucking baby. So alone. So vulnerable.

In the wrong fucking place.

· · ·

Too terrified and curious, I grab the letter from around her neck and rip open the red envelope, careful not to destroy the paper inside. Even with the lights on outside, it's too dark for me to read. When I stand up holding the letter, I look down at the kid on the ground and wonder where the fuck she came from.

How the fuck she got here.

And why she's reaching out to me with that look on her face. Like she *depends on me.*

For a split second, I don't want to bring her inside. But I'm not a monster. It doesn't matter who she is, or why the fuck she's here... it's just a baby. I don't think about the fact that I'm in over my head. I carry her inside and head to the living room so I can sit.

I have to push out the thought that I just brought a *random fucking baby* into my house and I don't know how she got here or if someone will come looking for her, or if I'll go to federal prison for having her. She's still quiet when I set her down. I have enough nieces and nephews to know that won't last, so I hurriedly scan the pages.

But I end up having to slow down and read them twice. Because holy shit.

Holy fucking shit.

This can't be real.

THREE
QUIN

The knife slashes at my chest. I roll onto my stomach, but no matter how much force I try to use to push myself back over... my body won't respond. I'm stuck. I grunt and press my palms to the floor, but it doesn't work. I feel searing heat across my shoulder.

When I feel the warm gush after, I know he cut me. He suddenly yanks me onto my back, and for a short second I make eye contact with him and see the insanity burning in his eyes.

He has his hands around my neck.

I'm trying to breathe, but nothing is getting into my lungs.

He dropped the knife.

I knee him in the balls. I feel the surge of adrenaline at this slight victory and then grasp the handle of the knife.

. . .

Everything after that is a flash of blood and a torrent of pain. But in the end, I'm crying and he...

Is dead at the bottom of the stairs.

I killed someone.

Holy fuck, I just killed someone.

Not just anyone. My brother. Eugene.

I scream so loudly I feel like the force will push my eyeballs out of my head. When my lungs nearly collapse from the force of my scream, I possess enough self-awareness to stifle my next scream with the crook of my arm.

The last fucking thing I need is the cops coming here and seeing this mess. Eugene dead. Me holding the knife. Our long history of having the cops called on the house by neighbors. I can't breathe. I wish I could, but it feels like someone is making a balloon animal out of my windpipe.

This doesn't look good. The cops have been here twice before. Both times, Eugene manipulated his way out of trouble and portrayed me as his mentally troubled *ethnic minority* sister who he needed to protect.

After the panicked screams come the loud sobs as my body moves on autopilot. I can't look at where he lies at the bottom of the stairs. It's not like in the movies. His eyes aren't closed or open. They're stuck frozen in between. His body lies in this unnatural, mangled position and his tongue pokes out of his mouth awkwardly.

Blood surrounds his head in a large, spreading pool that moves as slow as corn syrup across the hardwood floor.

I don't have to handle the body until the end of it. I need to clean the floor upstairs first, which is enough of a task with the gash on my shoulder and the pain all over my body from the rough beating Eugene delivered before I finally... whatever I did.

I must have pushed him.

And stabbed him.

Bitch, you are going to jail.

The thought forces me to clean where we fought like I need to eat off the floor. I scrub until my body aches. I have to take breaks. *Lots* of breaks. I am covered in a thick and extremely stinky layer of sweat when I'm done. I get most of the blood down the tub. I get the floor scrubbed with bleach. I wear through three pairs of gloves and I have a limited number left to finish the job.

But I still have the stairs, the body, and all of downstairs.

I don't even register that I can leave the house.

· · ·

I've been trapped here for so long hiding the abuse. Hiding my fear. It just doesn't feel real... I keep cleaning in that unreal state of mind, doing shit that will ensure I'll go to double jail or triple jail if I get caught.

When. When you get caught.

I ignore the lump in my throat and change out of my clothes, mostly because they're soaked in sweat and I can't handle all the smells going on right now. I still haven't figured out what to do with my adoptive brother's body.

Before I begin cleaning the stairs and look at my brother's body up close, I text my best friend. She's in Santa Fe... hours away from here. Hours away from the local police. *And she's involved with some thuggish biker who might know what to do with a body.*

The fact that I'm not thinking straight right now isn't even a thought in my mind.

Quin: Can I still come to Santa Fe?

She takes what feels like forever to respond, but I'm not ready to look at the corpse again, so I just... stare at my phone. I watch the three dots until Juliette sends a response.

Juliette: Of course! When?

It's Thursday. I can keep the body preserved for another day. Maybe. He hasn't worked since our parents died, so it's not like he has a boss or anyone to miss him. Maybe a girlfriend. I still think I can last a day. I don't want to seem suspicious.

Quin: This weekend.
    Juliette: Is something wrong?

She's my best friend. I might not tell her the details, but I have to tell her the truth. Especially since I might have to bring this problem to her doorstep.

Quin: Yes.
    Juliette: Call?

That sends me into a full blown panic. I can't call her and we can't talk about this on the phone.

Hell, we shouldn't even text each other. I leave her on *read*. I'm just going to show up to Santa Fe and we'll figure it out. Juliette and I used to joke about supporting each other if we ever needed to hide a body together.

I just didn't think that body would be... *his*.

FOUR
CASH

The second I walk into Hunter's place, I feel squeamish. Nothing wrong with the place. It's a nice condo in Santa Fe, it's just that Juliette's art makes me deeply uncomfortable. He calls out to me to come straight to the kitchen for the two of us to discuss business. Important business, according to him.

I'm just happy that I don't have to get involved in another one of Southpaw's gambling situations. The club needs money and we need *clean* money, so when Hunter calls me about an investment opportunity due to Wyatt's perpetual need for more cash, I jump at the opportunity.

I would much rather handle business with Hunter than with Wyatt. The man never met a game he wouldn't bet on. Part of you has to admire a man who has balls of steel. Another part of you has to wonder what kind of idiot is dumb enough to bet all the money they have on Little League games.

Since Hunter is sober, I bring my own liquor.

"Where is Juliette?" I ask him.

He rolls his eyes. "She's out with this friend of hers. Quin."

"She has time for friends with the baby?"

"That's what I said," Hunter grunts, sipping on a Dr. Pepper.

"She's a pain in my ass. I need a distraction and there's a great opportunity coming up."

"Clean money?"

He nods. "Yes, sir. Clean money."

"Okay."

Doesn't make too much of a difference to me, but it's much easier to work a job laundering clean money right about now. Our family has been through enough recently without one of us heading off to prison. Cody has enough problems out in Dallas with the IRS up his ass for five years of allegedly underpaid taxes.

"I s'pose I could use a little cash," I tell Hunter.

He smirks. "None of y'all ever turn down an opportunity to make money."

"What have you got?"

He pulls out a binder of pretty legit looking documents. I glance through them, but it doesn't take me long to figure out what he wants us to get invested in.

"This might be legal, but it's goddamn dangerous, Hunter. And un-Christian."

"When the fuck was the last time you went to church?"

"My mama is going to make my life a living hell if I invest in a titty bar."

"It's not just a titty bar," Hunter says. "We're also gonna sell shrimp."

"What does your old lady think about that idea?" I ask him.

"She hates it," he says. "That's why I need you to run it."

I laugh. Hunter ought to get back to drinking if these are the brilliant thoughts he comes up with outside of liquor's influence.

"I'm not running a titty bar."

"Fine," Hunter says. "Then get some lazy ass Hollingsworth to come up here from Texas and run it for us. I don't give a shit. Fact of the matter is, I crunched the numbers and the last three around here... all the girls got deported."

Running a strip club is far too much work. Deportations mean potential border control involvement and other bullshit if anything goes wrong. We can find money elsewhere. Hunter gives me the most serious look. This 'legal' business venture is already beginning to sound like far too much trouble.

"Is there a reason you want to get into this business?" I say.

"Why the fuck else?" He snaps. "Money."

I shift uncomfortably in my seat. Yes, money. The Hollingsworth family has always had enough of it since investing in gas stations along the old Route 66 highway and our whiskey distillery that produces Hollingsworth whiskey and other products, not like that ever stopped any of us from looking for the opportunity for more. I just didn't think Hunter Sinclair was hurting for cash.

"Didn't think you needed any."

He gives me a dark look and then lowers his voice as if his old lady might pop out from around the corner at any minute.

"This is about Wyatt. We need $750,000 for the Rebel's but... I have personal matters to attend to. I need another $100k on top of that."

These motherfuckers spend money like it's going out of style and they don't have the head for figures to keep up with the expenses. The Sinclairs are at least a little better than the Shaws.

"A strip club isn't going to get you $100 grand quickly," I try to explain. These kinds of things take time.

Hunter's face darkens again. "I know."

"I see."

"You don't have to be involved in the other business."

"Drugs are risky," I respond, perfectly interpreting Hunter's insinuation. Running drugs out of your own club is the perfect combination of risky and smart, but it's the kind of business you can get away with in your twenties. I don't know if Hunter really wants to risk jail with his wife and baby at home.

"I know," he says, taking a sip of Dr. Pepper that looks almost wistful. "But Juliette's pregnant again. And she's having twins."

Fuck.

. . .

I don't have to say the cuss word out loud. My face says it all. That's the thing about being born red, you never get the privilege of hiding your emotions. My cheeks are always quick to match the color of my hair.

Hunter tries to hide his emotions, although I can see how complicated this is for him. Bringing twins into the world on top of Mackenzie might be tough if he keeps up the habit of bailing out Southpaw's stupid ass.

"What if we come up with a better idea?"

"A legal idea?"

"I said a better idea," I reply. "Not a legal one."

The apartment door opens and it's clear that Juliette is home. I can hear her talking from the doorway along with a baby babbling along in an attempt to match the rhythm and cadence of her mother's speech. Hunter presses a finger to his lips, but I don't need to be told to keep club business away from an old lady.

I rise to my feet out of politeness, and Juliette turns the corner, not just holding Mackenzie, but with a woman. Holy shit, look at the ass on that woman. And the tits. She's full-figured all right. The entire room fades around me, if I'm honest.

I just see this woman standing next to Juliette and become fixated with her instantaneously.

"Hello, ma'am. I'm Tanner."

Juliette steps between us. "Don't look at her. Don't talk to her."

. . .

That makes me want to look and talk to her even more... Unlike me, this gorgeous woman has some type of respect for Juliette's command. She doesn't look at me, doesn't give me a second glance and that lack of attention feels like a purposeful jab. What the hell is wrong with Juliette? While Quin looks away, I get a damn good look at her and experience no remorse for doing so.

Quin looks like she has a nice, tight pussy. Women that big usually do. There is something about a plus-sized woman who is somewhere in the super-plus-sized range that does it for me. Quin gets my dick hard instantly. I don't even mind that Juliette can tell.

"*Hunter*," she says sternly. "Are you going to intervene or let him keep acting like a pervert?"

"Can you relax, Juliette? He's introducing himself."

That sexy ass chocolate cupcake with extra frosting steps aside from Juliette and I can tell immediately that everything about my appearance impresses her. That doesn't surprise me. I have meticulously built my body since I was sixteen-years-old.

I obsess over everything I eat and how I spend every minute of my day. I find a woman like this one... fasc*inating*. The race thing doesn't bother me. I know the rules. Screw black women, don't marry them. My father understood that sometimes a man has dark urges.

None of those urges are as dark as the ones that strike me in the presence of this voluptuous woman. I don't even care about her name. I just want her clothes off, my tongue in her pussy and my face squeezed between thick ass thighs.

"My name is Quin."

Juliette glares at me as I take Quin's hand. This is not the time for a normal handshake. I take her hand and kiss it. Fuck. She smells like an Oreo milkshake. I can't take my eyes off her, but her eyes dart away quickly.

"Okay, we're getting out of here," Juliette says, glaring at me.

"Stay *far* away from the studio. We're discussing women's business."

Hunter gives her a look that I don't quite catch. Juliette ignores him and walks off with Quin in tow. Her friend moves a lot more slowly than Juliette. I can't tell if it's because she's less athletic, less angry, or because she wishes she could stay in the kitchen with me. I don't bother hiding the fact that I'm watching her ass as she walks away.

Once they're out of earshot, Hunter chastises me like he's some fucking priest.

"You don't have to stare at her like you want to eat her."

"I want to do a little more than eat her."

He scoffs. "That's what you think. That chick is seventy shades of fucked up."

"She must be what... three hundred pounds?"

"Who gives a fuck?" Hunter says, sipping on his soda. "We're here to talk business, not pussy."

"Can't talk business until I talk pussy."

He knows I have the upper hand here and he hates it.

"There's nothing to talk about. She spent the past year stuck in a bed. Juliette says she barely recognizes the chick."

"She's gorgeous."

"She's fucked up. Don't even think about it, Cash."

"Why not?"

Hunter looks around like someone might come popping out around the corner.

"For one thing, she's black."

"So is Juliette," I say in a normal speaking tone. I'm not afraid of shit.

"Yeah, but she's light and well... I don't care about that stuff. Your mama is gonna hit the roof if you show up with a woman like Quin to Thanksgiving."

"I'm not going to bring her to Thanksgiving. I'm going to stuff her like a Thanksgiving–"

"Please. Spare me."

"What's wrong with her?"

"Nothing."

"You said she was fucked up."

"Oh. That. It's not important."

"Great. Then I can still sleep with her."

"She's Juliette's best friend, Tanner. So you can't."

I don't like Hunter's attitude. He used to be more of a go-getter.

"It's been at least a month since I've been with someone."

"That is a normal amount of time to be single."

"Not for me. Women crave my dick."

"Fuck, listen. I don't care what the fuck you do. But if you touch her and Juliette asks me to put a bullet in your head, I'm gonna listen to my old lady without question."

"Okay. We can talk business now that I have your explicit permission."

"Not what the fuck happened."

I have to calm him down. Hunter doesn't stand a chance of stopping me once I set my mind on something and it will be best for both of us if we don't argue about the chocolate cupcake his old lady just dragged into the back room.

I'll be back for her later.

FIVE
QUIN

I don't know what I thought would happen when I showed up in Santa Fe. The second I said one wrong word in front of Juliette, she ushered me out of the house and took me to some local place she says her husband goes to discuss "club business".

When I tell her everything, all she does is tell me to act normal. No other reaction to the dead body in my trunk or the steps I had to go through to get my brother into pieces. I went numb throughout the process, but I still had to do it.

I still had to butcher him.

Part of the reason it was so goddamn easy to get to Santa Fe is because I don't think I can close my eyes and fall asleep. I follow Juliette's direction not to give any reaction when we return home. I don't expect to see the giant in her kitchen.

Juliette immediately steps between us, but nothing could block me from seeing *Tanner*. He looks like... a model. I mean...

bigger than a model. He looks like he has the body of a comic book superhero.

I haven't seen many people in a *very* long time and I definitely haven't been this close to a man as attractive as Tanner. He has a gentle lilt to his accent that drives me crazy too. Juliette grabs my hand and drags me away so we can wait for him to leave.

"Is that your husband's friend?"

"Yeah, another racist biker," Juliette says. "They're talking business but I don't think we should get anyone involved who Hunter doesn't approve of."

"He looks like the type of person who could help move a body."

"Yeah, but I don't know if Hunter trusts him," Juliette explains. "This is serious."

I feel vomit clawing at my throat again.

"Sorry," Juliette says. "I didn't mean to freak you out. Don't worry. We'll get you out of this."

"What if someone reports him missing?"

"Stop," Juliette says. "Let's watch something on TV until they're done talking business."

We have to wait so long that I end up taking a nap and waking up to Juliette and Hunter talking in the kitchen.

"You are the craziest fucking person I have ever met," I hear Hunter saying to her. *Ouch.* I think he's abusing her until I hear what Juliette shoots back next.

"I'm crazy?" she says. "You're the one who thinks you can hide the fact that you're opening up a *strip club* from me when you made me do our taxes!"

"You were supposed to drop them off at Tylee's, not mind my damn business."

"You are out of your mind, you ignorant, brain-dead, mean ass, doo-doo farting ass clown."

"What the hell kind of insult is that?"

I hear a loud noise and Juliette squealing. Maybe I should go in there...

Slowly, I pull myself together and wipe the sleep out of my eyes before walking down the narrow condominium hallway to the kitchen where Juliette and Hunter are arguing. Well, I thought they were arguing. Juliette jumps away from him when I walk into the room, but he still has his hands cupping her ass and seemingly no intention of letting her go.

When he looks over at me, I can't help but think how cute they look together.

"Listen. Sorry if we woke you up."

"We?" Juliette says. "You were the one being loud."

Hunter squeezes her butt and glares a little bit. Juliette stifles a squeal and leans lovingly against his chest.

I've never had that with a guy.

I never had the chance.

"You have nothing to worry about, Quin," Hunter says. "That's all you need to know. I'll call a couple of my guys and they'll handle it. You're Juliette's best friend and... well... that makes you family."

It doesn't feel real.

·   ·   ·

"I don't want to open the trunk again..." I mutter numbly. I feel guilty. Dirty. Scared.

"You don't have to," Hunter says. "All I need is for you and Juliette to stay here and lay low for a few days. We'll handle the situation and burn the vehicle. It'll be your job to keep Juliette out of trouble."

"I do *not* get into trouble," Juliette says.

Well, we all know *that's* a lie. But maybe, just maybe, this will all go away.

And everything will be just fine.

And one day, hopefully soon, I can get some sleep...

Six
CASH

Nobody knows about the baby that showed up on my doorstep or the letter claiming the child is my daughter. I have folks in my family verifying the letter's claims. Sure, the letter came with DNA test results, but those could be doctored. We need something more specific. Until then, I have the child out at the adobe house, guarded by the only person I trust with this information — Wyatt's mom. My aunt.

Mom is too fragile to handle information like this. She will want this kid to be mine so fucking badly, she'll make it happen. I just want the truth.

Aunt Deborah makes me categorize the women I've slept with and I give her a list of names that I can remember. I know it doesn't portray me in the best light, but she takes down the names without judgment and plans to use discreet methods to track down the child's mother and how this two year old ended up on my doorstep.

I don't even know if she's two.

I don't even know her name. It feels wrong to give her one because she isn't mine and it also feels wrong not to give her one.

.   .   .

This bullshit couldn't have come at a worse time. Hunter and I need to iron out the details of this deal and then... the baby.

Even if I don't know her identity or how the hell she ended up on my doorstep, I feel this strange, unusual attachment to her. It's not like me. I don't get attached to anything. Not women. Not children.

If there's one thing I learned from my parents' marriage it's that love will fuck you up. They were crazy about each other... but I mean crazy. They fought as hard as they made up which is all well and good to acknowledge now that I'm a man.

But when I was a kid, most of what I remember is the fighting and how goddamn bad it would get. From the time I was twelve years old, I would steal whatever bikes I could get my hands on and just ride out until it was dark. Nobody even cared that I was out late.

As long as I made the varsity football team and kept my grades at a C average, neither of my parents gave a shit what I did.

If your own parents don't give a shit about you, it makes it hard to trust that anyone else will.

The longer I stay away from the baby, the worse I feel.

When I leave Hunter's place, I'm glad he doesn't notice any change in me. But believe me, there was one.

It's the only thing that has distracted me successfully from my anxious, clawing thoughts of the baby that showed up on my doorstep.

. . .

Quin Nash.

Hunter's warning to stay away from her doesn't stop me from conducting basic research from my hotel room. I have to check out before 11 a.m. tomorrow morning to head back to Arizona, leaving me plenty of time to think about Quin and what I'm going to do about her.

Because I have to do something.

She's beautiful.

Not just that... I could use her.

She clearly needs some help or she wouldn't be hiding away at Hunter and Juliette's place. There's nothing Hunter Sinclair can give her that I can't. And she has no real connections to the club. No reason to betray the fact that I have a child to anyone.

I can't stop myself from thinking about her for the next two hours in my hotel room. I find her on social media through Juliette's page and catch myself up on every possible detail about her. She's about Juliette's age — twenty years old.

So too young for me, but not illegal. And she's pretty. I like women who redefine the word thick and Quin fits the bill perfectly.

I convince myself that my primary desire for her isn't about sex. I have a baby problem on my hands and a mystery to solve. And that baby needs a nanny. Normal folks might consider hiring a nanny but that opens up someone in my line of work to a hell of a lot of risk.

I would much rather have someone I can trust. Someone I can control.

Someone like Quin.

My aunt Deb calls just after I take my tenth screenshot of a photo from Quin's public social media page.

"Hello?"

"Baby Avery is doing perfectly," she says. "I'm putting her to bed right now."

Avery? That's new.

"Avery? Is that what we're going with now?"

"Yes," she says. "It is. Wyatt called, but I didn't say anything."

I exhale. "Thanks. He has his hands full with Oske."

The Shaws have a secret there. I don't know what it is, but I know it's big because otherwise, Oske would be dead. Wyatt isn't the type to hold back against anyone who represents a threat. But Oske is still here... still causing problems. Still on the goddamn run. Maybe we should have listened to Reaper.

"Did you call Annie?" she asks.

She means my mother, Annabel. I haven't told my mother about the baby despite my aunt's insistence.

"We don't know if the kid is mine."

"She has red hair, Tanner."

"I know. So does everyone in the family. She might not be mine."

"This would be a lot easier if you had a theory about *who* she is."

I don't answer the question. I might not have a theory, I just know what my instincts are telling me.

She's not mine. But I can't tell if it's denial or just knowledge of where I planted my seed the past few years. I can't say I always used protection but... I can't think any of the women I've been with wouldn't have popped back up with that kid to demand child support the second they saw those two pink lines.

I took a picture of the note, so I open it up and read through it again.

Dear Tanner,

Okay. This person knows who I am. Not just my club name. That means they know exactly who I am and possibly have some connection to the family.

This is your child. I have attached the corresponding documentation and genetic testing to prove these claims. The child has family traits. I am sure you do not remember our encounter all those years ago.

If you do not care for this baby, she will face certain death at the hands of her mother.

.   .   .

You must not contact the police. Give her a good life.

No signature. *This is your child.* It doesn't sound like anyone I
know. That's the part that fucks with me. Aunt Deb believes the
kid is mine. She thinks I'm like my father. But I'm not. I'm
nothing like him. I'm not dumb enough to commit to a woman
knowing I can't keep my dick in my pants. And anyway, I'm not
like my father in the most important way.

I *can* keep my dick in my pants.

First, I read the letter quietly to myself and then I read it again for
my aunt. She listens and then she asks me to read it again before
repeating each line.

"Is there a chance it's Andy or Beau's kid?"

"He's married. So no."

"Your father was married and how many half-brothers do you
have?"

"If Avery was his, why did she end up on my doorstep?"

She sighs. "I don't know Tanner. Maybe we should tell Annie.
She could get the truth out of him."

Annie. That's my mother, and the last thing I want to do is
mention another baby my father had out of wedlock. His parting
gift, by the age of Avery. The back of my neck flushes with the
certainty that my father must have planted his seed days or weeks
before passing away. Fuck.

It would be just like him, but without proof, what's the point
in getting my mother all upset?

"I don't want to disappoint my mom. If this is some type of
hoax, she'll lose her mind. She's lost too much already with dad

gone."

"The baby is family, Tanner," Aunt Deb says with that guilt inducing voice she uses with her sons. That might work on a Shaw, but it won't work on me...

I don't know how she can be so sure.

"I guess. But I'm telling you, Aunt Deb. I would know the mama. I would remember."

"Right. Well, Tanner. When you get over here, you had better get yourself a nanny. Someone you can trust. I watched Wyatt handle Junior on his own and it isn't as easy as you think."

I never thought it was easy.

"I'll hire someone."

"Call June if you need help finding someone."

"I don't need help. I can get a nanny for my kid. Nothing to worry about."

I get off the phone with my aunt, but I can't stay in bed anymore. Not with Quin and the baby on my mind. Avery. Now who told Aunt Deb the baby needs a name now, huh? I thought we could get around to that when we actually had *answers*.

SEVEN
QUIN

Logically, I know I can get out of bed. I don't have to be here all morning, even if breakfast is finished. Old habits die hard. I make myself get up after forty minutes of staring at the ceiling.

Juliette and Hunter seem *normal* this morning, but I can't finish the eggs and toast Juliette cooks because watching her squirt ketchup all over her breakfast reminds me of Eugene and what he looked like lying there all mangled at the foot of the stairs.

I don't want to be gross, so I just pick at my food and pretend that I have a low appetite for a normal reason — not visions of dead people I can't get out of my head.

"Will you be okay on your own this morning?" Juliette asks. "We have to go to my OB this morning."

"The OB?" I know that's the doctor responsible for her baby and all of that, "Surprise," Juliette says with a smile. "I'm pregnant again."

"What?!"

"I know, and it might be twins," Juliette says. "I don't want to get over excited too soon and curse it or something."

I nod with understanding. It must be pretty early, so I can get why she didn't immediately announce it. I run over to my best friend and give her a congratulatory hug. Early or not, a pregnancy with twins is worth celebrating. Juliette hugs me back.

Holy shit. Mackenzie still seems like a new idea to me. When I met Juliette, I didn't think she would meet the love of her life and become a mother in such a short space of time. She seems crazy about Hunter, but I'm definitely surprised to hear her talking about more babies. *Wow.*

Life happens so quickly sometimes...

"I'll be fine on my own," I respond. "I'm not fragile or anything. I can hang out and wait..."

I'm desperate to look like I'm handling things. Juliette hands Mackenzie over to her dad and then wraps me up in a big hug.

"We'll be back before noon and we'll bring poke bowls, okay? Trust me, everything will be fine and you *will* get through this Quin."

Unless the cops show up. Unless I have to go to prison. Unless someone reports Eugene missing. I offer her a thin-lipped smile and try not to let every last one of my anxieties spill out.

I appreciate Juliette's support, but she has no idea what it's like to go through something like this alone. The second she left Kansas, she ran into a man like Hunter Sinclair — one willing to do anything to protect her. All the men I've known have either been entirely disinterested in me, like my adoptive father or terrifying, like Eugene.

That just means I have to take care of myself, but considering I spent the past several months as my brother's prisoner... I don't even know what that looks like. I feel scared. Embarrassed. Like he stole life from me that I don't even know how to get back. Juliette thinks I just need time to get through the shock and the trauma.

"Nothing will happen to you in Santa Fe... I promise..."

. . .

Juliette is one of those people who just automatically makes you feel better. She has a handle of her shit. She seems like she always did. It's how she ended up with a husband and a baby so quickly and I don't even know if I'll be able to keep my ass out of prison.

Unlike my high school days or those trade classes I took for a brief time before my parents died, I don't have any structure or anything motivating me to get started with my day so it took me forty-five minutes to throw on a red Kansas City Chiefs hoodie and a pair of black leggings with wide ankles after my shower. I hate how skinny leggings squeeze my thighs and force them into these uncomfortable shapes.

Then again, I've had a lot of time to hate shit while locked in my room. I even started a troll account to go after Jojo Siwa but eventually got a hold of myself and deleted it when they actually replied. My mind did not respond well to captivity.

But now that I'm free... I don't even know who I am.

After Juliette and Hunter leave, I stay in the kitchen scrolling through my phone. Juliette's kitchen is goddamn sterile compared to the one I used for the past three years. I'm almost afraid to touch anything. But I'm hungry. Juliette thankfully hasn't succumbed to any insane healthy eating trends so I don't have to go far to find something decent. I drop a few waffles in the toaster, pull out the butter and maple syrup before frying some sausages and getting some eggs together in a separate skillet. Yum.

The Eggos finish first, so I munch on them while I finish cooking up the sausage and eggs. By the time I'm done with the Eggo waffles, toast sounds good, so I put a couple slices in the toaster.

When I sit there with my full post-waffle breakfast, I feel relaxed. Really relaxed. Eugene can't hurt me anymore. The entire kitchen smells like a home. And there's food. Lots of it. I cut one of my breakfast sausages up and then shovel it onto a piece of toast with some scrambled eggs.

"That smells good."

I yelp and drop everything. It's more like I throw it, honestly. The voice behind me chuckles. I slowly turn around in my chair to see who it is. Not Hunter. But my instincts lean towards surprise more than they lean towards fear.

The man from the day before is standing right there in the kitchen like he lives here. He smiles when I look at him and a strange chill moves straight through me. But he's smiling, so there isn't anything about him that should scare me.

"Hunter and Juliette aren't here," I tell him.

"I know," he says, walking purposefully over to the kitchen sink. He takes a clear glass and begins to fill it with filtered water from the slower faucet on the sink. I can't help but watch as he fills the glass. His thick fingers seem big enough to break it just from the way he holds it. The man has huge arms too — gigantic, well-built arms that fill out and expand the tight black t-shirt he has on.

He has a light sunburn on the back of his neck, but I'm surprised he's not more red considering the climate in Santa Fe. His hair is a robust, scarlet color. Some ginger men look a little rough, no offense, but Tanner doesn't look like that at all. He sets the glass of water on the counter and turns to face me.

"How've you been?"

I give him a skeptical look. Why is this man talking to me? I'm pretty sure he's Hunter's best friend, so he must have a key to the place or something. Maybe he's just making small talk.

"It hasn't been that long since I last saw you. Everything's fine."

"What brings you out to Santa Fe?"

My eyes snap nervously to his. I have an immediate panicked thought that he knows everything and that he's the one Hunter called to bury the body. The breakfast I barely had two bites of suddenly feels extremely unsettled in my stomach.

"Visiting Juliette."

"Really? Couldn't pay me to visit anyone out here..."

Yet here you are...

But I don't say that out loud. I just keep looking at him.

"I'm getting paid," he says. "Just not to visit. But... business is almost over and I've got a place out in Arizona I'm heading back to."

"Cool..."

I don't know much about Arizona, honestly, so I try to eat a little more and pretend that talking to a guy who looks as sexy as Tanner Hollingsworth isn't making me nervous the longer the conversation lasts.

I'm the furthest thing from a natural flirt. I give all my Sims in the Sims 4 the "unflirty" trait, that's how serious it is.

Tanner smiles and a flush of red forms a funny pattern across his nose and cheeks, like a raccoon mask. I've known white boys before, but I've never seen any get all red this close.

"You ever think about going to Arizona?"

"Nope. Didn't even plan on leaving Kansas."

"Got a boyfriend back there? Family?"

I try not to give him a shifty look, but I know my ass must look suspicious as hell judging by the expression on Tanner's face. But maybe I have it all wrong.

. . .

I don't even know what to say.

"I asked you a question, ma'am," Tanner says. "Do you have a boyfriend back home where you're from?"

He means the question.

Our eyes lock as I stare at him for a few seconds to double check that he's serious. My opinions on my physical appearance are one thing but when you're a plus-sized black woman, random people feel extremely comfortable letting you know exactly how they feel about your looks. Old men make creepy comments about your "thickness" on the lighter end of things. A white guy at a gas station once said, "Damn that bitch is fat" right in front of me. Like I didn't have feelings.

It's like it says something about my worth as a person that I have extra weight. Tanner looks exactly like the type of guy who would typically target me, so I don't know what to say.

I would prefer not to be the target of some white guy's jokes.

"I don't have a boyfriend."

Tanner circles me a little and then takes a seat next to me. I can smell his cologne and damn, it smells good. He also has the largest arms I've ever seen. His biceps are insanely thick and muscular. I wish I didn't notice them. He has a tattoo of a red-tailed hawk on his shoulder.

I can tell because I used to love the Animorphs series growing up. I read every single book from my local library and I was absolutely obsessed with Tobias. I bet he has the hawk tattoo for some crazy redneck reason, but the feathers peeking out from beneath the sleeve of his t-shirt attract my attention.

"Well, Quin. I'm glad to hear you don't have a boyfriend."

"Why?"

He winks. "It means you have the perfect opportunity to run away with a cowboy."

"I don't think that's going to happen."

"Why not?"

"I'm not exactly built for running."

"That's funny," he says. But his expression doesn't change. "Can I get you a drink to wash down breakfast?"

"I already had orange juice."

"Water?"

His closeness and his pale blue eyes both make me nervous. Tanner walks towards the sink and again, I can't help but stare at him. He returns and sets down a glass of filtered water.

"There," he says. "I'll wait with you until Hunter and Juliette come back. You play cards?"

"Only spades."

"What about gin rummy?"

I shake my head and take a sip of water.

"I'll explain the rules," he says. "It's an easy two person game. I used to play with a buddy of mine and bet bike parts but he has somewhat of a gambling addiction, so we had to cut back."

Tanner pulls a deck of cards out of his leather cut which has the name CASH stitched across a tag on his chest. The cut has other patches sewn on with various symbols and a couple latin phrases. I get distracted from observing his patches when he shuffles the cards.

"So," Tanner says. "This is the goal of the game."

His eyes flicker towards mine and the second I make eye

contact with him, I get nervous again and bury myself in the glass of water, chugging the rest.

He waits for me to set the glass down before he continues explaining the rules. I fixate my gaze at a point on Tanner's forehead as he keeps shuffling and bridging the cards.

"You want to be the first one to run out of cards..."

I try to nod, but my limbs feel sluggish. The weird feeling sends a single jolt of panic to my brain. The primal state of panic is the last thing I remember before either slumping forward or falling backwards, completely unconscious.

EIGHT
CASH

I watch her sleep for three peaceful hours. I get up a couple times to check on Avery, but for the most part, I just watch Quin – my beautiful captive. Once Hunter and Juliette find out, they'll be pretty mad, but by the time they find out, it won't matter. I have what I need and more importantly, some type of understandable pretext for keeping this woman here.

She is beautiful as she sleeps, even in her hoodie and those leggings. Maybe the hoodie and leggings make her even hotter. Her breasts are so fucking big. I mean... everything about her is big. It's exactly what I like in a woman.

Her skin color isn't a problem for me. Our club charter voted to maintain our old rules for the safety and preservation of our culture, but that applies to new members. I don't let the club tell me who I allow into my bed. I'm not like my father. I don't like tramps who let any dude with a monkey wrench and a Harley pump cum in their pussy.

When I have a woman, she becomes entirely and completely mine.

. . .

The last woman I tatted my name on got it covered up and since then... I've been on my own, no interest in pressing a needle to skin until Quin. Not like I'll tell her that right away. No. For her to submit to this captivity, I have to appeal to this woman's sensitivity and make it seem like I have a *good reason* for bringing her that surpasses my depraved desire to conquer her voluptuous body.

Just the thought of inking her skin gets me rock hard. Quin emits a soft groan in her sleep as she comes down off the drugs I had to use to get her here. If she wasn't such a big woman, I wouldn't have needed drugs. It's not like I mind having to use what's in my toolkit, I'm just saying that Quin played a role in those circumstances.

Humans are stronger than you think, especially with adrenaline rushing through them. Physical violence won't get Quin to submit to me. I need... *something else.*

She groans again and I call her name to speed up the process.

"Quin, wake up. Everything will be fine. I just need you to wake up..."

Quin rolls over slightly, lying on her side and hiking her legs up. Her ass faces me with all its voluptuous glory making the hard-on in my jeans fucking impossible to control. She has the sweetest face when she's sleeping too. Soft. Full. Innocent. I've always had a thing for round, chubby faces. I don't know why.

"Quin. I need you to wake up now."

If I sound more firm and commanding, it'll scare her less.

She moves again. This time, her movement is a little more convincing. *Good.* Her fingers twitch and then her lashes flutter open. Her round cheeks move along with her lips as she yawns a little bit. Her lashes flutter more.

"What's happening?" she mutters. Her head tilts from side to side as she tries to get her eyes open and get a good look around the room. She might be able to get her eyes open, but I have her bedroom purposefully dark. I sit in a brown leather armchair across from her, an inherited vintage piece from my dad's office in Chicago. A small chrome lamp casts warm LED lighting over my face.

But not much.

"You're in Arizona, Quin," I say to her calmly. "You're at Tanner Hollingsworth's house."

I lean back in the chair, fighting the urge to pour an ounce of whiskey down my throat or light up a cigar, anything to quiet my mind from the rush of excitement I have from obtaining my prize so easily. Hunter and Juliette have their hands full with their family, anyway. Whatever big mystery brought Quin Nash to Santa Fe... I'm sure I can handle it.

"No..." she mutters. The groan and the immediate rejection send a pulse of anger straight through me. I don't even want her subconscious mind to feel the slightest disappointment.

"Wake up," I command firmly, hating myself for betraying such immediate irritation. We need to get this over with before Avery wakes up, which she usually does in the middle of the night.

"No... Juliette..."

"You are no longer in Juliette Sinclair's custody," I repeat. "Now wake up, Quin. I would rather not have to do it roughly."

My threatening tone forces her eyes to snap open and the fear cast all over her face nearly causes me to regret my tone.

"Tanner?" she says. The way she says my name gets me so hard. But she doesn't sound happy, which doesn't thrill me.

"Yes," I respond gruffly. "I rescued you from Santa Fe and brought you here."

"Rescued?" she groans. She tries to raise her head but the

drugs must still be in her system because she makes a loud, uncomfortable moan and then rests her head back against the pillow. It's for the best that she can't fight back yet. It will make convincing her to stay much easier if she doesn't have adrenaline coursing through her system.

"Hunter tells me you're in trouble and Arizona is much safer for you than Santa Fe. If you want... I can offer you a job until the dust settles."

"Job?"

"It's a lot," I say, but I don't stop talking because I don't want her to think too deeply. "But I'm in a situation myself. A secret baby situation."

"Secret baby?"

"Listen, I'm sorry for how I took you but... I don't want to get Hunter and Juliette involved in my problems. I don't want anyone in their family getting hurt."

"Getting hurt?"

Quin's repetitiveness gets under my skin. I have to remind myself that I'm the one who drugged her and fight the impatient urge to spank her ass awake.

"Listen, Quin. All you need to know is that if you help me, we keep Juliette and Hunter out of trouble while I solve my problems and you get paid... plus safety. Unconditional safety. I will protect you from... anything and everything."

"Everything?"

I grit my teeth.

"Yes."

"You have no idea what you're talking about."

I don't. But I need her to believe that I know *exactly* what I'm talking about.

"You're in big trouble. You wouldn't have come so far from home on such short notice if it weren't big. And it's big."

I stare at her until the fear hits her. Shit, maybe I'm not too far off.

"I don't want to get Hunter and Juliette in trouble," she says. "But you *drugged me.* Why should I trust you?"

"I drugged you for your own safety. That way no one can say you ran away from the trouble you got yourself into..."

Her fear is so intense that she doesn't notice how goddamn vague I am about "what she did". I feel bad for scaring her. A little.

"Listen," I say, softening my voice. "I have a problem and you have a problem. Work for me and we can help each other out. You're a grown woman. You don't need Hunter Sinclair to tell you what to do."

She considers it.

"I don't understand what you need," Quin says. I can tell she still doesn't trust me, but she really must be in ungodly amounts of trouble to give me a chance so quickly.

I stare at her until she breaks eye contact. These little moments of exerting control over her will make it easier to handle her later on. Quin appears unaware of my strategy as she looks at the floor.

"Before I drove to Santa Fe to visit Hunter, someone dropped a baby on my doorstep. I don't know who it is, or why, but they claim this baby is mine. While I investigate the situation, I have her here..."

"They claim the baby is yours?"

I wouldn't mind her skepticism if I didn't find the mystery behind the baby on my doorstep equally confusing and frustrating. I would much prefer having answers to this.

"Yes. I am conducting a thorough investigation. Until then, she needs a nanny."

Quin raises her eyebrows and then drops them slightly.

"I can barely take after myself."

"Nonsense. You have clearly been through some serious shit, Quin. But I can tell you're a good woman."

Truthfully, she could be a terrible person. But when I look at her face, I can't help but notice my immediate attraction to the soft roundness of her cheeks or the way her full figure affects the rest of her features.

I want to trust her without any reason stronger than my initial powerful attraction to her. I have always preferred the body type of a plus-sized woman on the larger end of that spectrum... but it's more than Quin's body.

Maybe it's the darkness behind her eyes.

Maybe it's that goddamn trouble she's running from, somehow pulling me in.

"I don't think I'm qualified."

"Neither am I," I tell her. "I'm not a father."

"Technically, you are."

"Right. Well, I didn't plan on it. I have no idea what's going on and frankly... you're a woman. It's instinctive."

"That's sexist," she says with an educator's tone of voice.

I grunt in response. Sexist or not, I need her to agree to be Avery's nanny. I can't bear to be around the kid alone for too long and my lifestyle isn't friendly to having some kid hanging off your arm. I need her as much as she needs me.

"Don't deny yourself protection and safety over bullshit politics, Quin. There's nothing sexist about the truth."

If I'm lucky, my so-called sexism will only inspire her to accept my offer and take Avery off my hands. I don't want to worry about the baby while I solve this mystery, make money, and handle club business.

And anyway, if she says yes, this will ensure I can get closer to her.

I haven't met a woman I want in a long time and I sense that once I get to know this one... I'll want her even more than before.

"I'll accept your offer," she says. "But only because I can't stand the thought of Avery developing your backwards notions on gender."

"You plan on staying here for a while then?"

"Did I say that?" She responds with a hint of panic.

"Avery won't be able to comprehend the concept of gender until she's at least seven years old."

"Whatever," Quin says, throwing up the single dismissive word to create distance between us that I desperately want to deconstruct.

"It's agreed. I'll draw up a contract and you can read it in the morning."

"Right," she says, gazing at me tentatively. "What about Juliette and my phone or whatever. I need to contact people."

"You can get your phone back when you sign the contract tomorrow."

"So you're blackmailing me?"

"I'm recommending you think about my offer and my capacity to provide what I promise."

I walk over to her and kiss her on the forehead, certain the small action will imbue her with a jumbled sense of desire, outrage and confusion. The last thing I want when Quin looks at that contract is for her to be in her right state of mind. *Legally* she should be there – naturally.

But I want this woman's emotions vibrating at a fever pitch so she comes running into my arms and never leaves.

NINE
SOUTHPAW

Anna stops my hand before I grab the handle of the basement door. Steel and Condom are already downstairs with Oske, but she can't help herself, my wife has to get involved. It feels fucking good calling her my wife. It doesn't feel good having her lecture me on how to conduct torture.

"Give her the benefit of the doubt, Wyatt."

Anna. The perfect woman. The second I laid eyes on her in that Flying J, I knew I had to have her. I knew I would kill *anyone* who stood in my way. Yet, for all the ways I had to have this woman, I have caused her immeasurable heartbreak too. It makes me want to obey her commands now that she has this twisted titanium ring on my finger and a tattoo on my chest.

"She coerced Tamiya into some hare-brained plot that could have ended with Mackenzie Sinclair killed or worse. Sold into some kind of infant sex slavery."

"That really isn't as common as you think," Anna says, although I'm not so sure. When I get to drinking and playing cards with the guys at the clubhouse, you hear stories about what they see on the highways and you wonder...

We know other clubs deal in human merchandise. Mostly immigrants and Indians. Sometimes black chicks from the inner city. People who most Americans don't give a fuck about, if I'm being honest. Anna's hand on mine stops me, but she can't prevent this from happening. When I offered Oske protection and promised to keep her secret, she promised to stay out of trouble. To keep her ass out of club business. She has higher status than the sluts who hang around the clubhouse... on this condition. Her goddamn loyalty.

If we need someone to break her tonight, at least we have Hog. While Cash lays low, Hog represents the Hollingsworth family. He got his club name because he'll fuck anything. I never wanted things to get to this point between us but after all I've done for her... I can't show weakness. I can't let Oske or anyone else think they can get away with this.

What if someone kidnapped Junior? I would burn down every square mile of the old Route 66 highway without a second thought.

"I won't kill her."

"That's the bare minimum, Wyatt," Anna says.

"She doesn't deserve your protection."

I grab Anna's face and pull her close for a kiss. The mother of my child is still so soft. So perfect. I want her lips so fucking badly. The ache spreads through me. I hold onto her from her hips and kiss her forehead. I would much rather spend the night making love to my wife but sometimes... you have to torture a family member instead.

This is my father's shame, not mine. But I can't bear looking at Oske's face. It's impossible for me not to see the family resemblance. How could he have done this? It would have been just once. Just one time. But that was enough.

"Go to your room, Anna," I command my wife as gently as I can. "I'll handle everything downstairs."

"It's not her fault. Her connection to your family isn't her fault."

But it feels like it is.

We all have our demons in this club but my father's demon haunts me in ways that others don't. She sits in my basement threatening to destroy all of us. He kept Oske's true connection to our family hidden from us for years. He lied to me. To my brothers. *To our mother.*

If she learned what he did now, it would kill her. I want her to have that perfect memory of him. Her honest husband.

"I love you, baby," I whisper to my wife. "I love you so fucking much."

I always say that to Anna before I do some fucked up shit. Just in case it's the last straw with her. I need her to know that I love her ass more than she will ever know and that is never gonna fucking change.

Magnum Sinclair somehow got the short end of the stick so when I get downstairs, he has a shotgun pointed right at Oske, who has her tongue stuck out and an expression on her face like she's trying to get her ass shot. What the fuck is wrong with this woman?

"Oske, stop that," I growl at her, which causes her to promptly suck her tongue back in. Condom and Steel must have worked on her a bit, because she doesn't look like she's in the best shape.

"Let me hit her, boss," Condom asks. "Please..."

"Minnow dick," Oske 'mutters' loudly enough for us to hear. She doesn't express the slightest shred of remorse when I glare at her. Condom turns bright red but I can't tell if he's pissed off or drunk. Maybe a mixture of both.

"Quiet, Oske. I have been more than generous with you but you have pushed it too far. What the hell possessed you to convince Tamiya Simmons to kidnap Juliette's baby? And I want a real answer."

Her expression falls away and thin-lipped stoicism returns. She's so full of shit, playing up the calm Indian stereotype as if I can't recognize the fire behind her dark eyes. I don't know what the hell my grandfather was thinking. It's not just that Oske's here... It's what he did after she was born.

"Is this about the past?" I growl at her. "Is that why you're fucking with me?"

Nothing.

"Give us an answer," Steel says. "You took my niece from the safety of her home and unlike my cousin... I won't ask the boss for permission if I get the urge to smack you across the face."

Oske ignores him, keeping her gaze angrily fixated on me. I don't want to stop them from punishing her. Being the bad guy often offers you the easy way out. One bullet would get rid of this problem and I wouldn't have to keep this unpredictable fucking firecracker on such a short leash.

It's my damn fault for having a heart.

For wanting to be a different man than my father.

Her mother didn't deserve what happened to her.

"You owe me," Oske says.

"I have given you everything I can. I promised I would look after you and I have kept that promise. Obviously, Oske, I have to reconsider my commitments to you now that you intimidated someone to kidnap an infant."

She remains cool despite the tension in my voice. Steel and Condom unconsciously respond to my firm tone, trained by years of riding and working together. They both tighten their grasp on their weapons. Oske feels the energy in the room shift.

"You could give me the benefit of the doubt instead of kidnapping me and tying me up in a basement."

"You ran," I remind her, gritting my teeth and reminding myself that she's still five years younger than me and less mature. That I owe her. She's right. Anna's right.

If Oske needs forgiveness... maybe I shouldn't deny her. After all, I have my share of screw ups.

Never hurting a child. Never something so fucked in the head.

· · ·

I need answers. Real answers.

"I can't imagine why I ran," Oske says. "You and your gang of thugs are all responding so rationally."

"How do you tolerate the mouth on this bitch?" Steel grunts, grabbing one of Oske's braids and yanking on it hard. She tries to bite his forearm like a rabid coyote as he laughs and stumbles back.

"Fuck you, you racist piece of shit," she says. Condom lunges forward to hit her across the face, but I step between them.

"Enough. All of you. Oske. If you insist on causing trouble, I will leave you down here without food until you speak. If you give me a good reason for what you did, I will give you the benefit of the doubt..."

"Why?" Condom grunts.

Steel and I make brief eye contact. He knows the Shaw family secret because his brother is my best friend, but I'm not close enough with Magnum Sinclair that I spilled my family's dirty secrets out to him.

"Because... if she lies to me, she knows we can track her down and kill her."

"White people," Oske spits with genuine disdain. "You think violence solves everything."

I glare at her.

"Fine," she says. "Although I should stay quiet and let you assholes figure it out."

"Oske..."

"I sent Tamiya to kidnap Juliette's daughter because I knew she would never hurt the baby, and it would create a diversion long enough to distract them."

"Distract who?!"

"I don't know," Oske says. "Something happened at The Fire

Spot during my girlfriend's shift. She recorded the conversation and sent it to me, but we couldn't make out all the details. But you dumbasses have enemies. Lots of enemies."

"Elaborate."

"Mackenzie's kidnapping pulled in all the senior members of the Rebel Barbarians. I think some or all of you are going to be targets of some kind of attack or assassination."

"Who would want to kill us?" Magnum asks.

Oske glares at him. "I can think of a few people who might want to."

It doesn't take long for her to turn her anger back to me. She's right about the club having enemies and the way she looks at me causes me to twist up with guilt that shouldn't be mine to bear.

Why should I have to pay for what white men did long before I was born? As much as I believe that, I can't look into Oske's eyes, know her story is true, and toss her into the Wild West with nothing. She might be trouble, but that girl is my trouble... Anna would never forgive me for abandoning her. Or for unjustly punishing her.

"Do you still have the recording?" I ask her.

"Right," Steel says. "Make sure the bitch ain't lying."

"I'm not lying," Oske says. "Someone is after you and I can prove it."

. . .

"Who?" Condom asks. "You keep saying this shit, but you can't say who."

"Don't you think I know that, asshole?" Oske says. "I can't help not having answers. All I know is that I stopped half of you from getting your asses shot at or blown up."

"Fine," I tell her. "Then prove it..."

TEN
QUIN

Terms of Employment
Quin Nash agrees to provide childcare services for Tanner
Hollingsworth's daughter, Avery Hollingsworth henceforth known
as AVERY for the duration of Tanner's inquest into Avery's
identity and parentage:

I can't help but wonder what happens if he finds out that Avery doesn't belong to him. What happens to the little girl then? So far, I haven't met her, but I sit across from Tanner in a leucite chair parked at a pristine leucite table, and stare at the contract he drew up for the care and protection of the daughter he isn't sure is his.

My curiosity is getting the better of me, I have to admit. And I have demons. Demons that I believe this man can protect me from. If he's enough of a psycho to drug my glass of water and drag me out to the middle of nowhere...

It feels like someone twisting a dagger in my chest. I suppress my fears and concerns about Tanner's sanity, focusing on his promises and the contract. We're even further away from what I did and he makes a good point about getting Hunter and Juliette involved. If he really wanted to hurt me, he could have done it already.

Maybe it's a weird way to think about things but I spent so much time in captivity that I can't help it. My mind feels in tune with predators and I don't know how I feel about that. Probably nothing. I haven't felt much of anything since the crime I committed.

The crime I'm desperate to bury.

I keep reading before the weight of what I've done closes around my heart. I have to expand my chest with deep breaths to keep the pressure at bay.

Confidentiality Agreement.

Quin agrees to keep the name, identity and all information about AVERY secret including her existence. This includes keeping this information from Juliette and Hunter Sinclair, all her family members, friends, and associates. Severing this confidentiality agreement will result in swift and merciless punishment decided by Tanner Hollingsworth or in his place, his aunt, Debbie Hollingsworth.

Quin requires written consent from Tanner Hollingsworth before disclosing any personal or identifying information whatsoever about AVERY.

I understand secrets. I don't get *why* Avery has to be a secret, but it shouldn't be that hard to keep her existence a secret. I can always tell Juliette that I'm working as Tanner's housekeeper or something that sounds believable since I wasn't exactly the tidiest person growing up.

The contract continues identifying my nannying responsibilities.

Quin Nash's Nannying Tasks
Quin agrees to care for AVERY as follows, completing each of these tasks daily and submitting a verbal report to Tanner Hollingsworth in person or over the phone at the end of each day. In rare cases, Tanner Hollingsworth will request Quin submit this report via email.
AVERY requires daily feeding, bathing, dressing and constant supervision. During her sleep times, AVERY must be monitored by the home's internal security system and the alarm must always be turned on.
Quin must maintain a safe and clean environment for AVERY at all times, subject to random inspection by Tanner Hollingsworth.
Quin must be responsible for age-appropriate educational activities for AVERY and must spend at least two hours a day engaged in active developmental play. AVERY must also maintain a consistent routine with naps, meals and bedtime.
AVERY is not to be put to bed after 8 p.m.
Quin must perform housekeeping tasks related to AVERY such as laundry, tidying her play areas, diaper duty and preparing meals for AVERY.

Written down, the tasks don't seem impossible. Tanner doesn't seem concerned with the fact that I have no experience with diaper duty or preparing meals for toddlers.

Quin Nash will be compensated for her work at a rate of $2,500 per week. This money will be dispensed every Sunday at 4 p.m. after her completed week of work.

I put my finger beneath that part of the contract and read it twice just in case I made some type of mistake. That doesn't seem to be the case. I glance up at Cash, whose round blue eyes haven't left my face since I began reading the contract.

"It's not a mistake," he says calmly. "This job simply requires discretion."

"Right."

"You have functional bank accounts, I presume?"

I glance up at him and not, trying not to betray my nerves.

"I can always pay you in cash."

"Maybe cash would be better."

It's not that I don't trust Hawk and Juliette to help with my problem, but I don't want infusions of cash into my bank account drawing the attention of law enforcement. It might be an unnecessary precaution, but I won't feel safe needing to interact with *any* bank to access money. Especially not a bank with video cameras.

"Cash it is," Tanner says. Relief floods through me, although maybe I should feel guilty instead. I didn't know how I would survive without access to any money, but Tanner's deal might not be so bad after all...

I tighten my lips and keep reading the contract. This all seems too good to be true.

This contract will extend until the day Tanner Hollingsworth discovers the true identity of Avery Hollingsworth, at which point, the contract will be terminated and Quin will either be free to go or may choose to extend the contract another year.

I wonder how long it's going to take him to find out Avery's identity. I don't know what the baby looks like so for all I know, this could be a matter of weeks. Would that be such a problem? In three weeks, I would have enough money to get an apartment in Santa Fe so I can be close to Juliette and have some support while I get on my feet.

There doesn't seem like a way to lose here... I suppress the nagging thought in the back of my head that there must be a catch here. That Tanner is too calm. Too sure of himself. I'm almost done with the contract, so I just keep going.

Termination of this contract is possible if Quin or Tanner break any aspect of the contract. Otherwise, this contract cannot be terminated for any reason.

The clause gives me a slight pause, but I can't think of anything that could possibly happen out here to give me cause to terminate the contract. Based on the previous terms, I doubt I'll be out here long.

This agreement will be governed in accordance with the laws of the state of Arizona.

He has space for both our signatures – employer and nanny.

. . .

My heart pounds. The same pounding throb that reverberated in my chest when Eugene lay dead on the floor at the base of the stairs. That rush of fear reminds me of that moment and the truth of my situation with Tanner hits me like a smack to the head.

This man has no idea I took a human life.

He can't possibly know that for all his pretense that he knows my secret. He can't. No sane man would ask a killer to become his nanny. It doesn't feel like my place to suggest he conduct a background check and that wouldn't exactly support my goals of staying out of trouble with the law.

"Seems pretty simple," Tanner says in a smooth, country accent. He sounds very Southwestern, a distinct voice that blends a Texan drawl with the nasally, flat intonations of Midwestern speech. A General American with a dash of sexy cowboy. It's hard for me to think logically when he speaks to me.

"Makes you think there's a catch."

His eyes flicker with an emotion I can't place when I search his face for deception but just as soon as I observe the flicker, it fades away, leaving Tanner's placid expression behind. That man has a *very* handsome face. I'll admit that.

"I'll sign it," I say to him. "But... if you fire me and send me back to Juliette's, I understand."

"Not gonna happen, sugar plum."

Sugar plum? Ew. I assume that's just some old-fashioned Southern thing and I pretend to review the contract again, even if I know exactly what I'm going to do.

. . .

What choice do I have? It's either this, or I find my way back to Juliette and Hunter's place to live off their generosity. At least now I have a chance to stand on my own two feet.

"Can I call Juliette once I sign this to let her know I'm okay? That I went with you willingly?"

He raises his eyebrows in surprise, and then he nods.

"Of course. Wouldn't want your new employment status causing any trouble."

I take the pen Tanner hands me and sign my name with a flourish. His shoulders depress slowly once I'm done.

"Perfect," he says with audible contentment and a slow exhale. "Let's take you to meet Avery, sugar plum."

Sugar plum.

Not exactly what you call your nanny...

Then again, maybe it's a Southern thing.

Eleven
CASH

For eight weeks, my mind claws at an escape from the troubles plaguing my sleep. Who is this child? Where did she come from? Who brought her here and why is any of this happening? Southpaw calls with answers about Oske, but those answers only seem to provoke more questions.

I have about half an hour before Quin comes for her weekly pay, so I want this club-related call with Southpaw to end quickly.

"Is it a wild goose chase or was the Indian girl onto something?" I ask him.

"Tamiya and Rebecca listened to the recording Oske's girlfriend picked up and analyzed it with their forensic audio software. They picked up three voices discussing some type of fucked up murder plot involving Barbarians, but we don't know who they were after, or why."

"Can we identify who the fuck has problems with us? As far as I know, I've kept my ass out of trouble," I respond.

"And I handled my shit with the gambling," Southpaw says. "Oske has some ideas about why this might be happening."

"Like what?"

"She's family, you know that, right?"

He means that he has some type of relationship to that crazy Indian girl that causes him to protect her no matter what shit she does. If she were my problem, I would have sent her ass to Canada or kept her locked in a basement somewhere for a very long time ago. Southpaw is too damn permissive.

"Yes."

"I value her perspective and even if she is a huge pain in my ass... she understands how the world works out here. Every battle is for land rights, water rights, cattle, or something of that nature."

As much as I find myself suspicious of Oske, my family has been out here for generations and she's damn right about the reasons folks out here all kill each other.

"Right. But as far as I know, no Barbarian territory is in dispute."

"Agreed," Southpaw says. "Oske thinks we have new challengers. The clubhouse blowing up and the situation with the Blue Blood Knights might have spread to other clubs around the country."

"Like who?"

"I'm still looking for answers," he says. "If you could stay out of trouble until I figure it out, I'll let you know."

Staying out of trouble should be easy. The business deal with Hunter worked out well enough and the money from that flows into my accounts at a slow, steady trickle that will avoid unnecessary attention from the IRS. We're going to have all the money we need in about ten months, right when we need it.

I don't bother pointing out that if anyone is prone to getting into unnecessary financial trouble, it's the man with the gambling addiction.

"I'll stay out of trouble if you do. No casinos. No card games. No shooting dice."

"I get the point," Southpaw says. "I'll stay away from liberal arts college Quidditch matches too."

"What the fuck are you talking about?"

"Nothing," he snaps. "I would never gamble about something so stupid and I don't know what Quidditch is."

"Maybe quit drinking while you're at it."

"I'll call you when I have more information," he says, pointedly ignoring my advice. "Steel is looking for information about other clubs who might be interested in what we have."

"Gotcha. Stay out of trouble. Easy peasy."

When I hang up, I can't help but think of how fucking different life has been, honestly. Juliette is pregnant again. Wyatt and Anna are most likely trying for their second, if I know Wyatt. Gideon's mom only has 18 months left on her sentence. Ruger's mom will be out in nine months. Tylee and her husband are moving into a different house in a couple months.

Before I know it, we'll have another club meeting out in New Mexico...

I hope I have answers about Avery by then. I brought Quin here with the worst intentions for her. But once I had her in my captivity, my desire to inflict my cruel control on her dwindled.

Temporarily.

My cravings for Quin Nash have risen again. Eight weeks in my custody and she has become nothing short of my singular obsession. It doesn't help that she's the only woman I have seen in the past eight weeks who isn't a blood relative. My balls are ready to fucking burst every time I have to watch her thick ass walk into a room, completely oblivious to her effect on me.

If she weren't holding Avery almost every time she enters a room, I surely would have acted on my desires for her by now. I find my urges overwhelming and nearly impossible to deal with.

Quin is everything I want in a woman and watching her tenderly handle Avery fucks with me completely.

Quin avoids me instinctively. Whatever dark past she's running from must scare the crap out of her because she's willing to live with a creature she fears just to get away from it. I know I captured her presence willingly, but only to an extent. Once she settles Avery for the night, she always disappears into her room and she *always* locks her door.

That lock on the door is going to be a problem soon.

I count out the twenty-five hundred dollar bills for Quin's eighth week working for me. I wish I could say I know her better now than when she moved in. I suppose I know her the way you know a dead person when you visit their house's estate sale after they die.

There are signs of Quin all over the house. She has a natural talent for childcare, just like I knew she would. For all her conviction that I have "sexist notions", my ability to identify her as a nurturing woman was pure instinct, not a stereotype. I can tell she's the type who would never allow anything to happen to Avery, even if I can tell she thinks Avery is mine.

Well, she said it explicitly.

But I'm not convinced. Not at all. And still waiting for explicit answers from the lab.

Quin knocks on my office door at 4 p.m. to collect her money. I look forward to our weekly meetings, but after eight weeks of visiting my office, she hasn't become more comfortable around me in the slightest. I find it endlessly frustrating.

"Come in," I call to her in the gentlest voice I can muster. Her continuous fear is becoming somewhat of a nuisance for me, as difficult as that is to admit. I have been more than patient in waiting for her to get comfortable around me and the longer I have to wait, the darker my fantasies become.

Masturbation doesn't help. Touching my dick only makes me want her more. I lack self control.

Quin makes it worse when she enters my office wearing... *that.*

What the fuck?

"Are you going somewhere?" I snap at her.

Last I checked, we agreed that having her wander around the neighborhood was dangerous. She doesn't have a car and I will only let her borrow mine to take Avery to the doctor, but right now, she looks like she's planning on a night out. We don't have an official agreement in the contract but... I don't like the looks of this.

"I'm tired of being stuck in the house. I'm just going to the Arby's drive thru."

"Dressed like that?"

She frowns at me, even if I'm making an excellent point about her outfit.

"It's a maxi dress," she says.

. . .

I have no idea what that means. All I know is I can see every last curve of Quin's body. This dress hugs her breasts and ass, highlighting how goddamn *big* she is all over. Her curves get me rock hard and any sane man with a functional dick would have the same response.

"You're not going out around men like that."

"Who said anything about men?" she says. "It's a drive thru. And it's none of your business if I want to talk to men."

"Are you talking to men?"

I look up from my desk, tapping my fingers on the stack of hundred dollar bills I should be handing over to Quin before sending her on her way. Yet here I am, staring at her in that dress and feeling fiercely possessive over her.

"I make $2,500 a week and I don't leave the house or pay rent," she says. "I bought one stupid dress and want to do one thing for myself and you're asking crazy questions. Can you just give me the money?"

My eyes flash to hers in complete surprise.

I've never heard Quin express anything but utter submissiveness towards me. Why is she acting so strangely over this dress and drive-thru trip...

"I'll take you out," I tell her. "If that's what you want."

"I don't want to go out with you," she responds quickly.

I smirk. "Well, you're either going out with me or you're not going out at all. That maxi dress or whatever you want to call it is a little too nice for Arby's."

"What about Avery?" she says, folding her arms over her chest, like mentioning how good she looks somehow offends her.

"I'll call my aunt. She's been staying nearby on standby for babysitting. Now come. I'd rather take you out myself than have you run off."

TWELVE
STEEL

After all these months out of prison, I finally switched back to cigarettes. Nothing tastes better than hand-rolled American Spirits. I know all the dangers, so I keep it to one cigarette in the morning with whatever coffee I pick up from the gas station, one cigarette with my liquor in the evening and a cigarette after sex.

Haven't fucked since before I went in. I don't feel like I'm missing much. All the chicks hanging around the club look worse for wear. Opioid addiction has fucked with every last inch of America and getting head from a cracked out chick about to pass out holds no interest to me.

It's not easy to find good women. Hawk lucked out by not getting his ass sent to prison. I find it funny he's the one who found a woman first. Women always preferred me. I was always the sober one, the one who could hold a conversation without embarrassing myself.

Now my brother has everything I thought I would have by his age and I'm a goddamn felon. It's hard not to feel like a screw up. Like my father would have been disappointed in me, even if he was the one who told me to accept the plea and promised me everything would be okay when I got out. I was only in prison to keep bigger charges away from Gideon – what he did to that woman in the desert. So I pled guilty and did my time for a good cause.

Dad promised everything would be fine.

Nothing could have been further from the truth. I was in prison while pieces of dad were getting put in the ground. Didn't see his grave until they had the stone finished. I've had to bury others since I got out. Friends. Family. I almost can't stand it. It's a part of life and I get that, but life might be worth all that shit if you had a good woman laying next to you. A woman with a nice tight pussy, big tits, and lips that fit perfectly around your dick.

Club rules won't stop me from letting a woman of any goddamn color suck me off if her lips are the ones I want.

Not like I've met a woman I want in a while...

Southpaw: Three clubs are suspects for the bodies in the desert. Got the list from Tamiya. Midnight *SS*. Blood Riders. Rebel Vipers.

He sends me the location of all three clubs. My job is simple. Ditch my Barbarian gear, wear a white button down shirt, dress like a more serious type of gangster and collect information in biker strongholds. Out of the three clubs Southpaw lists out, the obvious villains stand out.

Midnight SS.

. . .

I had my fair share of run-ins with the Aryan Brotherhood in prison, including some fucked up shit I had to do to secure my protection. Those memories from prison are the ones I want to push to the back of my head – the dark shit I had to do to survive. It doesn't matter where you're locked up in this country, you have to be strong to survive. Not just strong. You have to be cunning and willing to fuck shit up if necessary. I had to get so goddamn comfortable with hurting people that I sometimes scare myself.

I ride to the Rebel Vipers stronghold first. Their clubhouse is on the outskirts of Omaha, Nebraska around 5 hours away from the Old Route 66 highway entrypoint in Missouri. Several Blackwoods and Sinclairs own businesses at that point of the highway.

Magnum is one of the first Sinclairs to invest in businesses out west with his real estate ventures in Santa Fe. Mostly Blackwoods and Shaws have businesses out there. But our family owns a gas station near Joplin, MO, run by Caitlin Sinclair. Juliette was the target of the main attack, so Southpaw suspects the Sinclair family may be the target.

These folks might be just as likely as a bunch of Americans who run around calling themselves *SS* like they forgot what side of the damn war our granddads and great-granddads were on... I barely graduated high school and I know that. You get sick of their shit when you have to listen to the Aryan Brotherhood talk their shit in prison.

I park my bike in Omaha at the rental Southpaw arranged for me. It's a small double wide about ten miles away from the Vipers clubhouse with a small Ford Escape parked out front that he wants me to use for surveillance. The damn thing looks like a mom van. I don't care if Tylee "kindly" donated it to our cause... I suspect she just wanted her brother to fund a new F-150 truck for her.

I hang out at biker bars all week before one of the gang

members talks to me. He's a new recruit, easy to manipulate because of how green he is. Five years in prison teaches you how to spot the gullible. It starts as a matter of survival, but you can only pretend to be a predator for so long before you actually become one.

The recruit, Luke, drops his ID right in front of me and I read it in a flash. He's twenty-three years old, lives in Nebraska, and from the looks of that ID picture, he's been around bikes his entire life. I get him hammered, let him beat me at pool, and I find out everything I can about the Vipers.

His daddy is the gang leader and although they are into some messy shit... they have absolutely no issues at all with the Rebel Barbarians. I keep my identity a secret, giving him a fake name and a detailed backstory that I steal after one of my old cellmates. Thank you, George the tree cutter from Montana.

Luke must be the dumbest of his brothers, because he spills all the information I could possibly want. He even invites me back to the clubhouse, but I can't risk anyone older than him placing me from a charity ride or anything like that.

I just keep him drinking and then give the bartender $100 to get him home safe before I take my mostly-sobered-up ass back to my temporary housing. No leads here. The only thing I did was worsen my alcohol dependence. I don't see the point in contacting Southpaw until I get some sleep.

A sunbeam blasting warmth across my face wakes me up around 11 a.m. the next day. Drinking never keeps me asleep past noon. It's much better to treat a hangover with more alcohol than with sleep. Dad always used to say that. I piece together something moderately healthy and workout for forty-five minutes before I call Southpaw.

After prison, my routine for looking after myself has become both meticulous and non-negotiable. The only things I'm missing are a pair of pretty lips to cum on or to cum in. I'm not too picky.

Southpaw picks up after two rings. I can hear his son gurgling in the background, so he must be busy on dad duty or diaper duty. I can't tell which would be worse.

"What happened last night?"

He knows I've been tracking that recruit.

"Got the kid drunk. He spilled his deepest secrets. Typical bullshit. Nothing about the club."

"Fuck," Wyatt says with a frustrated groan. I hear Anna clear her throat disapprovingly in the background.

"I'll track down the Midnight SS next."

"Are you up for such a long trip?"

"I've got nothing better going on. After so much time in a cage, it feels pretty good to ride again."

"Enjoy that freedom," Wyatt says wistfully as Junior gurgles loudly. "I have Ruger watching Oske closely while we investigate to make sure she isn't up to any bullshit."

"You trust Ruger to watch a woman?"

"No. But if Oske finds out he's watching her, she'll know I'm not fucking around. One wrong move and I'll handle business the way our fathers would have wanted."

He doesn't know how much that comforts me to hear.

"I'll keep you posted on what happens when I get there."

"Midnight SS," he says wistfully. "Sounds fucked up. Doesn't ring a bell though."

"I'll call you when I get there."

"Stay safe, brother."

I take my time driving out there. In a hurry, I could make the drive in two days, but this time I drag it out to seven. It's something in me that doesn't want to get close to the Midnight SS motherfuckers.

It's this deep instinct I've got that they're the ones looking for trouble. But why? Putting the business with the Blue Blood

Knights behind us was supposed to mean an end to shit like this.

I don't want to do something that sends me back to prison. I would rather die than go back there and I'm too afraid to tell anyone. Especially not my twin brother. I can't help but think if he were the one behind bars, he would have handled it much better than me. I can't help thinking that he's always been better than me. Now, I suppose there's proof of that. I'm a felon. He isn't.

If I can do something to redeem myself and to make up for my mistakes, maybe it's helping the club to solve this mystery. Who wants to punish us? Who wants to hurt our families? And how can we stop them...

Thirteen
QUIN

This dinner with my boss is the first time I have ever gone out with a man. I know it's not a date. I'm not stupid. Actually, after eight weeks, I think I understand Tanner Hollingsworth quite well and he is in no way shape or form attracted to me. He stares at me like I'm a curiosity because like most of the cruel, tall, and dangerously attractive men I've met, he finds my plus-sized body to be some type of freak show. He likes having me around because I'm safe. There's no one I'll go to with his secret, so all my appeal to him centers around that — my ability to shut up and stay out of trouble.

Attraction doesn't factor into it at all.

Eliminating any chance of attraction between me and Tanner should make it easier when he opens the door to his GMC Sierra and offers his hand to help me up. I glance at his hand like it's a foreign object because I've never actually been in that situation before. I've had more doors intentionally slammed in my face than held open. If you're not a plus-sized black woman, it's hard to believe how fucking badly random people will treat you in public.

"Take my hand," Tanner says gently. "It's pretty high up."

I just keep gawking at his hand like a shelter dog who's never experienced kindness before. Shame rushes through me and I feel self-conscious about my reaction. Tanner has rough hands that still have engine grease beneath the nails, but are otherwise clean. He has a tattoo around his wrist — barbed wire — and then a date printed beneath that.

I wonder if he's spent time behind bars or if he knows someone who has. He has a black spade tattooed on one of his fingers and a knife tattooed on his forearm. I wish I wasn't noticing his tattoos. Nervously, I reach for his hand and he helps me up into the truck.

I'm surprised by how strong he is, although I shouldn't be surprised by that. He knocked me out and had to carry me somehow to get me here. I don't know the details.

"One day, I'll take you on the bike. But you look too pretty for a dirty ride."

Did my boss just call me pretty? He shuts the door to the truck and climbs in the driver's side before his words hit me. Tanner looks over at me and smiles. I quickly look away.

"Honestly. I haven't been out in a while either. If you enjoy dinner... We could make this some type of ritual. You get a break from cooking and get some real food in you and... I don't have to worry about your safety."

"Are you really worried about that?"

I scrutinize his face for the truth because I was pretty sure Tanner brought me here for his own selfish reasons. By now, I'm sure those reasons aren't sexual, but they are definitely still selfish.

"Yes," he says. "It would be a lot of trouble to find another nanny I trust. You are great with Avery."

I nod, pretending that I don't notice how he smuggled me out of the house without his Aunt Deb meeting me. I don't know if that's for his safety or another reason. I'm just the nanny, so it's not like he would be ashamed to be seen with me.

"Do you have a preference for food? I could use a rack of ribs," he says. "I miss Texas barbecue. Arizona barbecue isn't all bad or anything, but you can't beat Texas."

I don't know enough about barbecue varieties to compare and I'm simultaneously nervous as hell and unclear why Tanner is even doing any of this. I thought this would be a simple trip to the drive thru. Now, I have to eat steak in front of my boss. Is he going to fire me? My mind can't relax. But Tanner seems thrilled.

"Barbecue sounds fine."

"Great," he says. "Mind if I play some Luke Combs?"

"Not at all."

He turns up the music and I'm glad that for the next twenty minutes, I don't have to talk. Although it's not like thinking makes my situation here any better...

Everything in Arizona is so spread out, so it shouldn't surprise me that it takes that long to get to the steakhouse or that there are no other buildings around. It's like an oasis in the desert, decked out in lights outside and neon signs that hearken to that touristy Route 66 All-American aesthetic.

Tanner parks the truck in the front next to three other motorcycles. He notices my nervous glance over at the bikes.

"The only folks out here will be club affiliates. Family friends own this place."

He seems sure of himself, but I'm not sure I share his confidence. He comes around to help me out of the truck and again, I have to touch his hand to get out. He squeezes my hand with a strange firmness that sends an unfamiliar warmth shooting straight through me. It's a feeling I've never had before, probably because I've never had a man who looks like Tanner this close to me.

"I hope you have an appetite," he says. "Because I'm hungry."

He puts his hand on the small of my back to guide me towards the door. The flush of warmth spreads everywhere and I move as fast as I can to get away from his hand. He's just my boss and most likely doing this is a protective and fatherly way... So I don't want to mess it up by getting myself all confused.

"Table for two," he says to the hostess, who stares at me the entire time he talks to her. I don't want to make a big deal out of it but I can't help but feel self conscious. What exactly is she judging about me? I look away, but I can still feel her eyes on me and I hate how self-conscious I am. Tanner appears blissfully unaware and totally confident. We get a booth in the back of the restaurant, glasses of water and then order.

He leans back and a cheeky grin crosses his face once the waitress brings our order to the kitchen.

"It's nice to be out," he says. "I needed a break from Avery."

"Your daughter?"

"Alleged daughter."

Now that I know Avery, it's getting harder for me to deny the truth about her. She has to be his. The girl has red hair. She has his blue eyes. His chubby cheeks. If she isn't his baby... Why would someone drop her on his doorstep making that claim? A guy with a firm, ripped body like Tanner Hollingsworth must lose track of all the women he sleeps with.

It would be downright unrealistic for him to keep track. One of those women has done the humane thing and left the child with him instead of with the system. Well, it would be humane if Tanner had the slightest bit of empathy. He barely spends any time with Avery at all.

It's like he hates her.

"She has red hair."

"So?" He says. "Lots of people have red hair."

"Statistically, that's not true."

"She's just as likely to be your daughter as mine," he responds gruffly and that placid grin on his face vanishes. I don't mean to push him, but it's hard not to defend Avery from his coldness.

"Are you any closer to getting test results?" I ask him.

"This discussion is over," he says firmly. I open my mouth to say something else, but his expression darkens so severely that I think better of it and sip my water. The waitress returns with drinks and I feel relieved when Tanner chugs half his Michelo in half a minute.

I stay quiet because I have nothing else to discuss aside from Avery. It's not like I'm going to tell him about my nightmares or about the dark shadow I see hovering in the corner of my room sometimes at night when I'm trying to sleep. My adopted brother's ghost is haunting me. Or maybe it's just anxiety. PTSD. Something.

Either way, Avery has been my only source of light since the incident and Tanner's coldness towards her doesn't impress me.

"Do you like football?"

"Not really."

"I thought we could go to a game. College. Arizona State."

"With Avery?"

His auburn eyebrows get all furrowed and frustrated.

"Football will be too loud for Avery. I'll get Aunt Deb to babysit again."

"Can we do something that includes Avery?"

He exhales impatiently. I know I'm pushing his buttons but... I don't care. She's his daughter. He might not want to accept it, but it's the truth and I don't want to spend time buddying up to some man who won't claim his own child.

That's just not who I am.

FOURTEEN
STEEL

I'm a hot fucking mess when I roll into Globe, Arizona, home of the Midnight SS. The small town wasn't always packed to the gills with racist shitbags. I spend so much time making my way down the old Route 66 highway and getting drunk in every bar to get all the information possible.

It helps to be a conversationalist. It's one of the ways I'm better than my twin brother. He's a brooding alcoholic. I'm the chatty kind. It makes me better with women, better with people in general and so far, it's paying off.

Only thing is, the shit I'm learning about these Midnight SS motherfuckers makes me want to stay far away from them.

When you're dealing with folks like that, you want to strike first but striking first means risking time in prison. Time away from my brother. He already looks so much younger than me. He might be leaner, with less muscle on his frame, but prison aged me more than I thought it would. I don't want to go back.

The pressure pushes on the back of my head with total agony. I wait until midnight to scope out the Midnight SS clubhouse. I take my bike to a safe house pre-arranged by Magnum where he's also left me a car to tail the wannabe Nazis, even if it seems like a trap. A bright red Chevy Silverado. Seriously? It's what I have and I trust Magnum, so I take the truck. Red? He could have at least found a silver one...

I blast the air conditioning, but it barely seems effective against the Arizona heat. I know the entire family loves it out here, but I want the winds to blow me out across Route 66 all the way to Santa Monica. Somewhere with an ocean breeze and bikinis. Fuck this heat.

My conversations with various folks in the know in various bars across the country helps me to find the clubhouse. Bikers talk to bikers and I know how to play my cards. I talk felon shit with other felons, biker shit with bikers. You get the point. Everyone has their thing and you find out where to meet 'em and keep 'em until you get the information you need.

I know the Midnight SS clubhouse is off U.S. 60, about fifteen miles off-road in the middle of the desert. How you find your point depends on who you believe. I have my pick of the finest drunks in Texas... I leave their differing opinions up to a coin flip and head West off the highway.

There might be guards around the clubhouse tonight, although I was assured the Midnight SS are so secretive, they don't bother with guards. Not enough folks know of their existence. Yet, if they do exist, and if they do have any power, they know of ours. I don't like how that makes me feel.

Just when we got peace, I don't want to start a war. I want to lay my father's memory to rest. I want Hunter to raise his family. Shit, I have some catching up to do unless I want my twin brother to be the one who gets every damn thing in this life while I have nothing.

The winds need to change.

I turn off the headlights and try to get the engine as quiet as possible as I roll my way across the barely-marked roads towards the clubhouse. I suspect my coin flip has me pointed in the right direction because of the tire tracks pressed into the dirt.

This could just be a popular place for dirt bikes, but the hair on the back of my neck raises with the raw instinct that suggests I'm approaching something dark and dangerous. The first thing I notice, even before the Midnight SS club house, is a large towering something rising out of the desert.

Two willow trees. Big willow trees with large boughs. Every last inch of my body drips in sweat. I drive the truck behind one of the willow trees and park it there between the tree and the clubhouse. If there was anyone around, they would have shot me by now. Shit, this is Arizona. Anyone could shoot me.

I reach for my gun and hop out of the truck. Send the felon on the suicide mission... Who gives a fuck if he makes it out alive, right? I can't complain. I don't care if I make it out alive either.

The clubhouse is a lot cleaner than you would expect. No graffiti, even if you would expect a place like this left unguarded out in the desert to pick up a few tags. I suppose folks are too smart to fuck this clubhouse up if they even know it exists. I wish I felt safer because of my pistol, but it's just so fucking hot that I can't help but feel this low-level irritation.

It's not just the beads of sweat dripping down my neck. The air is thick, wet, and that makes it hard for it to enter my lungs. I stuff down the feeling I have that some shit could pop off at any minute. It would be pretty damn hard for any living thing to avoid detection out here – something I should take note of in case the folks who own this place come back.

But how often do bikers really use their clubhouse?

· · ·

After scanning the building for a security system, I find nothing. What I notice outside the clubhouse ends up being plenty to send a chill down my spine. The willow trees aren't as benign as I thought. When I get closer to them, I begin to smell a distinct metal smell before I notice blood at the foot and nooses hanging from the boughs. Two nooses from each large bough of the tree, each one about six feet apart.

What the fuck? I take my phone out and use the flash to get pictures to send to Wyatt. When the flash goes off, I can see brown splatter on the tree trunks. Blood. It has to be blood. I shove my phone in my pocket and walk back to the clubhouse. My breathing sounds heavier. It could just be the heat, but something about those trees makes my blood run cold.

You get a heightened sense of danger when you're in prison. I can smell a fight based on the noise levels at breakfast. I could always sense when to keep my shoes close.

I can tell something bad happened here. Bad shit happens here on a regular basis. The doors and windows are all latched, but I find a weakness in an unlatched basement window. It would be much easier for Hunter to fit through than me...

I did everything in my power to keep bulky muscle on my body in prison. Without guns, without my family, I needed my body to be my primary source of protection. I left with only three scars from fights. One long scar on the left side of my torso, one on my right leg, and another on the back of my neck.

The scars don't bother me because they just add another way I'm different from Hunter. We would always fight over who was tougher and usually, Hunter would win. After prison, that has most likely changed. I might even be the quiet one now... at least when I'm not drunk off my ass.

I have to suck my belly in and scrape my shoulder to slide into the Midnight SS clubhouse basement. I land in something sticky and have to stop myself from letting out a very unmanly yelp...

Something ain't right here.

I almost swear, but I just stabilize myself against the wall instead because... I'm pretty fucking sure I'm hearing something. It's dark. Too dark for me to see now that I'm blocked from the moonlight outside. I hold my breath. The noise gets louder. It's not just rats running around the basement, although I hear the familiar sound of their nasty fucking paws...

I hear breathing.

Slow. Human breathing.

I grab my pistol. Adrenaline courses through me so fucking fast, my night vision improves almost instantly. I can at least see movement. Three small figures that must be rats or mice running across the basement floor and then a large lump. The source of the human breathing.

Did you even load the pistol, you stupid motherfucker?

I can taste blood on the back of my tongue.

I don't like this.

"Put your hands up, or I'll blow your fucking head off," I growl with false confidence.

Fifteen

CASH

I almost cum in my pants watching Quin eat, making it very difficult to handle her anger with me throughout the rest of dinner. I have no desire to accept this so-called truth about Avery. My point about red hair stands. Lots of folks have red hair or at least carry the recessive gene. This has to be some plot.

I know exactly where I've put every load of cum I've ever shot.

Since this baby showed up on my doorstep, I have thought *very* carefully. She can't be mine. It's just not possible.

Not like it was some exciting revelation how long it's been for me.

But it's been a long time. Long enough that watching Quin accidentally drip barbecue sauce on the side of her face gets me rock hard. I love her cheeks. Her softness. The way her pink tongue looks when it slides out of her mouth and she licks up that barbecue sauce. I want to feel that sexy ass tongue sliding all over my dick. I'm losing my patience.

We barely make conversation throughout the rest of dinner and she won't let her disapproval of me slide. She won't stop drawing the conversation back to Avery, as if that baby is the most interesting thing in the world. The only thing she cares about is Avery, and she doesn't understand why I refuse to allow that child into my life.

The thing with attachments like that is people can use them against you. I don't know why anyone would want to do something like that, but I can guarantee their intentions are no good. I need my mind clear and spending all day with that baby won't keep my mind clear. Aunt Deb has the same opinion as Quin, but you can't run around letting women tell you what to do.

Our drive home is equally quiet. I relieve Aunt Deb of Avery, ensuring that she never sets eyes on Quin before she leaves. Once she drives away, I open the truck door. Quin hops out with her face set in a glare. Avery lights up and reaches for her and I don't hesitate to hand the baby off. Quin's face softens when she looks at Avery and my jealousy is heavy and immediate.

I know how pathetic it is to feel that kind of jealousy of a baby. She doesn't belong to Quin either. It doesn't matter how much dramatic cooing she does. Quin walks straight past me into the house, whispering sweet nothings to Avery. This isn't how I thought dinner would go. I thought she would look at me with stars in her eyes... not pure loathing.

She's human and presumably heterosexual, so she must be attracted to me physically. It's just that she can't stand to look me in the eye. I have a bit of a problem with that since half of what I want out here is companionship and somehow... I screwed that up.

. . .

I walk off to my office and leave Quin to her own devices. At least she enjoyed her dinner, even if she didn't enjoy me.

Reluctantly, I get started on accounting work. I studied business in college, although I really studied football and drinking with a minor in business. Accounting wasn't too hard to get a handle of, honestly.

I find the spreadsheets soothing.

But tonight, resizing and moving the numbers around does nothing to calm my mind.

I can't stop thinking about Quin. Her anger with me. Her frustration. How easy it would be for me to fix that.

Her disinterest in me only makes my desire for her more difficult to deal with. I want to wrap my hands around her throat. I want to press my dick between her ass cheeks, who make a goddamn statement any time she walks into a room. My dick stiffens at the mere thought of her ass. I can't control my erection.

And I don't want to anymore. I minimize my Excel spreadsheet and open up the house's security cameras. I don't have any installed in the bedrooms, but I can watch Quin walking around the house through the public areas if that's what she gets up to. I scan the cameras until I see her moving. She's putting Avery to bed. I have cameras in Avery's room, so I listen in.

Quin whispers to Avery that somebody loves her and that she's going to pray for her. She's just like my Aunt Deb... overly attached. I just can't let my mother find out about Avery before I get answers.

An email notification distracts me from the camera, which is perfectly trained on Quin's cleavage, unbeknownst to her. Each of her breasts are bigger than my head and I can't even imagine how fucking large and sexy her nipples must be. I love a woman with big nipples that are just begging for my tongue.

I'm losing myself watching her.

I don't want to hold back.

I watch her on camera for another hour until she disappears into her bedroom. All I have left to do is stroke my cock so I can get this woman off my mind. I try to talk myself out of it at first. Then I unzip my pants. I tell myself it won't get further than touching myself and trying to distract myself with the spreadsheets afterwards.

But then I get my dick out and I can't stop getting thoughts of Quin's lips wrapped around it. I don't know where the hell this craving comes from but it's strong. So goddamn intense. I really want control over myself, but I don't have that. The only thing I can control is my hand wrapped around my dick.

I close my eyes and lose myself thinking around her, pumping my shaft slowly. The fantasy starts with Quin's lips, but it doesn't take long for me to imagine her incredibly soft pussy wrapped around my dick. There is absolutely nothing like pumping your cock inside some soft pussy with a thick ass bouncing around it.

There is nothing like a plus-sized woman. I bite down hard on my lower lip as my cock grows in my hand. The veins around my shaft bulge in a lightning pattern that wraps around my dick all the way to the head. I want to drive this dick so far into Quin's pussy that she screams.

Imagining my cock spearing her delicious, soft pussy makes me feel the immediate urge to burst inside her. I won't last long. Holy shit. It can take me a long time to finish myself off but the thought of Quin turns me into a fucking teenager.

Maybe it has been too long since I got some pussy.

I groan and my dick erupts everywhere. I make a fucking mess. Thankfully, Quin is locked in her room so I can sneak out of my office and clean myself up. I fight the urge to check on Avery after I take a quick shower and change into something loose fitting and comfortable – black sweatpants with no shirt.

I shouldn't indulge in the fantasy that this child has anything to do with me. If someone comes and takes her away after that... I wouldn't be able to handle it. The last thing I need to do is bond with the girl. I'll leave that to Quin and Aunt Deb. My phone vibrates right as I'm about to climb into bed, continuing to fight the temptation to knock on Quin's door and do... *something*.

Mom: Is there something going on I should know about?
    Great. Did someone talk?
    Me: I love you, mom.

It's true. I love my mother. Which is exactly why I'm sparing her this senseless club related drama. She's having a hard enough time getting over my father's death, the last thing she needs is to go through the grief of attaching to a child that has nothing to do with us.

I turn my phone off after I send her that reply. My mother

isn't the type of woman to let things go. With my phone turned off, I climb into bed with nothing but my thoughts. Considering how easy it was to make myself cum in my office, I don't expect my dick to stiffen the second I slide beneath my top sheet.

Fuck. I'm not even thinking about Quin.

Until I am thinking about her. Obsessively.

She judges me harshly for the Avery situation.

Too harshly.

And she doesn't seem to understand how fucking hard it's been for me to lie here every night with a woman so goddamn fine beneath my roof and not slide my dick between her soft, dark brown pussy lips.

Control yourself, Tanner.

But tonight, I don't think I have it in me. I get out of bed and open the top drawer of my dresser to find something I haven't had to use in a *long* time. The last time I used this ski mask, Magnum paid me $100,000 to rob some asshole in Vegas who owed him money over poker games. It was an easy gig. No blood on the mask. Never got caught and the dickhead paid Magnum the $467,000 he owed him.

Crazy bastard.

· · ·

My hands feel like they're working without my permission as I slip the ski mask over my head. An eerie sense of calm settles over me, even if my dick doesn't settle.

This house was designed to fulfill my every need... including this one.

While a stranger couldn't make it past my security system, I know every inch of this house and the vulnerabilities that comprise it. One vulnerability in particular causes my dick to tent my pants even further. I look like a criminal. It isn't a bad thing, I guess, because that's exactly what I am.

This type of thing is dangerous without a plan, but I don't envision myself sleeping through another night without sliding my fingers and eventually my cock between my black nanny's pussy lips.

I'm too fucking impatient. I need Quin now.

Sixteen
Quin

It's amazing that Tanner hasn't noticed the fact that I only sleep three hours a night. He never comments on how tired I look. Maybe I'm good at hiding it. Whenever I get close to falling asleep, I see apparitions or get intense flashbacks to that night. The smell of bleach makes me want to throw up. I have to hide all the symptoms of my PTSD from Tanner, which is pretty easy.

But tonight, he was just pissing me off and getting under my skin. He's so goddamn selfish and wrapped up in his feelings about Avery, but he doesn't care about this poor baby's development beyond hiring me.

And did he really hire me? He kidnapped me before offering me a job.

I hear a thud against my window. My heart stops in my chest and cold fear spreads throughout my body, numbing all my limbs and freezing me in place. I've never heard a sound like that outside my window before. My bursting heart quickly interrupts the freeze. I sit up, but the window opens all on its own. The *locked* window.

I gasp and my first instincts are probably stupid. *Hide.* I rip

the gigantic down comforter over my head – completely unnecessary in Arizona if it weren't for the air-conditioning.

What the hell is hiding beneath the covers going to do for
me? I have never been in a situation like this before that has
ended well. I normally barricade my room and that has worked
perfectly well. The last time a man attacked me... I fought back. I
killed him. Going through that again scares me more than what
might happen to me.

The footsteps draw closer to me and my fear only grows more
intense. I can't move this time. I may have attacked my adoptive
brother, but I can't bring myself to do it again. Even when I start
hearing heavy breathing.

I feel a hand tugging at the comforter and dragging it away
from my body. I hold onto it, like I can possibly hide from this
intruder who already has his hand on the comforter. Instinctively,
I know it's a man. There's no way a woman could be doing this.

I drag the comforter around my body tightly. The hand drags
it away. Easily. Only a man could be that strong. I yelp as the
fabric nearly shreds my palms when he pulls it away. The
comforter falls to the ground with a thud and I can still hear the
intruder's slow, heavy breathing.

The last defense I have is burying my face in my pillow. It's
foolish, but hiding my face is the last instinct I have.

He's going to kill me. The thought pulses through my head
repeatedly. Every inch of my body feels like it's covered in sweat.

The last thought that pops into my head is Avery. And what's
going to happen to her after this intruder kills me.

By then, Tanner will have received an intruder alert and will
hopefully spring into action with a firearm. He keeps them out of

sight, but we're in Arizona, so I know he has some firearms around here.

But right after I have that thought about Avery, a knife doesn't slide across my throat. A hand touches my ass. I have a huge butt, and always have. The type of butt that never looks "appropriate", no matter what I wear. So his hand can't cover the entire cheek, but I can feel his hand exploring the soft, small patch of flesh it occupies.

I become utterly paralyzed. Even more than before. His hand moves up my ass and then the intruder groans.

The pillow smells like my bonnet. I'm desperate for fresh air but the groan that comes out of the intruder's mouth sends a jolt of fear through me that pushes me deeper into that impulse to hide. His hand moves up my ass. I can tell for sure the hand belongs to a man now.

It's too big. Too strong. He squeezes a handful of my ass cheek, which takes more than two hands to hold each one.

"Fuck," he groans and the voice sounds strangely familiar. Like a famous actor, or something. I'll have to remember that detail when I tell Tanner... If I survive to tell Tanner...

The hand moves all the way up my ass to my lower back. I have to breathe now. I tilt my head to the side, moving it away from my pillow but my instincts take control and when I suck in air intending to take a deep breath, what happens next is I let out a blood-curdling, uncontrolled scream.

I swear I scream so loud the walls shake and just as I fill my lungs to let out another concrete-cracking shriek, the hand moves from my ass to cover my mouth and the intruder's voice changes.

"You scream like that and let the man of the house hear you, I'll cut your ass up..."

Holding down my lips with one hand, he returns to stroking my ass with his other hand.

"Your ass feels fucking delicious..."

Half a strangled yelp makes an effort to escape my lips, but that only makes the intruder's hand clamp down tighter and he surprises me by using the hand on my ass to spank me. The hard smack shocks me and I try to bite down on his finger and fail as he blocks me from breathing and follows up his first hit with a second one before allowing me to take air in straight through my nose.

Pain. Immediate pain.

"You make one more sound and I'll keep whooping your ass until you can't sit down for a week. How the hell are you gonna explain that to your boss?"

Him mentioning Tanner sends my emotions into overdrive. I can't explain what exactly happens internally, but it's like all my feelings twist up and implode. I let out a sob, which the intruder's hand suffocates, and tears spill out of my eyes.

I hate that he mentions my boss.

I hate it so damn much...

I shudder and nod, mostly because I'm sobbing too hard to do anything but agree with this monstrous intruder in hopes that he doesn't end my life. That's my only goal at this point — survive.

Once he stops covering my mouth, he can hear me softly crying. His next exhalation is almost kind, although it's fucked up for me to attribute any form of humanity to this monster.

"I won't hurt you unless you make me, sugar plum," he says. "You have nothing to worry about."

I don't know why I can't recognize his voice. I try to turn my head a little to glimpse his body, but that offers me no hints. All I know is that the man is huge and his physique is clearly muscular. Not like that helps my prospects of escape or survival. The intruder is far too fixated on my ass and his intentions to notice me trying to see more of him.

He returns to touching my ass with both hands.

"What's a woman like you doing with all this ass?"

I don't think he really wants me to answer, but when I don't, he hits my ass again. I don't yelp. He scares me too damn much for me to scream. He chuckles when I flinch but doesn't make a sound.

"You're a good girl," he says with that buttery smooth voice. "I like a woman who knows her place. I'm old-fashioned like that."

Old-fashioned? Is there something old-fashioned about climbing into a woman's bedroom and groping her? I squeeze my legs shut as his palms rove over my butt cheek. Strange wetness between my legs makes it hard for my thighs to stick together. I don't understand the feeling.

The intruder's hands move to the separation between my ass cheeks and I squeeze my legs even tighter together. That doesn't work to deter him. He separates my legs easily and then he touches me between them forcefully.

He groans again.

"I want to touch you so fucking bad."

Is anything stopping him? I can't stop my racing heart. I can't stop him from touching me inappropriately. This intruder can do absolutely anything he wants with me and he knows it. The sound that comes out of my mouth is another unwilling whimper. I flinch, expecting him to hit me, but he's too distracted by touching between my legs slowly through my clothes.

My legs separate. If I give him this, he won't hit me...

"Yes, sugar plum," he groans. "I feel that pussy getting nice and wet for me..."

. . .

I can't believe this is happening.

I've never even been kissed.

"I want to put my dick in your pussy so fucking bad..."

I flinch again as my terror intensifies. I guessed the intruder's intentions when he started touching me but convinced myself that mildly touching me would satisfy him. I don't get lucky. He escalates from touching my ass cheek to touching me between my legs and now...

He can't do this to me.

I blurt out the only thing I can think to say.

"I'm a virgin..."

The words seem naive when he responds.

"Good," he says. "I always said if I ever made anyone my old lady... she would be mine and only mine..."

He presses one knee into the bed and I whimper as I clutch my pillow. From what little I can see of this man, he left no identifying features uncovered. He's even wearing a ski mask. If I scream loudly enough, Tanner might hear and stop him. Tanner would save me.

. . .

But if I screw that up, this man could kill me. He could kill Avery.

He could kill Tanner too if he's sleeping hard enough or locked up in his office worried about money.

The man kneeling on the bed presses his weight into me and I feel every pound leaning into me. He's heavy. Not heavier than me, but still a big, strong ass man. I can't get any air in as his body covers mine. He's almost cradling me as he joins me in the bed.

His hand gropes my ass cheek as he makes space to nestle his crotch against my butt. I yelp loudly and he has to cover my mouth. His dick. I can feel his dick and the terror forces an extremely unwise yelp out of my mouth. The intruder's hand tightens and his voice erupts, "I told you not to be loud."

Slickness pools between my thighs. More fear. Despite my frozen body, I do my best to nod in agreement. I don't want to anger this man. It's best to go along with whatever he wants... anything he wants.

"You have the softest ass," he whispers. "And since you're a good girl and kept your hymen safe... I'll go slow. No need to fuck you like a bad girl until I turn you into one."

I hate every implication in his statement but at this point, I'm too terrified to make a sound. I just nod and force myself to ignore the slickness between my legs. It's only making everything worse. I feel gross and distracted when I should be focused on one thing — survival.

The dick pressing into my ass feels huge. I'm no expert, but relative to my butt, that thing feels as big as this man's forearm — which is huge.

His body cradles mine as he kisses my neck. The kiss has the unfortunate effect of calming me a little. The physical sensation of soft, masculine lips against my neck sends a confusing river of calm straight through me. My terror subsides enough for me to tune into different sensations aside from the weight pressed on top of me and the gigantic dick weighing against my ass.

He smells good. And familiar. The familiar part doesn't stick in my head very long, but the pleasantness of this man's smell gives his invasion a confusing effect on me. I squirm as if that could possibly help me get away from this powerful specimen of a man who climbed in through my window and has me pinned to my bed.

SEVENTEEN
CASH

She has to know it's me. I speak to this woman in a similarly stern tone every day. I love that she's playing along. Acting like a stranger. I don't think she's acting about the virgin thing. Her body is stiff. Nervous. Probably because it's her first time. I meant what I said... I'll make it good for her.

Quin is everything I want in a woman and it's not just because she is a sexy black woman, insanely fucking thick in the way that makes a country ass white boy lose his goddamn mind. She has this way with Avery that makes me feel guilty for being such a piece of shit about the situation.

Most women irritate the hell out of me and nag me to the point where I can't see the point in them. With Quin, it's different. I don't listen? She stands up to me. She's strong. She's sexy. She has all the feminine features I love in a woman with even more to love of every last helping of flesh.

I want to put her big brown tits in my mouth and suck on her nipples until she cums. This woman has pushed me to the point of fucking insanity and going along with this stranger fantasy makes it even more likely that when I spread her legs apart, I'll cum nice and deep in her virgin pussy.

My hands reach for the waist of her pants which I slide off effortlessly with her underwear. She yelps in a mixture of arousal and despair, which I fail to punish with a hard smack on her ass because I am so fucking distracted by how goddamn perfect her exposed ass looks. There is absolutely nothing more delicious than a plus-sized woman's body. I work on my muscular physique with the intention of giving a nice, thick woman a night to remember with my body.

"You are so fucking beautiful," I growl before grabbing her ass gently on the spot where I smacked her earlier. She makes a low moaning sound, still in slight pain from where I spanked her earlier. That moan sends my desires into overdrive and my dick thumps against the inside of my pants, desperate to make contact with this fine woman's bare ass. The movement makes my sexy plus-sized nanny more nervous because her body stiffens and those thick thighs stick together again.

God damn, her skin is soft. I feel so fucking lost in my desire for her that I don't think about anything but touching her, kissing her, and getting my dick inside her so that she's no longer a virgin. Quin squirms like she's trying to get free and I keep her pressed into the bed with my weight.

Her reluctance sends a minor frustrated urge through me. This is a fun game but at some point, I need to get my dick in that pussy. I can't keep playing around. Breathing slowly, I massage her soft ass, enjoying the layout of her butt with my palm. I feel so rough in comparison. I've spent my whole life under bikes or getting my ass in trouble. I'm cut up and fucked up. Quin is soft all over.

"I want you so fucking bad," I whisper in her ear as I grind my dick into her ass. "Can you feel how bad I want you, sugar plum?"

She only answers with a moan. I reach my hand from her ass cheek between her legs and that's when I really drive her crazy. Her pussy lips are so slick that my fingers almost slide inside her, especially when she squeals and gives a resistant wriggle that inadvertently draws my fingers between her outer lips.

Once I'm in there, I don't stop. I rub every inch of Quin's slit while she fights me — fights her own goddamn pleasure. The poor virgin has no idea what's happening except for the fact that it feels fucking good and she is so desperate to play along with me that she hasn't let up for a second that she knows exactly who I am.

It's so fucking hot. Her pussy is warm. Soaking. She drips so damn much that her pussy lips and thighs are coated. Her warmth guides my fingers exactly where they need to be. I slide around her soft lips until I find her clit and then I move around it in slow circles that drive this woman absolutely fucking wild. Holy shit, she is perfect...

Quin has the softest pussy I've ever felt and is so fucking wet.

"I have to put a finger inside you, baby," I whisper. "I have to touch those sweet inner walls."

She whimpers something that almost sounds like a no, but it's too late. Her pussy is so wet that moving my fingers up and down her slit makes it easy to slide inside her. My index finger enters Quin first and the moan that comes out of her nearly makes me cum immediately. She sounds so fucking hot and her pussy grips my finger tight, surrounding me in heat and increasing my lust for her into deranged territory.

I have already gone way too far but Quin's tight pussy clamping around my single finger makes me want even more from her. Lost in my desire for her, I kiss her neck, tasting her fear as I push my finger deeper. I want another moan. She provides exactly what I crave when I thrust my finger deeper, tempting me to add a second one.

Once Quin feels the second finger pressed against her entrance, I can feel her fighting again. Her ass moves against my crotch with the clear intentional effect of getting me extremely fucking hard. There is so much precum oozing from my dick that it feels like I pissed myself.

I need this woman's pussy the way I need oxygen. If I don't get my dick inside her sloppy wet lips, I'll drive myself even crazier than I have already. I withdraw my two fingers slowly and then push them back in. Quin responds with a loud moan when I slide all the way back inside her. Fuck yes. I love that noise. She sounds perfect and every hot noise out of Quin's mouth just makes me more desperate to give her sweet black pussy every inch of my gigantic white dick.

I'm not being arrogant – just truthful.

The Hollingsworth men aren't just known for our red hair, but for our *unusual* family trait of all being extremely hung. I knew from the time I was a kid that I was a freak. I let the kids in my class pay $2 to see my dick in third grade – male or female. Dad beat my ass so hard when he found out that I couldn't sit for all of Memorial Day weekend – and we'd gone camping, so I had to sit at those hard ass picnic tables with my ass throbbing.

Of course, things only got worse from there. More freakish. Bigger. More veins. A huge cock head that looks about the size of a Macintosh apple. It's a personal condition that's damn near impossible to hide, but the older you get, the less you like being a freakshow.

Quin can feel me pressed against her ass. She knows what to expect. But only in theory. This poor virgin has no idea how much damage a dick this big could do to her tight pussy. I have to tease her open with my fingers to make sure she can handle it. Even if she squirms. Even if she cries. Her pussy needs this.

Finger fucking Quin turns her into a mewling mess within a short space of time. I love the way she reacts to my fingers pumping into her perfect slickness. I love the contours of her pussy and the way her lips get so fucking wet the more I finger fuck her pussy.

I want her to cum so bad. I use my thumb to massage her clit as I fuck her with two fingers, and the sounds coming out of Quin's mouth make my dick so hard that physical pain courses through the length of my shaft. Her responses teach me exactly how to touch her so she cums. Quin arches her back and moans as my fingers touch her sweet spot.

It doesn't take much longer of me playing with her clit before her body tightens and I can feel her having what I assume is her first orgasm at the hands of a man. I bite her neck as I push my fingers all the way inside her and Quin comes so fucking hard I can feel her pussy tighten around both fingers. I can't even move them as she cums until Quin is fully done having her waves of pleasure knock her ass over.

I slowly let go of the spot on her neck that I sucked on while removing my fingers from her pussy before moving my hand up to her lips. Quin fastens her lips stubbornly and makes an uncomfortable squeal.

"Taste yourself."

She grunts in protest.

I grab her ass hard with my dry hand and push my wet fingers against her lips.

"I said taste yourself," I repeat and press my fingers into Quin's mouth once her lips part slightly. She allows me to push my fingers into her mouth, but she doesn't put any effort into sucking on my fingers. Still. She can taste herself. Quin can taste her perfect pussy all over my hands.

I remove my fingers and then spank her ass lightly. She whimpers again.

"You took two fingers well," I whisper. "My dick is a little bigger than that."

On cue, my dick thumps against her ass again. Quin emits another weak yelp, but she's smart enough not to be loud. I love how fucking easy it is to train this woman to do what I want. I grope her ass again, spreading her cheeks apart and letting her slick ass juices spread all over.

If my dick wasn't so damn greedy for her pussy, I would taste her first. Unfortunately, I can't afford to wait anymore. I have to get my dick inside this woman. I slide my pants and underwear off, barely concerned with the rest of my clothes. I feel too fucking crazy to even get my lips on her tits, no matter how badly I want to suck her nipples.

That sweet ass pussy is my priority. I need to fuck my nanny. *Now...*

My dick is fucking desperate to get inside this woman's pussy.

Touching the soft skin on her ass with my dick drives me crazy. I don't give a shit about protection. The thought only enters my mind for a second before I quickly banish it. I spread her big ass cheeks to give myself room to enter her and press the head of my cock against Quin's entrance.

Instantly, she feels my size and responds with outright panic. I wouldn't expect such a big, sexy woman to freak the hell out at the presence of a big dick, but she's still a virgin. Still new to this. I nibble on Quin's neck with soft kisses and continue running just the head of my dick along the entrance of her pussy. She wriggles and squirms and then her fighting gets to be too much for me.

"Hold still or I'll put that whole dick inside you, woman..."

Quin holds still and my body relaxes. Fuck, she feels so good. Her pussy is so slick and I unload so much precum all over Quin's outer lips that it's almost like I already came. She makes one last whimpering plea for mercy.

"Please... it feels so big..."

Damn right. My dick is huge and Quin is definitely in for a surprise.

"You want me to go easy on you?" I whisper, warming her pretty neck with my breath. Fuck, this woman is a goddamn treat. I wish I could be here all night.

Shit. I wish I could be here every night...

Now that I have my dick nice and wet, I push just the head inside of Quin and she cries out so fucking loud that I have to clamp my hand around her mouth. I know it hurts her. The head of my dick is far larger than a couple fingers. But Quin's response indicates pure terror. I can feel her pussy stretching around my dick to its maximum capacity and I don't even have my shaft inside her.

Quin needs time to adjust. I run my tongue along the length of her neck. She tastes fucking good and that only makes my dick bigger and harder for her. I don't think it helps the situation, but

I can't stop kissing and sucking on her neck. Especially when she starts moaning. My hips move against my will and she makes a sexy fucking sound as I push into her more.

I grab her body and hold her against me so I can control the pace. Her pussy is so fucking tight that it's almost impossible not to burst with barely half my dick inside her. I can't tell if she's crying out in pain or pleasure, but I have gone way too fucking far for me to stop.

There is something insanely hot about fucking my nanny in the first place, especially after watching her act like a mom for all this time. I grab her tits, even if I promised myself I would save them for later. It's hard to get a good grip, but she has so much that it's hard for me to miss a handful. Once I have a good hold of her, I slide my dick even deeper.

How the fuck does this thick, curvy woman have a pussy this tight? She fits my dick perfectly and her tightness grips me with just the right amount of pressure. Almost too much pressure. I have to stop myself from immediately cumming inside her.

I want to cum in my black nanny so fucking badly it hurts...

She moves her ass a little and I have to stop touching her tits to press her deeper into the bed and stop those movements. Quin is so fucking sexy that those slight gyrations are more than enough to force me to cum before I'm ready. Her pussy already has a perfect grip on my dick.

I groan and slide inside her just a little more. Those inner walls grip me like a hand making a fist and I can feel Quin's sweet ass pussy drawing the cum straight out of my balls. I can't finish yet. Not until I make this woman cum again and not until I get every last inch of my dick inside her.

Reaching around the front of Quin's body, I add to her pleasure by slowly stroking her clit. The round nub grows with excitement as I rub her soaked pussy lips in slow circles. Her moans now are true signs of pleasure. Gentle. So fucking sexy. I kiss her cheek through my ski mask, careful to keep my features obscured but unable to prevent my three-day old beard from scraping against Quin's cheek as I kiss her.

Goddamn, her pussy feels good. I can't keep this slow pace any longer. I need every inch of this woman's pussy throbbing around my cock. I want to give her goddamn everything if it will just keep her pussy wrapped around my dick. She makes me feel out of fucking control. I can't stand it. I just want to touch her. To feel more of her. To have her.

And to mark her...

Sinking my teeth into Quin's throat, I surprise her by thrusting the rest of my dick deep into her pussy.

EIGHTEEN
QUIN

I have never felt anything so painful and pleasurable as this stranger's dick buried all the way inside me. His weight pins me to the bed and the immense girth of his dick keeps me so stretched out that I can't help but voluntarily remain completely still. Holy fuck, he feels amazing.

Hot shame flushes through me, but he thrusts his hips so his dick rams inside me all the way and I can't experience shame because the immediate sensations of pain and pleasure overwhelm my body. I grip the bedsheets and feel his hips cupping my ass as he buries himself inside me.

My first time. With a stranger. A monster. And the worst part about that is that having him inside me feels so good physically. It's better than anything I've felt in my life. Especially since the crime I committed. The weight of what I did formed this numbness around me which this man cracks open, allowing emotions to spill out.

"Fuck," he grunts as he bottoms out in my pussy. "You are so tight. You feel so good."

His lips are so soft on my ears and neck as he begins to move that I nearly cum just from his kisses. My pleasure heightens when the stranger moves his hands to my breasts. He doesn't have to tell me that he likes them. I can feel his appreciation in the way he touches me and even if I know how fucked up it is... his desires make me want to push back against him.

I just wouldn't want Tanner to find me like this... betraying him...

The man kisses my neck and his rough stubble sends pleasure shooting through me again. I moan loudly, which provokes an immediate response from the intruder. His hips move faster behind me and his breathing gets heavier. With each thrust, the friction between my legs pushes me closer to a multi-orgasmic climax. Holy fuck.

This just feels too good...

"I want you," he growls. "I want you so fucking bad."

Those three words break me. "I want you."

Maybe it would be hard for anyone else to understand, but I went my whole life feeling like nobody wanted me. Not my birth parents. Not the white folks who adopted me... nobody. I've never been allowed to feel anything about it. To just snap and go fucking crazy. Until now...

His fingers brush against my clit again and he rubs slowly as he keeps fucking me. He wants me to want him back. I don't know why because I don't even know who he is. But his deep voice with its light, commanding Southern twang bends me to his will. I feel the dark and immediate urge to obey.

I push my hips back against him and I don't fight. I let the man who broke into my bedroom and fuck me with a ski mask take my pussy like it belongs to him. I moan. I thrust back as he strokes my clit and allow myself to feel everything. The orgasm that hits me nearly knocks me the fuck out.

The intruder pushes his big dick inside me all the way, stretching me out as he rubs my clit and holds my body against his like I belong to him. It's intimate. Hot. Impossible for me to stop myself from responding. The next moan out of my mouth is embarrassingly loud and prompts him to slam his hands over my mouth again.

"Now it's my turn," he growls in my ear and then he resumes fucking me from behind at a steady, faster pace. He doesn't care about my pleasure anymore, just satisfying himself. The masculine grunts he makes as he fucks me expose just how much he's enjoying himself and I can't stop myself from cumming again just hearing how much this man wants me.

"You're so hot," he whispers. "Hot enough to make a baby with…"

I nearly scream because… instinct. This man is a stranger. It's bad enough that I'm throwing it back like Megan Thee Stallion on him. The pressure against my lips prevents any sound from coming out as this 'baby' comment brings a different drive out of this intruder.

He fucks me harder. Deeper. I can't scream. I can't stop him. He's going to put a baby in me and there's nothing I can do about it. All I know is that this man is someone strong. Muscular. Sexy. A psychopath with a big dick…

Before I can find any way out of my panic, he thrusts forward one last time and empties himself inside me. Thick hot liquid gushes inside me, and my traitorous body responds with slow waves of pleasure. Cum leaks out of my pussy, but he keeps spilling more between my legs.

I can't stop this from happening. Except if I get Plan B…

. . .

But how the hell could I possibly get Plan B tomorrow without Tanner finding out...

The stranger bites my neck, yanking me away from panicked thoughts about Tanner. I shouldn't be thinking of him right now... It's wrong for so many reasons. The bite on my neck forces goosebumps all over my skin. I still can't scream. I just yield to the monster who climbed in through my window and emptied his cum inside me.

"You're already fucking sexy," he murmurs. "I can't wait to watch you get bigger."

"Who are you?" I whisper weakly.

He chuckles and kisses my cheek.

"Go to sleep. Don't follow me. Don't get off that bed or I'll fuck you senseless again. Wait for me to leave and lock the window once I'm gone. Do you understand?"

He's so close to me that his scent invades my nostrils. The powerful dominance he just exerted over my body bleeds into my consciousness, making me bonded enough to this beast to obey him. The man slowly removes his dick from between my legs.

I feel empty without him but so fucking blissful with all the cum he emptied inside me. I don't know why it makes me feel so good, but it's a light, gentle high that strips me of any will to fight or disobey him. Maybe it's exhaustion. Fear. The throbbing in my ass and thighs.

. . .

But I don't move. He climbs out of bed, slides his clothes on and disappears.

I get up, just like he asked, and lock the window behind him. I don't even see where he disappears when he climbs out of the window. There aren't even any trees around, so it's a real mystery. I'm too scared to run outside and go after this stranger. He could be anyone... I don't know why the hell he seemed so familiar.

I climb back into bed and in the morning when I wake up, nothing that happened the night before feels real. When I get out of bed into my slippers, cum dribbles out of my pussy all over my inner thighs and I have confirmation that the insane situation the night before actually happened.

I'm no longer a virgin — and I don't know who fucked me without a condom, possibly getting me pregnant. This is an emergency — and it's one I don't have time for because I have a full time job of looking after a biker's infant daughter. Avery's baby monitor sends a couple alerts to my phone and my day as a nanny begins...

Although I hate admitting it, Tanner was right about the job coming naturally to me. Avery is half awake by the time I get to her room and it doesn't take much for me to gently wake her. She smiles whenever she sees me and it makes me so angry that Tanner doesn't appreciate those little moments with her.

Avery clings to me and gurgles when I take her to the changing station for a desperately needed morning diaper change. This is the hardest part of the morning and often an experience of disgusting discoveries about babies and digestive systems. I'm lucky that this morning's diaper change isn't the worst I've seen.

While I change Avery's diaper, it's like nothing that happened the night before actually happened. I can stuff everything into this compartment in the back of my mind until my boss manifests out of nowhere, knocking on Avery's bedroom door with his ham fists. I freeze and Avery finds my sudden reaction entertaining.

"He he he!" she cackles dramatically while I debate the merits of pretending I don't hear the door and letting Tanner cook outside for a little.

"Quin? Are you in there?"

He has cameras everywhere, so he knows I'm here. I guess my plan to ignore him won't work then. I sigh and while holding Avery, I open the door. The look on Tanner's face is... different. Very different. I only notice it for that first minute of eye contact. Just as soon as I notice the difference, it fades away and he offers a gentle smile.

"I just thought I would check in."

I'm not wrong to be suspicious. I can't remember the last time Tanner has "checked in" on the baby he wants nothing to do with.

"Everything's fine," I say, no longer concerned with reading my boss's emotions and far more worried about hiding mine. Last night, a man climbed into my bedroom window and if Tanner finds out about that, I doubt he'll react well. At all.

Right now, I'm the only one available for him to hurt so the best course of action seems to be keeping my mouth shut.

"Okay," he says, those pale ass cheeks of his turning a suspicious shade of dusky pink. I hold Avery closer to me, but Tanner shocks me by reaching his hands out for her.

"Why don't you let me hold her? I can manage her while you make breakfast. I'm sure you're hungry."

I don't immediately let go of Avery. Nothing like this has ever happened before since I moved in with Tanner and I won't let his suspicious behavior go unchecked. He looks out at me beneath unfairly luscious blond and ginger eyelashes with an expression that I could easily mistake for warmth if I didn't know any better about his persistent insensitivity.

"I normally eat after Avery. I don't need you to step in," I say as politely as possible. Although my suspicions and my own guilty conscience are making this room genuinely difficult to remain in. It feels like Tanner is getting bigger and taking up more of the room. I try to sidestep around him, but he gets in my way and holds his hands out for Avery.

"I'm telling you as your boss. I'll take Avery."

Reluctantly, I hand her over. She gazes at Tanner with immediate suspicion and then smacks him in the face with her fist. I bite on my lower lip hard to stop myself from laughing. He turns bright red again and then takes her little fist, pressing it to his lips.

"I get it," he mutters. "I've been a dick. Come on. Quin says she's going to make you the finest baby formula money can buy... Or whatever kids eat at this age."

Avery makes more confused sounds, but she doesn't start crying, so I let my boss hold her and follow him out to the kitchen. Each step towards the kitchen only increases my anxiety. I have to watch Tanner's muscular ass (literally) walking in front of me as he does something that's so unfairly sexy.

I've never seen him hold Avery before like this. He looks so protective. So damn good.

The thought enters my head and guilt follows. It's all well and good to notice Tanner's muscular ass, but I had sex last night. Unprotected sex. I need to get Tanner's muscular ass out of the way so I can get Plan B and stop this from becoming a much bigger problem.

If he notices my agitation when we enter the kitchen, he doesn't show it. He actually seems like he's in a better mood than usual, so I get it in my head to take advantage of his good mood and get him out of the way so I can buy Plan B. My strategy is simple. He lets me take Avery on a short walk around 11:30 a.m. before lunch. Her stroller has a tracker on it and I have to keep my phone location on so he can watch vigilantly.

There's a CVS on our short route so I can just pop inside, get Plan B on one receipt and a popsicle on the other. Once Avery comes home with blue lips, he won't ask any further questions and I'll be safe. No pregnancy.

Of course, possible pregnancy is only my most immediate problem. The stranger might come back. He got into the house so easily the first time... what the hell would stop him from entering the house again?

I pull ingredients out of the fridge as Tanner sits with Avery and sings her some weird ass lullaby I've never heard the words to before. I try not to smile at how goofy he sounds singing to her. This isn't the time for smiling – this is the time for plotting how I'm going to stop myself from getting knocked up by a stranger...

NINETEEN
STEEL

Investigating club business in the desert...

I keep my gun trained on the woman curled up beneath a couple blankets and making some desperate effort to hide herself behind three kegs of beer. She makes a terrified yelping noise and then sits up, drawing her knees to her chest. I can tell that she's a grown woman, but this little thing is damn petite.

"What are you?" I ask her. "Some type of Nazi whore?"

She makes another yelping sound and sticks her hands up in the air. Immediate surrender. Judging by the way her ass is shaking and looking at my gun, she's never been in a situation like this before. Even with the moonlight, it's too dim for me to get a good look at her.

Her skin is dark, but her eyes look all Chinese. I don't think she's an Indian. They have a particular way about them that seems completely absent here. This woman is something else entirely, but I don't know what. Her hair has the same texture as

Juliette's... thick and bushy. But she can't be black with eyes like that.

She has to be some type of Asian or Indian.

Her whimpering and surrender don't mean she's entirely innocent. For all I know, it could all be an act. After all, I found her here hiding in some Nazi compound in the middle of the desert. It would be stupid as hell to let my guard down.

"Stop crying and stand up."

She cries harder. Christ. I don't want this woman getting under my skin, but there's something about watching one of them cry that has always melted me. This place is too fucking creepy for me to chill.

"I said stand up."

When she stands up, I get a good look at her, not like I get much information from looking at her. Keeping my gun trained on her, I use the flashlight I brought to scan her from head to toe. It's not just so I can get a better idea of her ethnic origins — although I want to know if she has any relation to Oske, or someone else we have problems with.

A woman this color can't be welcome out here. But she's not a cop. She doesn't have the smell on her.

"What are you doing out here?"

She doesn't answer. It's so fucking quiet that I hear a coyote howl. Scares the fucking crap out of me.

"I asked you a question. Don't make me put you in the ground."

"I don't know where I am," she says with a shaky voice. Shaky, but sexy. I keep the gun trained on her even if she has a voice that could make my dick hard under any other circumstances. "I left my car ten miles west. I tried to find somewhere before sundown but there were these —

Christ. She breaks down crying again and I struggle to keep my shit together. The more time we stand around having emotions, the more danger we're both in. Unless this bitch is the danger. All 5-fucking-feet of her.

"Stop crying," I growl. "What did you see? Tell me."

"T-they had a man..." she says, sobbing uncontrollably and then nearly falling over. I almost think it's a ploy, but I see her headed straight for the ground with no chance of bracing herself so I catch her — against my better judgment. Shit. She's really unconscious. Scared out of her fucking mind.

Neither of us have the privilege of falling unconscious around here.

"Hey," I snap at her. "Wake up. Wake up and tell me everything you saw."

I have to shake her pretty hard to get her awake and I start to get scared that I rattle something loose in the pretty woman's head from shaking her around so hard. But her eyelashes flutter open around those strange Asian-looking eyes.

She braces herself against my chest. The brief contact sends a surge of something dead wrong straight through me. My body tightens and I offer absolutely no resistance when she shoves me away and stumbles back to a position of standing on her own feet.

I don't have the gun trained on her anymore, which seems to make her a little more relaxed. She doesn't fight. She doesn't run. But she looks scared out of her mind.

"I watched them beat two men naked and cut their heads off," she says. "One of them saw me, but I managed to hide and the others convinced him he'd done too much cocaine but... they're going to come back. They're going to find my stupid Jeep and—

Here we go again... another fucking breakdown. This time, we definitely don't have time because I hear noises. Engines. She must hear them too because the skinny thing gives me one horrified look and just as senseless as a doe in the highway, she takes off. It's instinct — but a stupid fucking instinct.

"Hey! Get back here!"

It surprises me that she's so fast, but we don't have time for tricks and antics right now. I yell at her to get back here one more time, but she doesn't fucking listen, so I take off after her. Doesn't matter how fast she is, I have much longer legs and once I get going, it doesn't take long to get close to her.

I skid to dead stop when the woman screams and then she flies forward and seemingly disappears off the face of the earth. What the fuck?!

The next scream sounds even louder than the first. If the men on the bikes heading our way didn't hear us before, they sure as shit heard that ear-splitting scream coming out of this woman's mouth. Fuck. I scan the ground with my flashlight, struggling to get a stable beam of light through my shaking limbs. Too much adrenaline isn't always a good thing. In the army, they train you how to deal with that rush. In prison, your best bet is giving in to every fucking impulse that comes through your head if you want to survive the mentally ill motherfuckers trying to end your life.

I think like a prisoner, not a soldier. But you don't have to be a soldier to see a big fucking hole in the ground. I jog to the edge and see her down there screaming her fucking head off and surrounded by two dead bodies.

Bodies that I recognize. Club members. And if I don't recognize the bodies, I recognize the severed heads. I categorize the dead in my head as I lean over the edge of the hole and reach for the woman stuck inside.

"Grab my hand. Now," I command her.

The engines get louder and I need to get this woman out of that hole and back to the truck. I don't have time to react. Even if I have family in that hole. She stumbles over a severed head as she keeps screaming her head off and scratching her way through mud and worse towards the wall of the mass grave.

When I get hold of her hand, it takes no effort to lift her out of the grave, she's that fucking small. What takes the effort is calming her ass down. Her screaming nearly blows out my eardrums once I get my hands on her and try hugging her close so she can feel that human warmth and calm her ass down.

That doesn't work.

"You have to calm down," I growl at her. "CALM. DOWN. My own fucking brothers are in that hole and if you want to survive, you need to listen to me."

She wraps her arms around my neck. Good. Then she kicks me, almost hitting my balls. Bad. I pinch her hard on the leg for that and she yelps loudly, biting into my shoulder. Doesn't matter. I have her attention and she's not screaming her head off. She sinks her teeth into my shoulder as I make every effort possible not to make a sound.

If I have to calm her down, I have to *be* the source of her calm. Even if this little menace has her teeth deep into my shoulder. I breathe slowly. Waiting for her to catch up. Ignoring the engines growing louder and telling myself it's just because the desert is so damn empty I can hear them.

You have time.

"Bite me all you want, brat," I growl at her. "You're coming with me."

I drag her to the truck and toss her in the passenger side. She sits back limply staring ahead. Shock. Terror. Some fucked up combination of both. *She's pretty.* I hurry around to the other side of the truck and start it up. She looks over at me bewildered and terrified.

"Don't kill me."

"I'm not going to kill you."

She glances at the tattoos on my forearm. Scared. And she finally realizes I'm a biker.

"You can call me Steel."

"Joslin," she says. Then her brow furrows. "Is that your real name?"

"It's the name you need to know."

· · ·

I gotta get us out of here before we end up headless in a hole somewhere.

The two of us will have plenty of time to get to know each other...

TWENTY
CASH

She acts like nothing happened between us.

What the hell is wrong with Quin? She has to be pretending. Playing a game with me... But she just looks so damn earnest. I don't understand.

I have never fucked a woman in my life who hasn't become immediately and permanently attached to me. Instead, Quin has me sitting here holding this baby and watching her cook like she didn't have my dick coating every inch of her inner walls with my baby juices.

This is wrong. Completely fucking wrong.

"Avery and I are going for our walk at the usual time today," she says after a painfully long silence. Well, I assume it was painful for Quin because I was trying to make it that way. I need her to talk to me. To give me some acknowledgement that last night happened between us.

That she felt how fucking good it was to finally relieve the obvious tension between us. The tension she's currently pretending doesn't exist. This is so much worse than having a teenage crush. I used to just get one of my sisters to manipulate the truth out of my teenage crushes. With Quin, I have to stare at her beautiful, blank, emotionless face and guess how she feels.

Every second of guessing kills me.

"I'll come with you," I offer desperately. Quin immediately frowns.

"Why?"

I have to come up with an answer that a woman will want to hear that serves the second function of keeping my concerns private.

"I am taking your criticisms seriously. I need to be there for Avery."

Quin's scowl deepens.

"You don't have to come on a walk with us."

"I could take Avery and leave you here," I offer. She turns around and keeps cooking angrily.

I didn't know a woman could cook angrily until Quin, but I'm almost certain she's going to chop my balls off next the way she's slamming that knife into the cutting board.

"I didn't know babies ate onions."

"That's for my breakfast," she says snappily.

What the hell did I do wrong?

I don't fucking understand this woman at all, honestly. We share a beautiful and incredibly hot night together and she acts like I'm fucking nothing to her.

"It looks good."

. . .

She doesn't answer that. Once she feeds Avery, she flips her omelet and I offer to take Avery again. This time, the baby is fussy when she gets in my arms and I know her hesitation is due to her following Quin's cues. What the hell is wrong with her?

"Is everything okay?"

"Why wouldn't it be?" She says in a low, steady voice. Nothing suspicious there. Maybe that's the problem. She's too damn good at hiding and I don't like it.

"Just wondering if you slept okay."

"I slept fine," she says sharply, giving me an unmistakable glare. What the hell? I pretend I don't notice it and mumble something about getting Avery a bath before the walk.

Quin says that it's a good idea and then I disappear to turn over in my head again and again what the hell is going on.

At first I was concerned, but now I'm just pissed off. I made her cum. I kissed her neck. We connected. I don't understand...

Getting Avery dressed is harder than I expected it would be because she doesn't like that I'm not Quin. I try to be gentle with her and almost find myself bonding with her as I get her clothes on...

I can't let myself latch onto those little traits that I think makes her a Hollingsworth. She's not mine. She can't be... and when she has to leave this place, I'll get hurt if I get attached. It's smart to stay distant. It's what dad would have recommended and Aunt Deb knows it, which is why she doesn't put up too much of a fight when I make my point.

Once I leave Avery's room and return to the living room, Quin's body folds in on itself again. She considers me warily as I bounce Avery a little, but her looking at me like that just frustrates the hell out of me after a morning of trying to get close to her and meeting a stoic brick wall.

. . .

I knew Quin wasn't like other women when I met her, but this is something I've never experienced before. I took her virginity and she doesn't seem to care if I live or die. She doesn't seem to care that I'm taking her feelings into consideration and looking after Avery the way she wants me to.

"You go alone," she says with a tight voice. "It's nice that you're spending more time with Avery."

This isn't what I wanted, but she barely looks at me as I get the rest of Avery's clothes on. I give her another chance to join us and she turns me down definitively.

What the hell did I do wrong?

When I get back, Quin is nowhere to be seen until I summon her. She has a big ass lunch spread made for me. I wonder if she's trying to appease me or something but again, there are absolutely no emotions on this woman's face. I find it fascinating.

She could get away with murder if she wanted to...

The only time I truly made her lose control is when I had her pressed beneath me in bed. A desire that grows the longer she turns her nose up at me and ignores me. She can't ignore me when I have my dick buried to the hilt in her pussy.

I'm about to confront Quin about her attitude when I get a phone call that I wasn't expecting.

Not a good sign considering my situation, but at least it's not Southpaw calling.

. . .

"Aunt Deb? Good news for me?"

"I knew that baby was family."

My heart drops into my ass.

"So..."

"Not yours," she says, exhaling with deep, deep sadness. "That baby is your father's. She's your *sister* Tanner."

"That's not possible."

"Your father knocked up a 16-year-old the night the club-house blew up."

That sounds like dad. Our mutual silence tells me Aunt Deb is thinking the same thing.

"My mom can't find out," I say. Maybe it's fucked up but my first thought is protecting her. She had enough misery with my dad's running around when he was alive. The last thing she needs is this baby.

"That's not the worst part."

"What's the worst part?"

"Tamiya tells me this took so long because they were tracking down the child's mother. She's the daughter of some Neo-nazi. Not someone high level but a member of some group called the Midnight SS. Have you heard of them?"

The Shaws tend to keep their women informed on club business. I think that's why Aunt Deb fled our grandfather's iron fist into the arms of Harlan Shaw the second she got a chance. She fits in well with the Shaws. Unlike a lot of women involved in our lifestyle, Aunt Deb can handle the hard shit. And unlike the Blackwood women, she handles it without getting her ass stuck in prison on a bullshit charge.

"Can't say I've heard of them."

It's a lie, obviously. But I prefer to keep certain things private.

"What about Wyatt?"

"I haven't told him about this."

"I know," she says. I understand her implications. I've kept this secret for too long and she thinks it's time I tell the club. I suppose the idea doesn't seem so terrible now that I know the baby isn't mine. But this can't get back to my mother.

"What the fuck do I tell him? He'll know you kept the secret from him."

"He understands how the club works," she says calmly. Aunt Deb talks like she's been in control of this situation the entire time. I can't help but give in to her desire to pull some strings around here. When it comes to babies and family... I'm lost. Most of us are lost.

None of us expected our dads to leave this earth so soon. I don't know if the club can handle more loss without everyone losing their shit. Especially not any of the crazy ass Blackwoods.

"I'll call him tonight."

"Good," she says. "And how is that girl you've been hiding from me?"

"What girl?"

"I raised three sons, Tanner. I know you've been sneaking some girl past me and you haven't needed me to watch Avery as much for the past couple months. Is it serious?"

"It's just the nanny, Aunt Deb. I'll call Wyatt and then get back to you."

She spills out more affection than I can handle, so I have to hurry and get off the phone before the sentiment causes me to sink into the ground. I don't look forward to telling Wyatt about this. He can keep a secret, but it's the nature of the secret that I don't enjoy.

And who the hell is supposed to look after Avery in the long term now that we know my dad had a cheap night with an underage girl and now... *this baby is all alone if I don't take full custody of her.*

I don't know why the thought makes me feel so damn cold. I never planned on keeping this child. I planned on discovering her true father and sending Avery off to *him* – the irresponsible motherfucker who knocked up some biker trash. I can't abandon Avery. The thought sends me immediately into deep, bitter brooding. At everyone. At everything. At myself.

A knock at my office door startles me, but it can only be one person, so I gruffly invite her in, despite my increasingly sour mood.

She lost some of that fire she had earlier, which I certainly appreciate because I was finding that fire quite damn frustrating. I like seeing her on her toes like this. Not only is it sexy as hell watching her approach me with her head bowed in some mixture of defeat and submission, it makes me feel like she actually needs me. I like that feeling.

Considering her continuing this pretense that our night together meant nothing, I don't mind this dominated behavior.

"I have to ask you something," she says, her voice heavy and dark. I meet her gaze, waiting for her to confess that she remembers everything and that our night together was the most special she's ever experienced. My gaze doesn't leave hers as I wait for her to fulfill my expectations.

"Anything you want, Quin."

It's hard to stop myself from running my tongue over my lips, imagining how delicious her cunt might be right now.

"I need to get Plan B."

My hand clenches into a fist almost unconsciously. I have to stop myself from slamming my hand into the desk like a caveman. If we're going to play this game. Fine. Let's play.

"Why would you need Plan B?"

I'm sure I can barely contain the anger in my voice. I've never been good at hiding my feelings. It's the red hair and damn near translucent skin constantly betraying everything in my head and heart.

"I-I met someone and I've been seeing him secretly on Avery's walks. That's why I was so uncomfortable earlier but... I'm sorry, okay? I just really need this."

Her wide brown eyes are so earnest when she looks at me that it's hard for me to believe that this little brat is lying through her teeth.

"Met someone?"

"Yes," she says confidently. "It was quick and passionate but... I'm committed to taking care of Avery. I don't want to have another baby."

I must do a terrible job of hiding my anger because she begins blustering through an apology.

"I know I put Avery in danger but I promise it won't happen again."

She promises, does she?

Quin shuts up when I give her a furious glare.
"That's enough. The answer is no."
"What?"

There's her fire again. Not like it makes any difference. The audacity of this woman to demand that I give her birth control after our night together is beyond insane. What game is she playing with that lie? Passionate love affair?

If I hadn't taken her virginity myself, this lie would have utterly devastated me and sent me on a wild goose chase to murder this alleged lover.

"I said no," I repeat calmly, and then to fuck with her. "And when I find out whoever put his hands on you, I'll kill him myself."

Quin shocks me by meeting my gaze with absolute fire and fury. "I'd like that, honestly."

"I see."

Our argument has a downright fucked up effect on me. I'm rock hard and fucking grateful that Quin can't see it. Everything about her attitude right now is completely messing with my head. It's not just that she doesn't give a fuck, she's actively coming to me with this Plan B bullshit like I'm going to allow her to stop me from knocking her up.

My cock loses its stiffness when Quin's cheeks tighten and tears well up in her eyes.

. . .

"Please, Mr. Hollingsworth. I know I made a mistake. I know I did but... I can't have a baby..."

"Why not?"

She buries her face in her hands and her sobbing gets so intense that I can't stop myself from rising and wrapping my arms around her. Quin doesn't stop me from holding onto her, but she doesn't hug me back either. It's hard to stop myself from getting hard now that I have her in my arms.

"Listen," I say sternly. "I know you made a mistake but the chances of you ending up pregnant are very slim."

"How can you even say that?"

I'm lying, that's how.

"Because. I'm older. I know things."

"Like how to defy biology without Plan B?"

Defying common sense, I touch the top of Quin's head.

"Like you said, you made a mistake. You have more than enough money to deal with the consequences."

I pull away from her, my protective instinct passing once her sobbing subsides. I still don't understand this woman's game here. Once I let go of her, Quin considers me with a new expression on her face. Once I definitely don't understand.

"What about Avery?"

What is that face hiding?

. . .

"What about her?" I say sternly. "She still has you now. There's nothing to worry about."

My words clearly do nothing to comfort her. I don't need her comforted as much as I need to rid her of this foolish "Plan B" idea.

I'll have to handle that later.

Touching her gently on the shoulder, I give my sweet, confused nanny a stern command. "Return to your room, Quin. I have to make a business call."

TWENTY-ONE
QUIN

8 days ago, I walked into Mr. Hollingsworth's office to ask for Plan B. I didn't have the best lie prepared, but it was the best one I could think of on such short notice. I was so focused on my lie that I wasn't thinking about any other possible lies.

Every fiber of my being was entirely fixated on hiding my secrets from Tanner.

I never thought he might have more secrets than the ones I already know about. I should have known better. I thought this man was just a run-of-the-mill business man at best with the occasional dabbling in less-than-legal activities. Nothing as bad as murder.

That is... until he hugged me.

Until I smelled him.

. . .

The scent that I only catch when he has me pressed into his chest draws me back to the incident with the intruder in my bedroom and how he smelled when he pressed up against me and slid his cock all the way inside me while sucking on my neck and whispering the filthies phrases imaginable into my ear until I came.

Tanner smells like the intruder. I don't want to consider the unthinkable but eight days ago, I started to take notes.

Reasons Tanner could be the intruder – a document of Tanner's suspicious activities.

But eight days go by and nothing happens. Tanner seems moodier than usual and more withdrawn, but I have no more incidents with the intruder and Tanner acting withdrawn isn't exactly out of the ordinary.

The light of my life is honestly, Avery. Since our chat in his office, Tanner takes her walking, so I'm barely allowed to leave the house anymore. It's not an official rule but with cameras everywhere and Tanner's generally controlling behavior, I don't even dare to try. I can tell he's watching me because every time I wander into a room close to the front door, he suddenly appears.

I just tell myself that it's better than being in *federal* prison which is where I would be if anyone found out I killed my adopted brother. This prison has delicious food, unlimited television, and a beautiful view of the landscape. Tanner doesn't have neighbors for a quarter mile on either side, so his plot of land is beautiful, isolated, and entirely under his control.

Doesn't it make sense that the intruder could only be him, then?

. . .

For eight days, avoiding Tanner was pretty easy outside of situations related to Avery. Then, he calls me to his office after lunch and considering our last office conversation – I'm scared out of my mind.

I put Avery down for her nap and the one day I need her to stay up and throw tantrums over Cocomelon, she immediately falls asleep. Since Mr. Hollingsworth has the camera trained on Avery's bedroom, I can't waste another thirty minutes in here without him noticing. The best I can do is waste an extra ten minutes tidying the place up before I walk to his office.

Each step is so damn heavy, it's like I'm wearing platform boots instead of socks. The door of Tanner's office looks even more cold and uninviting than usual. Maybe that's just my projection of his feelings and attitude. I knock, although he obviously knows I'm outside because he invites me in when my hand barely grazes the door.

Tanner doesn't seem like he's in a bad mood, but he doesn't exactly seem happy either. Just serious. And handsome. I try not to make it obvious that I'm breathing deeply to see if I can inhale that identifying scent from earlier. I just smell whiskey. Way too much whiskey for this hour.

"I've known something for a while that I ought to tell you," he says. "Sit."

He has a chair for me this time, which is a lot more comfortable than standing in the middle of Tanner's office having a cry session, I suppose. He doesn't take his eyes off me as I sit down and when I'm seated, he still stares.

"I'm not Avery's father," he says. Then he stares at me and

waits for a response. I don't know what he expects me to say. The baby certainly looks like his...

"I'm her brother," he says.

Okay. Is that why he's been so weird the past eight days?

He sighs and drinks some more whiskey from the bottle. When he sets it down, his face seems even more red than before. Not just from drunkenness.

"Given the news, we should renegotiate your contract."

"If she's your sister then–

"My father is dead," he replies. "My mother can't know about this."

We make pointed eye contact and he doesn't have to say more for me to understand. His father stepped out on his mom and had another kid. Maybe even more. Damn.

"Okay. What does that mean?"

"It means Avery stays here until I sort out a better custody agreement."

My heart drops into my stomach. He's going to get rid of her. I knew theoretically I couldn't spend the rest of my life with Avery. She's not mine. I logically know that. But when you bond with a kid like that, the love never really goes away. Especially an innocent sweetheart like Avery. All we've had for the past few weeks is each other.

It's not like either of us could rely on Tanner...

I try to ask innocently, "Are there better options?"

There's a flash of frustration which quickly falls away.

"Not right now. She stays here with you. But given the change in circumstances, I need to update your contract."

"What about her mother?"

Tanner turns red. "She's a Nazi whore."

Okay. That sounds a little extreme. I'm guessing he doesn't want to tell me the truth because that can't possibly *be* the exact truth. When I keep staring at him, Tanner just looks impatient.

"So," he says. "Are you ready for our new contract?"

I nod. For Avery, obviously. Since the first night, the intruder hasn't come back, so I tell myself that won't be a problem anymore. And anyway, I have my suspicions about the intruder.

I just need to find a way to trap him...

Oblivious to my plans, Tanner slides a stack of papers across his desk. Clearly, he's known about this updated contract for a *long* time.

"What are the new conditions? Can you summarize?"

"Everythings highlighted," he says calmly.

My eyes scan the highlighted sections for changes.

. . .

Terms of Employment

Quin Nash agrees to provide childcare services for Tanner Hollingsworth's sister, Avery Hollingsworth henceforth known as AVERY for the duration of the next 39 weeks.

The first change hits me immediately, highlighted in orange. He wants to give our contract a definitive end in 39 weeks. Okay. I find the specificity strange, but notice nothing particularly unusual about it. All the tasks pertaining to Avery remain the same, which doesn't surprise me. The confidentiality agreement remains the same, not like that has been relevant.

This contract will be terminated at the end of the 39 week period unless Quin Nash produces a positive pregnancy test, in which case, she will remain in Tanner Hollingsworth's custody until he can assure the child's parentage.

What. The. Fuck.

"Tanner. Why did you put this section in?"

His glare strikes me as unnecessarily fierce.

"You confessed to running around getting fucked by strangers," he says harshly. "I have enough problems. Trust me, this is for your own good."

I want to argue with him, but I'm the one who came up with that stupid lie to try to get my hands on Plan B. My period isn't due for a little bit, so maybe I'll be just fine.

Right. I'll get my period and be completely fine, making this part of the contract unimportant enough that it doesn't matter if I sign or not. At this point... *I can't leave Avery.*

"It seems a little controlling."

"You don't have to sign it," he says. "I would happily let you go to get fucked by another stranger if that's what you want."

This is the second time my boss has used the word 'fuck' like that in front of me and I know he's drunk off his ass but damn... I give him a disapproving look and that gives Tanner enough motivation to stifle whatever rude comment might have popped out of his mouth next.

"I'll sign it," I say softly, putting my signature down for Avery's sake only. Tanner slowly sips more whiskey as he watches me sign the document. Once I'm done he exhales with relief and sets the whiskey bottle down.

"Good," he says. "I have to go out of town for a funeral tomorrow. My aunt will be here at 9 a.m. sharp and she'll be here with you until I get back."

"A funeral?"

"I don't want to talk about it," Tanner says gruffly. "I'll see you before I leave."

He gazes pointedly at the door to his office. Message received.

· · ·

"Great," I respond, desperately trying to hold together my professionalism. "I'll have Avery ready in time to say goodbye."

TWENTY-TWO
SOUTHPAW

Modern men don't get it. Chasing pussy will never be worth the trouble. Marriage on the other hand? Worth every fight. Worth every fucking hard moment – even when I'm the one causing most of those hard moments. I never thought I would have to bring something like this to Anna again. A list of the dead.

Hawk is on his way to Missouri. This time, Juliette agreed to a safehouse. Anna did too, but she hasn't left yet. Part of me doesn't want her to leave. If it weren't for the kids... I would keep this woman right by my side where she belongs.

"Your mom says it's the nicest spot you could hope for in Arizona," Anna says as she packs the last of her things in the Louis Vuitton suitcase I bought her last Christmas. She told me that she didn't have a real need for anything so fancy, but I insisted. I'm beginning to regret that sentimental purchase wrapped up in an apology for being a degenerate gambler...

"My mother lied to me three damn times about the Hollingsworth love-child situation. Excuse me if I'm not so quick to trust her."

"She started a college fund for Junior three months ago," Anna says, tossing a Ziploc bag of her weird womanly creams and potions into her suitcase. "She loves you. She also loves Tanner. I think she did the right thing."

She packs in silence. Tylee has Junior for the next hour so that I can say a proper goodbye to Anna. We don't get much time like this with the baby, but I appreciate every last one of these precious stolen moments. But the silence allows the weight of the latest news from Steel to weigh between us.

"I don't want to be here again," I tell her. "I'm sorry."

"You didn't kill six Barbarians in the desert," she says. "Just stay away from temptation while I'm gone."

Defensively, I come up behind her and wrap my arms around her. I hate even the slightest reminder that we have to be separate. Anna leans into my embrace. I love everything about my wife. I knew she would be mine the second I saw her walking around that gas station convenience store. From the second I met her, I proved I would do anything for her.

I kiss her neck, hoping she can't feel my sadness. I just want the gorgeous dark-skinned mother of my child to feel my love. Anna sighs and leans against me.

"Wyatt," she whispers sadly. I love how she says my name but this time, her concern fills me with guilt. I never wanted her in this position. But we can't let this go.

Jairus and Jotham Blackwood were both found beheaded in a ditch in the middle of the desert along with Tanner's cousins, Gage and Mason Hollingsworth. My second cousin, Christian Shaw and Hawk's first-cousin Coleton Sinclair were also in that ditch. Beheaded. Steel doesn't have much information and apparently, he got himself into trouble out there with some "witness" who he refuses to give details about.

. . .

All we know now is that we have closed casket funerals to arrange and an emergency club meeting to decide what we do about the Nazis. This shit is all connected: Oske and her baby kidnapping stunt, Tanner's infant half-sister and everything uncovered in the desert. As far as we know, Jairus and Jotham were out on a job when the neo-nazi fucks killed them.

There must have been some other reason, but our club meeting will determine all of that...

I squeeze Anna tighter.

"I will come back to you in one piece, woman. I promise."

She stops packing (finally) and turns to face me. Anna still has the incredible effect of making me rock fucking hard the second I properly look at her. The longer we're together, the more I fall in love with her.

"You can't promise that," she says, touching my cheek gently. She doesn't seem to blame me for it. Getting up on her tiptoes, my beautiful wife kisses me on the lips. She's so soft. So perfect...

"Maybe not," I whisper. "But I can promise other things."

"Like what?" she says.

"I can get you pregnant again."

Anna laughs. I'm not joking. I want more than anything to fill this woman with my seed again.

I thought once we were married and after our son was born that we would lose our passion for each other. I heard that's what would happen and I prepared myself to fight every temptation for the sake of loyalty to Anna. Nothing could have been further from the truth.

Every day I'm with this woman, I want her more. Just inhaling her scent and feeling her closeness makes me want her.

And we're already here. With a bed. I reach around the front of her clothes and slip my hand down the front of Anna's underwear. She gasps, accepting my fingers between her already soaked pussy lips. It helps knowing this woman wants me with every fiber of her being as much as I want her.

The mutual desire for each other burns both of us up and as I rub her clit in slow circles, she soaks my fingers in her juices and my dick gets impossibly stiff as I press into her ass. We have enough time to say goodbye if I'm quick.

Anna's pussy is too fucking good for me to do anything but take my sweet ass time. I keep rubbing her pussy lips until she moans and then I kiss all over her butt as I drop to my knees and pull those yoga pants and thong all the way off her ass. Anna's body changed once she had the baby and I became addicted to all the ways she got so damn thick.

Her ass cheeks got even bigger and I was already completely weak in the presence of her ass. I kiss each of her fluffy butt cheeks, fighting the temptation to bite her hard before sliding my tongue between her pussy lips. Anna's breathing slows once I kiss the back of her thighs as she accepts my desire to taste every inch of her before I take her.

It doesn't matter how many times I make love to her, she never stops tasting fucking delicious. I never stop wanting her just as much as I did when I killed that monster who thought he could touch a woman like this without proving his worth. I spread Anna's pussy lips open from behind, causing clear sticky juices to dribble out of her cunt before I even get my tongue inside her.

My dick wants to jump out of my pants she gets me so fucking hard. I thrust my tongue between her spread lower lips, getting deep inside her as I rub her outer lips with my fingers. She moans, pushing back against me and thrusting her ass and pussy against my face so she can feel more of my tongue.

I love how goddamn greedy she gets for having her pussy licked and I love the sounds she makes each time I hit one of her sweet spots and truly push her over the edge past that point of control.

Her orgasm builds slowly and I push my tongue into her deeper, letting her wet lips get sloppy all over my beard and nose as she cries out in pleasure and finally cums all over me. Her pussy tastes fucking delicious, so I can't stop myself from continuing to eat her out even past her point of climax. Her breathing is high-pitched and shallow, her pleasure too intense for her to form any words, but I can't stop myself.

It will be a long time before I get to eat my wife's pussy like this.

I need her.

I eat Anna's pussy like it's my last fucking meal until she loses her balance and leans over the bed with her ass exposed while I kneel there with my tongue in her pussy, just about ready to taste even more. I run my tongue over her ass, poking it into her asshole until she screams and attempts to desperately push me away from her puckered back door.

Nothing she does can stop me from pushing my tongue in her sweet black ass, so I keep eating her ass and rubbing her clit until she reaches another intense climax that gets my face and the bed soaked with her juices. To give her the slightest bit of a break, I lick her cum off her thighs while she gasps for breath.

Then I stand behind her and drop my pants and underwear in one swift motion. She's still so out of it that she barely realizes what happens until the head of my dick probes her soaked entrance. I slowly move between her lower lips, feeling every inch of her softness before I enter her. The first inch of her pussy is a mixture of bliss and torture as I hold back every instinct to cum inside her immediately.

Anna emits the hottest moan, making it even harder for me to hold back. Gasping for breath and holding onto my wife's hips, I plunge the rest of my cock into her with one sharp motion. I'm too desperate for her cunt to wait a second longer. We moan together as I rock my hips and fuck her hard into my bed. I made her cum so much that I can afford to be this impatient without any guilt.

Slamming my dick into Anna feels like heaven. I rub her clit to another orgasm and this time when she climaxes, the euphoria is too much for me to display any restraint. I push my cock all the way inside her and erupt. The animalistic groan that escapes my lips almost shakes the walls of my damn house it's so uncouth.

In the moment, the only thing I care about is Anna's soft hips, her wet pussy and the way her heat clamps down on my dick, drawing every last drop of cum from my balls.

I kiss her neck, completely unwilling to withdraw from her right away.

"I'm going to miss you," I growl.

"I can tell," Anna whispers, pushing her hips back against me slightly, beckoning me not to leave her right away...

TWENTY-THREE
QUIN

Tanner will be back in a day. I don't know where he is, but the woman Tanner assigned to stay with me — a nice white lady named Deborah — keeps me informed as much as she sees fit. Deborah is his aunt, but I would like her even if she wasn't related to Tanner.

She hasn't said anything to me in the past seven days but today she tells me in no uncertain terms, "Tanner will be back tomorrow."

I don't know how to feel about that. To describe the energy between us as weird would be an understatement. The new contract made me extremely suspicious and then Tanner has been strange ever since the whole Plan B incident. He acts like he doesn't trust me and then there's the incident with his hug.

His scent.

My suspicions.

I can't make any plans to test my suspicions until he gets back.

Until then, I have to just keep living the way I have been since Tanner left.

I would have appreciated the heads up that I would be in charge of his so-called safe house, but at least the guests are easy to get along with. Apparently, our place out in Arizona is the only one the bikers can send their wives and children to, so I won't be staying here alone.

I don't have any say in the situation – of course. Deb announces it to me at the last minute.

Juliette is stashed away somewhere else, but Anna Shaw, Deborah Shaw, Tamiya Blackwood and Rebecca Knight are here. Avery is still with us, as well as Juliette's baby. They have a good baby routine going together and it's nice to have Juliette for company.

Tamiya and Rebecca are private investigators and most of the conversations we've had since they all arrived have surrounded the mysterious incident that called the Rebel Barbarians to this unplanned meeting in the desert. Rebecca also suspects that Tamiya is pregnant, but she keeps brushing off the subject and turning everything back to the dead bodies found in the desert and the private investigation they have done into potential motorcycle clubs that might be involved.

I don't know enough about Tanner's club to guess about anything, but I absorb as much information as I can from their conversations and ask questions whenever I get confused. The way I understand it, they all suspect that Avery has something to do with the "situation" out in the desert. Tanner told me he had to go to a funeral.

I had to find out from Deb that this "funeral" wasn't something so casual, but the death of six bikers who were found headless in a mass grave out in the desert. I don't like talking about death and murder, but I try to act normal throughout the conversation, pushing out thoughts of blood. Death. The scent of bleach which always lingers in my mind when I draw those memories forward.

The night before Tanner gets back, Anna insists we have one last dinner together. The babies are all asleep and Rebecca has been rubbing it in everyone's face that she's not pregnant and can drink all the espresso martinis she wants. Deb Shaw joins her in project espresso martini, so they're both drunk as hell.

Considering the lack-of-Plan-B situation, I'm too scared to drink any alcohol. If I end up pregnant, I don't want the baby to have three spines or whatever happens when you drink early in pregnancy. Something bad. I remember that much from my health classes.

While the ladies without risk of pregnancy get slightly tipsy and a little energetic off the espresso martinis, Anna and I work on our spread for dinner. None of us have had a traditional black Thanksgiving in ages, so we get the crazy idea to have a Thanksgiving dinner on some random day in the middle of the year. Despite my white adoptive parents, I had Juliette, who had the best Thanksgiving dinners at her place growing up until her mom died. I can't wait to recreate the experience, even if nobody can throw down in the kitchen quite like Juliette. She has a talent.

We all love cooking and eating — except for Tamiya, who only loves cooking and clearly doesn't eat very much. She offers to make the sweet potato pie for dessert which makes me a little nervous because she's a little skinny to be trusted with dessert, but I have the responsibility of the greens and the baked Mac and cheese, so I have to let go and let God when it comes to the dessert.

Our fake "Thanksgiving" ends up being the most fun I've had in a *long* time. The espresso martinis and the atmosphere brings out the private investigator in everyone. Tamiya leads the conversation, unable to let go of the deaths in the desert.

"After Oske blackmailed me to kidnap a baby, Gideon is *not* going to let me get away with something like that again. I'd rather us feel safe."

Anna scoffs. "When have you ever felt completely safe since meeting one of those bikers?"

"Fair point," Rebecca says, slurring a bit. "But *I* don't have any biases and I have a list of suspects."

Tamiya gives her a warning look. Rebecca shrugs. "What? There aren't any bikers here."

Tamiya looks at Deb Shaw suspiciously.

"Deb and I got white girl wasted together. She's not going to snitch."

Deb Shaw laughs hysterically and throws her arm over Rebecca's shoulder. She's definitely wasted.

"I am *not* wasted," she says. "But I promise, I won't tell. I *promise.*"

"These men take loyalty seriously," Tamiya says. "Just make sure you know what you're doing before you end a life."

Rebecca clears her throat, clearly unconcerned. Deb giggles uncomfortably because of the alcohol, but that doesn't discourage Rebecca either.

"I have four main suspects with connections to the club who I believe should have their loyalty questioned."

Deb perks up and I wonder if Tamiya had a point about Rebecca being careful. Since I barely know what's going on, I want to know her theories, just out of curiosity. And, in the back of my mind, I might have to use this information as a bargaining chip with Tanner later. If I can't trick him into telling me the truth... maybe I can convince him.

Thankfully, I don't have to worry about his return until tomorrow.

"Spill," Anna says. "Because I don't know anyone stupid enough to cross my husband."

"Exactly," Rebecca says with a sparkle in her eye. "It wouldn't be someone close to the four co-presidents. Not *exceedingly close.*"

"They would have to have connections to the club to know about Oske. Or Avery."

"My first suspect is Savannah Hollingsworth."

Deb rolls her eyes. "She's a whore and a junkie. She's not smart enough to pull off something like this."

Rebecca nods. "Fair enough. I looked her up and she's been stripping in Florida right around the spot where Don Hollingsworth met her mom. Junkies might not plan something this elaborate, but if she has information, she might sell it."

"Is she sleeping with anyone in the club?" Anna asks.

"I don't know," Rebecca says. "That's why she's just a suspect."

"Next?" Deb presses her, clearly unimpressed with the Savannah theory. The next one really gets Deb Shaw's attention.

"Ruger's wife. Darlene Song."

Tamiya sighs. "Say that in front of Gideon and you're going to start a war."

"I heard Gideon beat his ass in a Taco Bell," Anna says knowingly. Deb Shaw erupts into peals of laughter at that revelation, making it hard for me not to smile because of her contagious ass drunken laughter.

"Is that what you're so worried about telling me?" Deb says.

"Yes," Tamiya says. "But she started it. So keep your ass going."

Rebecca looks smug, so clearly, *she* thinks this is the most likely theory.

"What type of woman would marry Ruger Blackwood?" Anna asks, wrinkling her nose. Rebecca might be impressed, but Anna isn't. I don't know enough about any of those people to even understand who might betray the Barbarians to a rival biker gang of killer Nazis.

"He got married to some piece of white trash when he was eighteen," Deb says, clearly unfiltered due to her martini. Tamiya tops off her glass from the martini shaker, at least half as entertained as I am.

"Where is the piece of white trash?" Anna says, hesitating over the more offensive words.

"Prison," Tamiya and Deb say together.

"*Unless*," Rebecca says. "She secretly got out early and she's on the run with the guy she dated before Ruger, who happens to be an Enforcer on the Midnight SS."

Even if you *want* to disagree with Rebecca's theory, it's the most concrete connection that any of us have heard.

"What's the Midnight SS?" I ask. I don't think I'm the only one who needs more information about that. Rebecca explains vaguely that they're a gang of dangerous bikers potentially after Tanner – and the entire family – but nobody in the room seems to know why.

"How is that even possible?" Anna says. "Wouldn't the Barbarians have heard of this club with such a close connection?"

"Do they seem like they're paying close attention to anything?" Rebecca says. "It sounds like there has been one problem after another the past year or so."

Anna shrugs. "I guess so."

"Are there any other theories?" I ask.

"Sure," Rebecca says. "Magnum Sinclair might have rented an apartment in Santa Monica to a Midnight SS member."

Anna shrugs. "He's a landlord. He doesn't know his tenants."

"It's still a connection," Tamiya says.

"Right," Anna says. "But maybe you had a point about being careful what we insinuate."

"I'll talk to Gideon," Tamiya says. "I can reason with him."

Anna raises her eyebrow. "Is Gideon the most rational option here?

"I know," Tamiya says with a smirk that is definitely more proud than remorseful. "But I can still reason with him."

"Nobody on that list is a Shaw," Deb says. "My son can handle this information objectively. Instead of involving your beloved hotheads... take it to him."

It's the comment only a drunken mother-in-law can get away with and everyone in the room must think she's lowkey right, because after about a minute of silence, Tamiya says. "Well. I can't argue with that."

We discuss our theories until late into the night. I'm the first one who can't seem to keep my eyes open, so Anna suggests I head to bed. The only comfortable sleep outfit that matches my vibe I can find to change into is some giant t-shirt that appeared in my laundry after Deb helped me out the other day. I throw that on over some underwear and climb into bed, ready to pass out.

All the club stuff they talk about should scare me more, but it just doesn't.

After the hell I went through...

I'm just happy to be free. I don't think I'll ever feel that unsafe.

Not with Tanner around.

It's weird but... I miss him. And the t-shirt I found in my laundry kind of smells familiar. The scent makes it easy to feel comfortable, which in turn makes it easy to fall asleep. Tomorrow.

I'll see Tanner tomorrow.

TWENTY-FOUR
REAPER

THE NEXT DAY...

I wouldn't call what I'm bringing home to Tamiya good news. The only good news I have for her is my solidified ideas for our matching tattoos to commemorate our first child once she's born. We finally know – *it's a girl.*

Rebecca dropped Tamiya off a few hours before I got home and she has the place cleaned up and dinner ready even if I've already told her a hundred times she doesn't have to do that.

"You think I shouldn't do anything," she says with annoyance every time I mention it. She's just mad that I think she doesn't have to be a fake cop with Rebecca Knight for money. Which she doesn't. But I let her do almost everything she wants as long as it keeps her from committing felony kidnapping again.

I don't even have my hand on the front door handle before Tamiya swings it open and jumps into my arms with a loud, excited screech. Even with a baby growing inside her, she's so damn tiny that I cup her ass cheeks and easily grip her and swing her around while she screams excitedly.

"You actually survived," she says, barely holding back her

doubt that I would make it through the emergency club meeting and "whatever mess we have planned".

"I promised I would come back."

Tamiya buries her face in my neck and I stroke her hair as I hold her close. Every time I hold her close, I think about our baby. I never thought I would become a father, but with Tamiya, it just feels right. She's my woman. My property. The only person I can imagine handling Gideon Blackwood's baby.

I imagine her growing, what it will be like to watch her swell with my kid, feel the baby moving around inside her... All that only makes me want to hold her closer – and get her ass into bed. We have a lot to discuss before I can get to that. I'm still happy just to hold her pretty ass close to me.

"I know," she says. "I know..."

Slowly, I set her down, but only because I want to kiss her. Our eyes meet and instead of having a rational conversation about my serious expedition, I grab this woman's cheeks and kiss her like we're at the end of a movie. I grab her cheeks, thrust my tongue into her mouth and suck on her lower lip, getting myself hot and ready for her before pulling away and gazing into Tamiya's eyes.

The glimmer of mischief across her face tells me she's thinking the same thing.

"I missed you, dirty girl," I whisper, running my thumb over her lip, which I just sucked on until it turned dark with blood.

"I missed you too, *Reaper.*"

My cock jumps in my pants when she calls me by my club nickname. This woman is so goddamn perfect. I kiss her again, pressing her up against the wall in the foyer and forgetting that we have anything to discuss except our raw physical needs for each other. Tamiya moans when my lips move to her neck. She's so soft. So ready for me.

"Take your pants off," I growl. "I want to fuck you right here..."

"Gideon..." she says sternly, switching to my government name. "The front door is open."

Shit. I barely noticed. I shut the front door with my foot and hike Tamiya up against the wall so I can follow through on my instinct to fuck this woman hard against the wall. She knows exactly what to expect since we always seem to find ourselves stripping each other's clothes off and making love like this.

We slide each other's pants off just enough that I can touch her bare pussy with the head of my dick. There isn't any getting her ready this time. Just desire. I touch her lower lips just to make sure.

"No," Tamiya says with a strained voice. "I'm pregnant and horny. Just fuck me."

There is nothing hotter than fucking a woman who's pregnant with your baby. I rub my dick over her pussy lips to feel her for the first time in what feels like forever.

"Did you touch yourself and think about me," I whisper as I suck her neck and slowly press the head of my dick against her entrance.

"Just like you told me to, daddy."

"Fuck, you feel so good," I whisper as I slide inside her an inch, cupping Tamiya's small round ass cheeks as I hold her up against the wall. Her pussy is so fucking tight and fits my dick perfectly.

I groan as I press my forearm into the wall and bottom out inside her as I kiss her neck. Tamiya moans from the way I stretch her out and this woman goes crazy when I kiss her neck, so the way I taste her possessively gets her riled up as much as anything else.

She moves her hips to meet my thrusts as I grab her butt and pump into her, fucking her hard against the wall.

"I missed you so fucking bad," I groan as I listen to Tamiya's breathing and watch her body react with the familiar undulations. I love watching her cum.

"Yes, baby," I murmur, encouraging her as I drive my dick into her. "Oh, yes baby. Take my big dick."

Tamiya moans louder and I can feel her cresting just over the edge of an intense orgasm. I push myself deeper inside her, enjoying every fucking part of joining with this woman. My woman. I bite down on her neck instinctively as she cums, marking her with my teeth, letting her know through shared pain how fucking much I missed her.

She clings to my shoulders, gripping my muscles fiercely as the waves of her orgasm render her completely vulnerable. My dick is ready to burst from watching her moan and surrender completely to me. The trust she has in me to spread her legs wide and lose herself like this is enough to drive me over the edge.

I hold her close to me and kiss her neck softly as I grunt, pressing into Tamiya with slow, short thrusts.

"I love you," she gasps as my quick thrusting forces another climax out of her. "I love you so much..."

I tease her nipples after her second I love you for the sheer pleasure of touching every inch of Tamiya's skinny body. Once I get my fingers around her nipples, she lets out the hottest moan that ends me for the night. My balls tighten and my cum shoots out of my dick like a goddamn volcano.

The noise I make is pure pleasure and surprise because I thought I could hold myself back, even red-faced and struggling to thrust into Tamiya's tightness. I push into her all the way, allowing ropes of my cum to coat her inner walls. Her pussy pulses desperately around my dick, clinging onto me and drawing me even deeper into her.

We're both covered in a slick layer of sweat and the last fucking thing I want to do is let go of this woman. But she shudders and presses her palms against my chest, begging for some relief as she gasps for breath. Poor thing needs air. I gently set Tamiya down and watch in complete awe as she presses her back against the wall and stares at me with a glimmer of excitement.

"That was intense."

"Yup."

"Skinny men," she says with a grin. "All the fat goes to their dick."

"Who the hell are you calling skinny?" I grunt, lunging towards her to swat her ass playfully. Tamiya skillfully dodges me but then returns to my arms for a hug. I kiss her and push her up against the wall again. It would be so goddamn easy to get lost in her again.

With the immediate tension out of the way, the business lingering between us makes it harder for us to get lost in another round of lovemaking. Tamiya is the first to pull away with the typical thoughtful sighing sound she makes when she has her mind all twisted up in an investigation.

"Did you learn anything out there?" she asks, getting straight to the point like her cop friend Rebecca taught her.

"That they're really dead."

My twin brothers -- Jairus and Jotham -- were killed out in the desert by the Midnight SS motorcycle gang for some unknown reason. After everything my mother went through, she shouldn't have to go through this. Not when she's almost out of prison. Not after just losing dad.

I didn't want to believe they were really dead, but I had to accept the truth.

I saw their bodies. Southpaw spared me seeing their heads but... he confirmed their identities himself. The mission to retrieve the bodies from the desert wasn't entirely successful.

Southpaw sent Ruger with a group of new recruits out to get the bodies and they couldn't get all the parts. Midnight SS must have been keeping watch or had a lookout. Gunfire popped out across the desert as they were loading the bodies up and with bullets flying, their priority shifted to getting the fuck out of there.

There were two bodies left behind – Ruger only got the heads of Christian and Coleton. So they brought those back to the clubhouse for the funeral in the new cemetery plot Hawk dug out himself.

Ruger still has a bullet in his right arm from loading up the heads in his escape attempt, and the doctor we got thinks he waited too long to have it treated. He hasn't listened to any advice Anna has given him through Wyatt over the phone, even if the boss's old lady is a smart cookie and knows her shit about nursing.

Ruger is just an idiot, plain and simple.

We still have no idea what the fuck is going on and the situation with the secret Hollingsworth love-child gives me a bad feeling.

It doesn't make any sense for a man to leave children all over the place. Those old bitter grudges over love and land can rip families apart. Don Hollingsworth should have known better and kept his dick in his pants. Now, Tanner has this baby who might be better off left to the Nazis and we don't have a goddamn clue how any of this connects to the deaths out in the desert, or Oske's fucked up plan to stop the Midnight SS from implementing a successful full-force attack against the club.

Silence lingers between me and Tamiya. She nods and grabs my cheeks, forcing me to look her in the eye.

"I'm sorry, baby," she says.
"That's life, isn't it?"

She runs her thumb over my lower lip.

"Rebecca and I have suspects."

"Who?"

"I don't want this to turn violent if it doesn't have to."

My eyes flicker to hers.

"It's going to get violent, Tamiya," I say to her sternly. "That's what we decided at the clubhouse. All out fucking war. Unanimous vote."

She doesn't look happy. But it doesn't matter. This is about blood and loyalty. I won't rest at night knowing those Nazi fucks are out there. What the fuck could people like that do to Tamiya if they got their hands on her?

I won't let that happen.

"What do you mean war?" Tamiya asks. I can hear the fear in her voice and I wish I could make it go away. But I can't.

Not until our work is done...

TWENTY-FIVE
CASH

I shouldn't be back here until tomorrow morning. That's what I told Aunt Deb. Everyone else is gone except her. Well, Avery is still in there and of course, Quin. That's who I'm making time for tonight. The shit I saw out there at the clubhouse is the type of shit that gives you a stronger appreciation for family.

For what matters.

The thought of Quin having any type of involvement in the mess I saw out there scares the crap out of me. Since I left Tucumcari, I've had it in my head that we ought to get ready to move. There are places I could rent in Santa Monica, or we could go somewhere far away from all club related activities -- avoid Route 66, where anyone might track her down and connect her to the club.

Every thought that crosses my mind on the long ride back home involves protecting Quin and Avery. Mostly Quin. I know I ought to be better at giving a crap about Avery, and it's not like I don't give a crap about her but... She's my father's mistake. She's not my daughter. Hell, that goddamn kid might be half the reason we have a bunch of Nazis up our asses.

Avery might be the reason we lost six club members.

Quin won't like the way I see things but... she doesn't like very much about me unless I have my mask on and I keep my interactions with her strictly to pleasuring her. I wonder if she really doesn't know it's me... or if she's pretending. I can't tell what's real anymore.

As much as I yearn for her company in the daytime, she's just not that type of woman... She only sleeps with me because I constructed an elaborate situation to make her feel like she has no choice.

Without my mask, without hiding the darkest parts of myself from her, she would never fall in love with a heartless biker. I might make her cum, but I can't make Quin fall enough. I'm not a good enough father, by her determination, just because I don't share her ability to fall in love with strange infants who bring trouble and expense...

Avery might be cute, but she can barely walk and she has already become a menace. I'll have to do everything in my power to protect her from the whore my father made her mother. Quin has a bigger heart than I ever will.

I run my hand along the seam of the window for the latch. I use a magnetic device to open it. Air-conditioning flows out of her bedroom into the muggy Arizona night. I don't have to climb much to get into her bedroom, but I have to raise one leg above my knees.

Once I get one leg into Quin's room, I can hear her breathing. By the time I'm standing in the middle of her bedroom floor, I can see her lying in bed. She looks like an adorable damn marshmallow sleeping peacefully.

. . .

It's a shame I have to violate that peaceful sleep and fuck that sexy marshmallow until I cream inside her.

I take one more step and Quin wakes up. I don't know which one of us regrets her waking up more since what alerts me to her awakened state is a sharp, surprised gasp.

Shit. I thought I would get a lot further before she woke up. Rushing forward, I throw what parts of Quin she managed to throw over the edge of her bed back onto the mattress and fling the covers off her.

My cock nearly jumps out of my jeans when I see what she's wearing beneath the covers. I don't think she means to tempt me with this, but she's wearing my old t-shirt and a pair of some boring cotton underwear that could never quite be boring on Quin because of how deeply her ass cheeks swallow every pair of underwear she wears.

I watch her closely. And her pantylines. And anything about her I can observe. She squirms and grunts in protest as I pin her body to the bed and immediately begin feeling up every inch of the woman I yearned for every goddamn night on the road. I couldn't wait one more night. I couldn't wait to exchange pleasantries with Aunt Deb and I definitely don't want Avery getting in the way of enjoying a nice slow fuck session with Quin.

"The people here are armed and dangerous," she grunts, trying desperately to fight me off. "You shouldn't be here..."

I don't know how the hell she stays so damn convincing.

"I can handle everyone in this house," I whisper. "Plus, maybe some pussy is worth dying over."

She grunts and throws an elbow at my chest. Aggressive. She's way more aggressive than she was in our first interaction. I take the hit to my stomach but pin her down so she can't pull any shit like that again. Quin grunts and keeps fighting me as I pin her down and finally stop groping every last inch of her body so I can get to the point. Kissing her.

Because I have her pinned face down, she can't see my face. She wouldn't be able to with the mask I have on, but this way, I leave nothing up to chance. When I kiss her, she makes a frustrated if not disgusted grunt. Subduing her is taking much longer than I thought and she isn't immediately yielding to my kisses the way I want.

With my dick begging for release, I don't have much patience for Quin's fussing, so I handle her the best way I know how. She yelps loudly as my palm makes contact with her ass. I take my chances that she won't wake anyone else and pretend that I don't give a fuck when I hit her again. This time she makes her best effort to stifle her yelping in her pillow.

"Fight me again when I come for your pussy and I'll tie you to the bed and pierce your clit until you remember exactly who you belong to."

My words are extreme considering I don't even have her clothes off, but I find myself not giving a fuck... Scaring the crap out of her works. Quin freezes and when I kiss her, instead of making a disgusted yelp, she whimpers softly. This is much better.

"I like you better when you're soft, Quin. This is the woman I miss."

She doesn't answer, but that doesn't surprise me. I touch her breasts. Her hips. I run my hand over the flesh on her ass that I just spanked senselessly. I doubt she'll be able to sit tomorrow. She winces just from my light touch. Maybe she's worried I'll hit her again, but I won't have to do that if she listens to me.

I kiss her neck, suddenly bothered by her silence.

"Did you miss me?"

"No," she says emphatically.

"I'll test that."

She grunts gently and then does her best to stifle the protest, remembering my previous response. The squirming picks up again when my hand travels to her mound and I gently rest my palm against the outside of her underwear. I barely have to touch her to have my answer about her arousal. The patch of her underwear I touch soaks my fingers instantly. For her panties to be this wet, her pussy must have been gushing like a waterfall the second her eyes snapped open.

"I knew it," I whisper. "You get so goddamn turned on when I sneak in through your window and dominate the fuck out of you..."

I pinch her lower lips, emphasizing my complete domination of her body and provoking Quin to emit a low, unwilling moan. She can't help but get turned on from every fucked up thing I do to her. This pushes every last one of her buttons and as much as I love this fucked up dynamic between us... she loves it too.

How hard did she really fight for that birth control?

"I love how soft your pussy feels," I whisper, pinching her lips a little harder, demonstrating my complete control more forcefully. Juices gush out the sides of her underwear, proving Quin's vulnerability to my forceful touch.

I feel like a goddamn monster. I don't care what she wants right now -- I need to cum inside this woman. Right. Fucking. Now.

Twenty-Six
Quin

I know last night happened because I wake up with cum all over my thighs and spilling out of my pussy from the multiple rounds of sex I had with the masked stranger. I can't admit to myself who I want it to be. I just know that it can't be my reserved boss, who keeps all his emotions so incredibly cool that he doesn't even let a baby's cuteness affect him.

It's *not* Tanner.

The thought makes me more uncomfortable than I want to admit.

After last night, everything just feels so wrong and confusing. I don't want to get out of bed.

Why did I let him fuck me? Why did I let him cum inside me?

. . .

This stranger put my legs behind my head and blocked my vision so he could raise that mask and eat my pussy with uncontrolled lust until I tapped out from pleasure. I tried to see his face but every time I came close to some small discovery about his identity, he would slip his tongue all the way into my asshole and make me scream.

This man violated every inch of me.

And made me cum even more than the first time.

I kept trying to draw him closer to me so I could smell him and get some fucking clue about his identity. Tanner shouldn't have been back here but... I still think this masked stranger smells like him.

If I get out of bed, I can search for evidence but if there's one thing I learned about Tanner Hollingsworth during his absence – and believe me I learned a lot – it's that he has one hell of a poker face. Anna told me so many gambling stories where her husband lost to him just because of his ability to button everything up and suppress any potential tempest of emotions with a cool exterior.

It must be a good trait for a redhead, otherwise likely to betray every thought in his head from the changes in his skin tone.

There were other people in the house last night, but none of them must have heard anything because none of them came to the door. I can't help but panic, thinking about what could have happened to Avery. Logically, I know the stranger left through my window and Avery's bedroom is practically fortressed off from the rest of the house.

This man didn't come for Avery, anyway. He came for me. Cum leaks all over my thighs as I climb out of bed, completely humiliated that I'm still wearing the gigantic t-shirt that must belong to my boss. The stranger pushed the shirt up over my breasts and marked them with dark purple hickies before pulling Tanner's shirt back over them.

Every inch of me is completely sore this morning. I turn over the events of the previous night in my head -- what little I remember through my exhausted haze, at least. I remember that man's scent. His strength. The combination of humiliation and pleasure as he made me cum.

But realistically? I don't know if this man could be Tanner. The man in my bed is passionate. Emotional. Rough but... he shares everything. Tanner on the other hand is completely buttoned up and reserved. He barely shows any emotion except frustration.

He isn't supposed to be back from his biker "club" meeting yet. From everything I've heard and certainly everything I've experienced with Juliette and her husband, this club sounds more like a gang than anything else. But I have my own dirt, so I don't want to judge folks on their activities outside the scope of the law.

People in glass houses and all that.

If Tanner hasn't returned yet... who climbed in through my window?

Hearing shuffling down the hall, I finally feel ready to leave my bedroom. I wipe myself clean as best as I can without taking a shower and change into normal full-coverage pajamas before I follow the sound of voices at the end of the hall. I don't know why I half-expect to see Tanner there waiting for me. Instead, Deb has Avery and the 'voices' are just Avery talking to her.

"I gave her a morning change and fed her for you," Deb says, smiling as she bounces Avery on her hip. I see the slight family resemblance between Deb and Avery when they're close like this.

Avery barely has any hair yet and what she has is light enough that it could go either way -- blond, pale brown or maybe some auburn.

"Thanks," I answer Deb, trying to act like a normal woman who didn't have a strange sexual experience with a masked stranger the night before.

"Did you sleep well?"

She looks alarmed when I meet her very normal question with startled eye contact. I get a hold of myself.

"Yeah. Nothing weird," I reply. "Is Mr. Hollingsworth back yet? I thought I heard male voices."

"No," she says. "He's far out. He'll be back around lunch."

My stomach drops. Far out? If Tanner is far out... who the hell came through my bedroom window?

Deb continues. "I was talking to my son on speaker phone."

"Wyatt?"

"No," Deb says, her face darkening. "I wish. It's Owen."

I never heard of or met anyone named Owen Shaw, so I just nod politely.

"He's my baby," she says. "Well. If you can call a 28 year old man a baby..."

The way I see it, Avery will always be my baby. Even if she's someone else's. Even if she's fifty-years-old. I might not be a mother but... I get it.

"Is everything okay?" I ask her, sensing she wants someone to reach out to. I learned from Anna that members of a rival biker gang killed her husband. I can't imagine losing the love of my life like that.

"It's not a good time for trouble," Deb says somberly. "But it's nothing for you to worry about..."

She kisses Avery's cheek and the mood shifts as we focus our attention away from the actions of criminal bikers and towards Avery's round, pink cheeks. Just when I completely forget bikers, gangs, or anything like that, I hear the distant roar of a motor-cycle engine.

Deb must hear it too, because she stops kissing Avery.

"Tanner?" I ask her.

I can't tell if I'm hopeful or scared. A stranger climbed into my window and came inside me. Twice. I could handle the idea that this person might be Tanner but... if it's not Tanner... I could be pregnant with a monster's baby. A real monster -- not just some fucked up guy who can't get in touch with his feelings.

Right now, I don't know what to think, especially when Deb Shaw's face turns white.

"No," she says. "I know the sound of a Honda. It's not that loud. This is someone else."

"I'll check."

Deb shakes her head and hands me Avery.

"No," she says. "You take the baby and I'll get a gun..."

Twenty-Seven
HAWK

Scratch marks sting my face from the last violent fight I had with Juliette before I left Santa Fe again. She has made me the subject of several paintings due to her separation anxiety. I don't see why she has to paint me stripped naked and getting eaten by mountain lions to feel better, but she claims it's her "artist's process" and there ain't shit I can do about it...

But fuck, the wind makes my face sting more. And maybe it's not so bad that she cut me up like that because you had better believe I grabbed her chubby behind and flung her into our bed so I could have one last moment of intimacy with her before disappearing...

War.

That's what Southpaw promised. It's what we all agreed on. War is nice in theory. In reality, you're on edge all the fucking time. You miss drinking.

There are only two people in the world keeping me away from liquor this time -- Mackenzie and Juliette. Mackenzie because of how much I love her and I want her to know how much I've done for my baby girl. Juliette because I'm downright terrified of what might happen to me if she thinks I'm drinking.

Ryder's drunken ass left half a flask of whiskey over at our place one time and the volcanic argument between me and Juliette nearly brought down half the buildings on our street. I never knew the word 'redneck' could be advanced into such a specific set of slurs until that little incident.

Condom pulls his bike right up next to mine as we watch the front door of the shitty double wide where we've been tracking Bucky's mother-in-law for the past five days.

He pulls a flask from his breast pocket and takes a swig that makes me downright envious. We only use our club names out here since we're on the road... Ruger Blackwood becomes Bucky - a tame ass nickname for a motherfucker that's goddamn crazy.

Sensing my envy as I stare at him drinking, Condom passes me a welcome cigarette. I set a good example for Mackenzie but considering each cigarette out here might be my last, I'm not too particular about staying on the wagon.

"It's a good sign we haven't seen her," Bucky says. "If she were here with her mama, we would have seen her."

Condom grunts. "Keep telling yourself that. She was a whore when you met her, a whore when you married her... Didn't she fuck Priest?"

Ruger glares at him from his murky green eyes. He has always had the general appearance of a serial killer in my opinion. Not the type of man you get close to. Typical Blackwood temper and stubbornness. Fixed in his ways -- especially about race. It's no surprise he got himself entangled with a chick like Darlene.

My opinion on Ruger's wife isn't worth much, but I'm not interrupting Condom to correct him, I'll say that much.

"My old lady is not a whore," Ruger says. I almost feel bad for him. I've heard him defend the Kansas City Chiefs with more enthusiasm and he was raised a Las Vegas Raiders fan. "Call her a whore one more time, Condom."

"I'm not saying she is a whore," my cousin says, stumbling into more trouble than necessary by not backing out of the whole goddamn discussion. "But if she were to be disloyal... that would be the act of a whore."

"She is not a goddamn whore."

Ruger drops his cigarette butt on the ground and stomps on it directly. Anyone else would have picked up on the subtle cue and let it go.

"I know," Condom says. "I know. But didn't half the football team pay her to blo--

Ruger's glare shuts him up. Finally. Then I get to shut them both up before the quiet tension picks up into a psychotic argument.

"Fuck. There's movement. New movement."

Five days of watching and I was starting to believe Tamiya fed our asses bad info. Gideon nearly kicked all our asses for doubting his old lady. I guess he was right because the flash of blond hair that leaves the double wide is a particular bleached shade that looks familiar now that I see it on the head of the five-foot tall woman glancing around anxiously before she darts to the old souped up Challenger parked out front the trailer and revs it up.

Condom puts his hand on his holster. Instead of rushing to action, I stay quiet and watch the whole scene unfold. The questions I have are more important than the emotions I feel. Ruger Blackwood is all emotion, especially for Darlene Song Blackwood, the woman he married when they were both eighteen-years-old.

Hardly feels fair to call either of them grown but the Blackwoods are religious, Ruger had his military service all planned out and honestly, both their parents wanted to get rid of them. Especially Darlene's.

"I ought to cut that bitch's throat," Ruger growls, his hands clenching and unclenching the handlebars of his motorcycle as fury emanates from his body. I don't have to look right at him to feel the anger coursing through him. The Blackwoods don't handle betrayal well. The recent losses in the family have all those boys rubbed way too raw.

Life fucked Gideon Blackwood up worse than prison could ever do to my brother. Ruger doesn't have Gideon's discipline. He never became an Army Ranger. Shit, I think he lost his benefits doing some crazy shit out in Hawaii. I don't know the details...

Condom pulls him back before I have to say anything. "Don't lose your shit, Bucky. We don't know she's a rat. All we know is she lied to your stupid ass."

If Condom weren't six foot eight and twice the size of any Blackwood, he would find himself at the wrong end of Ruger's fist. His sheer size stops just about anything that doesn't have wheels or hooves from messing with him.

Ruger glares, but he doesn't dare escalate things. Yet. Our personal problems have a way of coming out towards the end of a ride or during our club meetings.

The Dodge makes a distinct sound when Darlene starts the engine. Five days of watching have been boring as fuck, but they haven't been worthless. Reaper was here on our third night watching so he could install a tracker on that Dodge, so we don't have to risk detection to follow the woman behind the wheel.

We just needed a confirmation of her identity.

They both wait for my command before we follow the car. Condom has the GPS, a better sense of direction, and he spent more time around these parts riding after high school, so he leads.

I follow Ruger, partly because I have to make sure he doesn't veer off and do anything stupid but also because I have to send a quick message to Southpaw and Reaper, let them know our progress.

We might not know for sure Darlene is our rat, but what are the odds she's been lying to Reaper for her health? The Dodge stops outside a Love's travel stop twenty miles along Route 40 – the site of the old Route 66 highway. I like the open road, but parts of Oklahoma are hot, too shitty for words, and give you this unnerving feeling that you don't belong there and you had better get out quick before something gets you.

It's just a weird feeling.

A couple Sinclairs own gas stations in this part of the state – most along the highway – but this Love's isn't owned by anyone we know. We park our bikes as close to the travel stop exit and straight-shot highway on-ramp as possible before we get off and swap numbing agents. I take a cigarette from Condom and light up before glancing around the parking lot while my comrades take their own survey of the situation.

Darlene parked the Dodge at the pump. Ruger finishes off Condom's flask, handing it back to him with fire behind his idiotic green eyes. Condom punches him in the chest and snatches back the flask.

"What the fuck is wrong with you?" he growls. "That was my supply for the rest of the day."

"I'm going to kill that whore."

"She's your wife, Bucky. Relax," Condom says, clearly still seething over the indulgence with liquor. "I'm sure she has a reasonable explanation for lying to you and hiding out in Oklahoma with her mama."

"That bitch," he sneers, spitting on the ground. The last thing I need is this idiot getting out of hand.

"Bucky, chill," I reply, feeling goddamn blessed that I'm not gone off some type of liquor myself. "She's your property. I don't care what you do with her as long as you do it after we question her."

"We can question her after I shoot the bitch in the head."

"So we question a corpse, you dumb fuck?" Condom growls. "You can't let some woman get under your skin like this. Toughen the fuck up."

Ruger spits on the ground again, this time dangerously close to Condom, who leans with his arms folded, looking ready to burst if necessary. Lyle Blackwood was just about the only person who could get Ruger's crazy ass under control. Since he died that country boy has been a goddamn nightmare.

. "She's my property. If I want to tie her to a tree and shove a shotgun up her ass, I can do it."

"Shove your shotgun wherever you have to after we question her. I have shit to do that doesn't involve burying a body without getting anything out of it."

"Fine," Bucky says. "I'll go in there first and talk to her calmly."

"Like fuck you will," I snap at him. He already has his hand on his holster.

"I'll get her out of there," I tell him. "And I won't leave any witnesses."

I promised Juliette I would stay away from this kind of trouble... but all I've thought about the entire ride here is how I can keep this woman safe and if I have to fire a couple bullets to protect Juliette and Mackenzie... that's what I'll do.

"I'll watch him," Condom says, gesturing towards Bucky.

"I don't need your ass watching me like a fucking kid," Bucky replies.

We both ignore him. Everyone knows the Blackwoods are hot-tempered. I hope that woman enjoyed her freedom while it lasted because I believe him when he says he'll kill her. I just don't want it to happen on my watch.

TWENTY-EIGHT
CASH

I enter my house to an unexpected arrangement of women gathered around my kitchen counter that immediately puts me in a sour mood.

"What the hell are you doing here?" I grumble at Tylee before greeting anyone. Tylee's presence immediately irks me and I don't remember having her name on the list of approved people for the safehouse. She's a troublemaker.

Tylee Sinclair leans over the counter drinking milk out of a wine glass while Aunt Deb bounces Avery, and Quin acts like she doesn't notice me enter the room. Why the fuck isn't she looking at me? Quin has her arm around Tylee's waist like they're best friends.

And there's a pistol on the counter.

"Is that gun loaded?" I snap, striding over towards it and quickly demonstrating basic gun safety for the women in the room who stare at me like I have two heads.

. . .

"He thinks he's so cool," Tylee says. "I remember when he was a skinny little ginger kid you could fit in a suitcase."

After verifying the gun isn't loaded,. I slam it on the table in front of Tylee threateningly, provoking Deb and Quin to chastise me.

"Not in front of Avery!" they both yell in unison. When did all these women join some kind of cult and why do I immediately feel attacked? I glare at both of them, more specifically at Quin, who still won't look me directly in the eye.

"Okay. Fine. Sorry. Why is Tylee in my house."

"We're cousins and I miss you."

"I miss you too. The way someone might miss cancer or total body paralysis."

"Tanner!" Aunt Deb says. "Tylee came here with important information. I need you to sit down and listen to it."

My cheeks glow with frustration. After all the mess I just got into with the club, the last thing I want to concern myself with is having a discussion with women. I want to see Quin but having a discussion with her is the last thing on my mind.

"I just got back from a long road trip. I don't have time for this."

"Your mom found out about Avery," Tylee says.

Fuck.

"What do you mean, she found out?"

"Listen. We all know your mother. I did the smart thing and came straight here."

"Where is she?" I growl.

Aunt Deb scoffs. "She's your mother. You know where she is."

"She's hunting down the whore my father knocked up with a shotgun in the front seat?" I respond with a sigh.

My mom has been chasing down my father's various "whores" and affair partners throughout my entire life. I thought after Doc passed away, she would at least have some peace of mind that the man she stayed faithful to her entire life couldn't screw with her again.

He just had to leave her with one last screw up on the way out.

"I got here as fast as I could," Tylee says. "Literally booked a flight and rented that Honda to get out here from the airport. Isaac is pissed."

"You left your husband?" I snap at her. Tylee is constantly doing foolish, impulsive things like this and it's a damn miracle that Isaac Sinclair hasn't tied her ass up. Tylee's eyes narrow and she starts yammering at me like I'm the one out of pocket here.

"She called me," Tylee says. "I think she's going to blow that woman's brains out."

Yes. We all know my mother is crazy. She has a temper – always has. Right now, I don't want to deal with it. If she wants to keep fighting my father's ghosts, I don't want to stop her.

"I don't have time for this," I growl. "If my mother wants to shoot someone in the head and spend the rest of her life in prison... so be it."

"After what my husband did for Quin, I think you owe me."

My eyes dart to Quin who looks suddenly suspicious and uncomfortable. She's still ignoring my eye contact.

"Yes..." I reply, though I don't have a clue what she's talking about aside from the fact that it relates to Quin's big secret. "Your husband helped her out significantly. I remember."

"She's going to kill that woman, Tanner. You have to do something."

"The only thing I can do is keep Avery out of trouble."

Aunt Deb stands up and gives me a knowing look. We discussed this in the past and I promised her that I wouldn't let it come to that.

"What's happening?" Quin asks, sensing the secretive communication between me and Aunt Deb with only our facial expressions.

"I'm taking Avery back to Missouri to Wyatt's little place for me," she says. "It's the deal I made with Tanner if anyone comes after her."

"Wait, what?" Quin says. "I can come with you."

Obviously there's no chance in hell I would ever let Quin do something like that, but the fact that she could even think about leaving her unsettles my stomach.

"No," I snap impulsively, betraying my emotions to everyone in the room – not like any of them care. "You're staying here. Avery will go with Deb."

"What about your mother!" Tylee yells.

I turn to her sharply. "I already told you that I have enough problems. If my mother wants to shoot some white trash whore, that's her choice."

Tylee looks like she's about to slap me, so I make some effort to soften her temper.

"But thank you," I continue, calming my tone down so she doesn't follow through on her impulse. "We can get Avery out of trouble in case my mother truly loses her marbles."

"She lost her marbles a while ago, Tanner. What if she thinks you helped your dad hide it, huh? What if she turns on you?"

I sigh and rub my forehead.

"Tylee. Let me handle it. Right now, I want all you damn women out of my house. And Avery somewhere safe."

"You can't just send Avery away," Quin pipes up.

"It has nothing to do with you," I snap at her. "I'm the one who knows what's best for Avery and I don't require input from the nanny."

Quin's nostrils flare and I see her face change unlike anything I've seen before.

"How. Dare. You."

Her voice vibrates with anger that she doesn't bother concealing.

"Don't have a tantrum," I respond firmly, self-satisfied at my ability to keep my cool while she trembles.

"I'm not having a tantrum, you asshole. I *love* Avery and if you gave a crap about her you wouldn't send her away like a badly behaved dog from a shelter."

Everyone in the room is quiet. Too quiet. Deb and Tylee are both looking at me like I have two heads – and they hate both of them. Quin's little hands ball up into fists and I don't know why, but her fury is getting a rise out of me like nothing has been able to. Just because I don't simper around Avery showing every form of weakness imaginable doesn't mean I don't love her.

"This is not a debate."

"You can't send her away!" Quin yells. "I won't let you."

"You won't do a damn thing but go to your room," I yell at her.

. . .

If I thought it was quiet before, my house sounds like a goddamn graveyard. On cue, Avery begins her howling from another room. Fuck...

Deb glares at me. "I'll get her."

Tylee gives me an equally cruel look. "I'll help."

They walk away hurriedly, leaving me and Quin alone. She looks at me like she has so much more to say on the tip of her tongue. Heat rises beneath my cheeks and spreads over the back of my neck. I feel hot-tempered and humiliated. This is exactly what I never wanted to happen between the two of us.

After last night, what I wanted today was...

"I hate you," Quin says, scowling firmly. "I hate you more than I've hated anyone."

"Good," I snarl at her. "Because once Avery's gone, I'll have you out on your ass to fend for yourself."

She raises her eyebrows and then seems to stop herself from saying something before she turns on her heel and storms off down the hallway. Quin slams her bedroom door.

Tylee and Deb emerge with Avery all packed up. I can't stand to look at them.

"I hope you apologized," Aunt Deb says.

Tylee scoffs. "When have you ever heard a Hollingsworth man apologize?"

. . .

"Two weeks. Mom should be done with her revenge in two weeks and then... she can come back," I tell Aunt Deb.

"Tell Quin that," She says. "You can't expect her not to get attached."

"Not everyone can be a heartless monster," Tylee says.

"I'll be in touch," I grunt, ushering these annoying, meddlesome women out of my goddamn house.

TWENTY-NINE
QUIN

Tanner is an asshole and now I'm stuck here with him. I don't know what to think about that. Hopefully I'll only be stuck here for another twenty-four hours considering he just threatened to kick me out.

I hate him so much. How could he just send Avery away like she's nothing? How could he expect me not to get attached? Human beings aren't perfectly rational creatures and contracts can't stop you from falling in love.

I hear the noise of vehicle engines rise and fall as my new friends leave me behind with the cold, red-headed monster and the intruder who comes at night when he's asleep. The man I still suspect might be Tanner Hollingsworth. If it is him, I hate him even more for being that person. For making me cum while being such a demon.

For a few minutes, the house is eerily quiet and I almost convince myself that Tanner fell asleep on the couch or something. Then I hear his footsteps and briefly consider jumping out the window and escaping just so I can avoid him.

He knocks on my door and I pretend to fall asleep. It's a

tried and true classic in the Nash house, although it didn't exactly work on Eugene. He can't hear me move and Tanner's hearing isn't so incredible that he can hear my breath. But that doesn't mean he gives up...

"I'm still your boss and I command your presence."

Jeez. Straight to the stupid commanding presence.

I climb out of bed and walk to the door before opening it. Glaring. This is an official conversation, not a personal one. And considering what just happened out there, I'm pretty sure I'm about to get fired from... maybe the weirdest job I've ever even heard about.

Tanner gazes down at me beneath pale, strawberry blond lashes that frame his unnaturally blue eyes. The rest of his skin and hair draw your attention to the intensity of the blue -- more glacier than ocean. As cool as Tanner himself.

"I apologize for the way I spoke to you," he says. I might not have believed him if his cheeks didn't darken earnestly.

"When is Avery coming back?" I answer stubbornly.

"When my mother's temper settles. When I can be sure that Avery's mother doesn't come looking for her."

"I... I won't know what to do here without her," I answer. He keeps looking at me with the most bewildered expression on his face, reminding me of what he said. "I guess our contract is over."

"I said I was sorry," he says.

"But you didn't say I could stay," I reply. "I'll message Juliette. If Avery comes back then–"

He interrupts me. "I want you to stay."

"Why?"

Our eyes meet again.

. . .

"Because there's a lot of work to get done around here," he says. There his face starts looking all weird again. Tanner runs his tongue along his lower lips.

"I don't think there is..."

"How can you stand it?" he growls.

"Stand what?"

"I haven't seen you in days."

"I know..."

He's acting so weird. Tanner scowls and then he grabs my cheeks. What the hell? I freeze. He keeps looking at me. The strange expression only grows more confusing.

"Fuck," he whispers. "You're probably already pregnant. There's no point in hiding anything anymore."

I've never heard Tanner say anything like that, so I just freeze as he holds me in place. I freeze until he slowly runs his thumb over my lower lip and a familiar sensation grasps me at my core. I suck in a sharp breath of air which Tanner stops me from exhaling with his lips.

Instinctively, my hands press against his chest and find a firm, solid wall of muscle. Instead of pushing, I cling to his shirt and I let my chaotic, red-headed boss kiss me. Worse than that... I kiss him back.

His lips. I'm feeling his lips. All the times the stranger has broken into my room, I've never kissed him on the lips so I have nothing to compare to Tanner's kisses. All I know is that right now, these kisses feel so damn good. Rivers of pleasure flow through me starting at my lips and shooting straight through my core.

He lets go of my cheeks and stumbles a couple feet out of my door frame. He's so big that he can't stand upright in the door frame and his shoulders are so broad that he can hardly fit through it. Gasping and looking at him like this right after he kissed me, I almost forget how badly I want to kill him.

Then he opens his mouth.

"I need to fuck you again."

Again?

My brow furrows in confusion.

"Come on," he says with frustration. "I'm done playing games, Quin. There's no one here. It's been way too long..."

He gives me a quick once over then continues like he didn't just shake my world. "Take your clothes off..."

I don't immediately obey him.

"Clothes. Off," he growls.

I can't move without asking more questions. He acts like I should be used to this, but I'm not. I still have questions.

"It was you the whole time?"

He scowls. "We're done with the games Quin. I can't anymore. I can't..."

"I'm not playing a game."

I don't mean to sound shrill, but I can't help my reaction. Every emotion I've felt hits me like a late Amtrak train. I'm definitely not playing a game. I have spent so many nights obsessing over this stranger to the point where I worry about break-ins more than I worry about the police catching up to me for my own mistakes.

Then he says it so casually. Like I should have known that my boss would be psychopathic enough to put on a ski mask and climb in through my bedroom window to take my virginity.

Tanner chuckles. "Okay. No game. You can't expect me to believe you didn't know it was me, Quin... Come on."

There's an almost boyish mischief behind his lashes. Confusion hits me. He actually thinks I knew it was him. Our interactions all seem colored by this revelation and I'm too stunned to move or say anything that makes any sense. I just start stammering until Tanner puts his hand over my mouth firmly and then furrows his brow again.

"Fuck," he whispers, looking down at me, taking in all my panic and then perhaps... realizing his mistake. Or at least realizing that he interpreted everything wrong. Tanner doesn't admit faults from what I know about him.

I glare at him because that's all I can do with his hand over my mouth. He bites down on his lower lip nervously.

"So you haven't been fucking with my head?"

I swat his hand away from my mouth because this part I can't hold back.

"Fucking with you?" I say, my voice coming out as a very annoying sounding squeak. "You're the one climbing in through my window and-- doing things to me!"

"Doing things? What types of things are you accusing me of doing?" he says, suddenly seeming physically larger and more imposing. There are only two ways I can even get out of this situation with Tanner. I can step backwards into my bedroom towards my bed, which is a definite danger zone for us. Getting past Tanner might prove even more difficult. He played football in high school and college.

Even if Eugene sometimes told me I was built like a linebacker, most of them are a little taller than 5'2". My throat constricts.

"You know what you did," I respond weakly. "You hurt me."

Now his face goes from red to purple, like I've somehow said something untrue.

"I made you cum," he snarls. "I didn't... I never meant to hurt you."

"Well you did," I snap at him. How could he seriously think this wouldn't hurt me? My heart races as I stare at his face, confusion coursing through me. He's so handsome. So *evil*. He scared the crap out of me, made me feel so damn crazy, yet now that he's here in front of me, all of those angry feelings twist up in a ball and turn into something else.

He's a monster... why do I want him to touch me?

He grabs my cheeks again and kisses me. Is that what he thinks counts for an apology? I squirm and try to shove his chest again but when my hands contact his chest, I drag him towards me instead and my frustrated whimper turns into a moan.

I pull away from him in surprise, still holding onto his shirt. Tanner looks down at me in confusion...

"You kissed me," he accuses. We're way too close to each other for me to entertain any genuinely intelligent thoughts. The smell filling my nostrils now is dangerously familiar and even without Tanner's confession, there isn't any doubt about his identity.

I should run.

This man kidnapped me. He made me sign a contract under false pretenses. He's a horrible person. He climbed into my bedroom window and fucked me without a condom.

Any sane woman would run.

. . .

Unless she could feel Tanner's chest muscles. And looking into his blue eyes. And feeling his bulge pressing against her as he held her close.

He wraps his arms around me and draws my body against his. There isn't any escape from this tension between us. Not anymore.

"If you hate me so much," he whispers, running his thumb over my lower lip again as he looks me in the eye. "Why did you kiss me?"

Tanner doesn't wait for me to answer. He possessively grips my cheeks again and gives me a big, romantic kiss just like the ones in the movies, only better because it's happening to me and it's happening with my sexy, red-headed boss.

Thirty
CASH

Kissing her gets dangerous quickly. Grabbing onto bits of her flesh and holding Quin's body close to mine gets me rock hard in a second. I never even looked at another woman all those days away from her and I'm pent up something fierce. Having to argue with half my damn family to get this woman near a bed has me riled up and impossible to control. Technically, it hasn't been long but it feels like forever.

Pushing her back into her bedroom, I slide her ass back on the bed and join her, my body on top of hers as we kiss face to face for the first time. The harshness of my week-old beard against her skin only furthers my drive to lose myself in her softness. Since Quin doesn't obey my immediate commands to take her clothing off, I follow through on my own, stripping her down to nothing with enthusiasm while she paws desperately at my shirt for some gratification of her own.

To stop her from clawing at me so desperately, I grab hold of one of her enormous breasts and plop her dark brown nipple into my mouth. Quin has deliciously dark brown areolas and any time I come into contact with her impressive breasts, I get so fucking hard at the contrast between the two of us.

. . .

I flick my tongue over Quin's nipple until she moans and her hands fall to her sides so she can't get my shirt off. I'm not ready yet. Not until I explore every curve on her thick body and make this woman feel totally appreciated for every inch of her full figure. I kiss her soft shoulders, her arms and then return to her nipples again, thoroughly distracted by their appearance.

"You taste so fucking good," I growl as I suck on her nipples until they get incredibly wet and Quin can't stop herself from moaning when my tongue touches any part of her bare, dark-brown skin. This woman is the exact color of a milk chocolate bar and I fucking love it. Her taste. Her scent... how goddamn soft she is.

I want those ass cheeks in my hands and that perfect pussy wrapped tightly around my dick. Impatience for Quin's pussy drives me to move away from her nipples more than exhaustion. I could suck on those tits forever if my cock could stand the pain of waiting for her.

Quin's body tightens nervously as I kiss her stomach and belly button. She feels good, so I don't want to stop kissing this part of her, but she suddenly pushes her hand against my head with enough force that I can't allow myself any pleasure at the sensation of her fingers sliding through my hair.

"No..."

"I want to kiss you," I growl, running my tongue over her bare navel. Quin yelps out in panic and makes some half-hearted attempt to kick me.

I kiss her again.

"It's so embarrassing..."

"What's embarrassing about it?"

"I'm fat."

"I noticed," I grunt. "I like it."

. . .

I kiss her stomach again and Quin throws out her remarkably thick legs again in an effort to kick me in some undirected place. I grab her legs, holding both of them up in a v-shape as I stare down at her from in between them.

She just glares at me but from this position... this woman looks downright adorable. She looks like a MILF... a Marsh-mallow I'd Like to Fuck...

"I love your body," I say to her. Earnestly. "You should love it too. Anyone who doesn't love your belly fat doesn't deserve to fuck you. Now get your hand out of the way..."

Since Quin won't remove her hand on her own, I take it and move it out of the way so I can kiss her stomach with my original intentions. She sighs, but she doesn't push me away and after a few kisses, both her hands relax at her sides again and her breathing turns soft and desperate.

Once she feels relaxed, she can let go completely. I want to get her to that point where she experiences something even better than what happened the nights I climbed through her window. Every inch of Quin drives me into a deep and dangerous obses-sion. I kiss every bit of her flesh, unrestrained in my desire to touch and own her.

"You taste delicious," I murmur soft encouragement to her which settles her down. I move lower between her legs, preparing myself to put my tongue between her legs and eat her out. I already feel drunk off the scent of her pussy. I haven't even tasted her yet, but my lust feels somehow beyond my control. My chest tightens and tingling lust spreads through me.

I have to have her. Taking Quin's underwear off is a project because of her voluptuous curves, but I manage to pry the fabric from against her dark brown skin and her soaking wet pussy lips. My dick jumps at the realization of how wet she is. Eager to do more than strip her naked, I part her slippery lower lips with my index finger and rub along her soft wet folds, indulging in every-thing about her that she keeps hidden.

My mouth draws closer to her lower lips and my warm breath causes Quin's legs to spread open and before my tongue enters her urgently. I can't stop myself, nor do I want to stop myself. Juices explode from Quin's pussy the second my tongue makes contact and I respond by pushing her thighs up as far back as I can fold them to give me complete access to her soaked lower lips.

Lifting Quin's legs is a pleasurable challenge but allows me to flatten my tongue and taste every inch of the flesh between her legs. Her creamy juices have a downright addictive flavor and my desperation for more drives me to push my tongue inside her and rub her clit until her soft moans become more desperate. Fuck, I don't want to stop eating her pussy.

Every time she responds to a movement of my tongue, I repeat the action until Quin's thighs tremble and I feel her getting closer to a big climax. I slide my tongue over the length of her pussy and then wrap it around her clit and suck on her softly and slowly until she finally finishes. Her eruption is goddamn beautiful. She loses complete control over her body as she cums in my arms.

I still taste like her when I pull away from her pussy. Cumming all over my face calms her down and for the time being, she seems to have stopped her assault. Her toes curl as I lower her legs and everything about Quin Nash is soft. Sensitive. Beautiful. I kiss her pussy once more before I make my way back up her body with kisses, over her soft stomach, over those perfect tits until I can see her face again.

She looks away from me instantly. No. My instinctive need for control over her takes over and I instantly lose the softness I had. I grab Quin's cheeks, forcing her to look at me. Properly. I need her to see how I feel about her. To watch her cum dripping from my lips before I kiss her. Quin wrinkles her eyebrows like she's looking at something gross.

"What you did was criminal."

"Wouldn't be the first or the last thing."

"Is that an apology?" she says, clearly forgetting her orgasm and squirming against my grasp as my body pins her to the bed. I wonder if she's ever met a man strong enough to hold her down like this. Fuck, I could lift her over my head and eat her pussy if I wanted to.

"Why would I apologize when I'm not sorry?"

She wrinkles up her face more, so I hold her cheeks tighter, quietly reminding her of my control.

"You are sick..."

"I'm not."

"You kidnapped me here just so you could do this. You don't even care about Avery..."

"I have done everything in my power to save my father's bastard child. Who knows... I should have left her to the goddamn coyotes."

Quin kicks me. Hard. It's so damn hard that I actually roll off her. Not because of her strength but because of the fucking surprise.

"You are a monster!" she shrieks. I nearly fall off the fucking bed but luckily, I land on my feet.

Luckily for Quin.

"What do you want from me?" I growl at her. "To be happy that I have this... *responsibility*?"

"I want you to be a human being. *Care about her.*"

"What makes you think I don't care about her?" I snap. "Because I don't act like a foolish woman around her?"

"You are such a pig," Quin says, glaring at me. "Just because you can make me cum doesn't mean I like you."

. . .

It's like she knows how to piss me off.

"Who said I need you to like me?"

"Your red face," she says, glaring even harder.

"You're lucky I don't put my dick in your mouth and teach you a little respect."

I move closer to her, hoping to threaten her, or convince her. Whichever works. Instead, she just glares harder, but she doesn't budge. She feared the masked stranger, but she isn't afraid of me. I don't know if I like that. Her fear made this fun...It made her smell better. Taste better. Fuck better.

Maybe I'm sick in the head for being alone too long and Quin is right.

"You *stole* my virginity," she says, trembling and getting me so damn hard. But she doesn't show any fear, even if she must feel it.

I'm close enough to touch her again, despite her scrambling to the other side of the bed. I set one knee on it. Then another. Cornering Quin against the headboard where she lacks the coordination to escape. I keep searching her face for honesty, fighting the urge to grope her even more.

"I think you are scared," I whisper. "Or you would have confronted me a long time ago. You knew it was me."

"I didn't."

"Who the fuck else could it have been, Quin. This place has ironclad security."

Her lower lip trembles. Maybe a part of her wanted to deny the truth. But she had to have known it was me. She must have smelled me. Felt the way my beard scraped her flesh. Heard my goddamn voice. I refuse to let her get away with this. But the more I stare at her, the more she trembles. Tears well in her eyes and I smile.

There it is. The truth. Just because she doesn't like the truth, doesn't make it any different.

"We're all a little fucked up, Quin. You don't have to cry about it."

My dick gets hard as that first tear falls. She might act like she doesn't give a fuck about me most of the time but this single tear is proof that she cares. I wipe it away with my thumb as her lower lip trembles. Yes... the truth hurts, doesn't it?

"I'm not fucked up," she says, her voice sounding tighter and more tense than usual. It's not just her crying.

"Are you sure?"

"How dare you..." she whispers. "You have no idea what I went through. What he did to me..."

Okay.

Now... I don't know what the fuck she's talking about. But I have my suspicions. I know that a dark secret brought Quin to her best friend Juliette. I *pretended* to know exactly what she was talking about. Maybe it's this.

"I don't," I whisper. "You're right. All I know is... we all have dark shit inside us, Quin... Even a beautiful girl like you."

"I didn't mean to," she whispers. "I really didn't..."

Then she turns into a woman I don't recognize. Someone vulnerable. Quin wraps her arms around me and then she just bursts into tears against my shoulders. What the fuck?

. . .

Did I do this?

I wrap my arms around her, grateful to have her close. But I have no idea what to do with a crying woman...

THIRTY-ONE
QUIN

I don't know what comes over me. The urge to cling to Tanner Hollingsworth overwhelms me and nothing feels more important than wrapping my arms around him and being close to him. Despite his harshness, his cruelty, and his arrogant refusal to admit he loves Avery... he understands me.

On some deep, depraved level, he understands my darkness. I don't have to be afraid of anything with him. It feels safe enough to cry about the fact that I murdered my step-brother. That for the rest of my life, I'll have this nagging thought that I could go to prison. After this much time... who the hell is going to believe it's self-defense?

His arms are so strong and muscular. He squeezes me tighter, making me feel like I don't have to let go.

I don't even notice that I stop crying.

"There," he whispers, although Tanner didn't exactly do anything. "That's exactly what you need... Let it all out."

I sigh. "That doesn't make it go away though."

"I'll make it go away," he whispers. "I don't know what could reduce a strong woman like you to tears but... I will protect you, Quin. I promise."

"You're a..."

A freak? A monster? My boss? I can't define anything about Tanner that doesn't exist in the present moment. I can see his face. How fucking handsome he is. He even looks like he cares about me. But... how can he make this go away...

He grins. "I've done some fucked up things. I know. But the second I saw you, Quin... Well, I knew I was prepared to do a few more fucked up things to have you."

"That's what I mean," I say after a few long moments of silence. "You're...weird."

"Why?"

"No guy has ever done anything crazy like that over me. I don't know why you would."

"Other guys are stupid," he says, pushing braids out of my face. "That's simple. And you... are worth all the trouble in the world. I like fluffy women. But out of all the ones I've met, you're my favorite."

No more tears, but I have that strange flutter in my stomach again. He touches my shoulders. Then my hips. Then Tanner kisses me. His lips are perfect. He still tastes like me, which is weird at first, but then it becomes almost freeing to just not give a fuck. To be a little bit more like Tanner. I get more into kissing him.

Then, I do something I've never done before. I reach for his dick. He chuckles as his dick jerks in my hand.

"Fuck," he says. "I like the way your hand feels on my dick."

I have no idea what I'm doing. Only instinct fuels me to move forward. I slowly cup his cock, touching him along the outside of his trousers, completely unsure of what exactly I crave from this man, but knowing that I want him.

My boss. The freakishly gigantic redhead who terrifies me and turns me on equally. Tanner exposes the dark side of me effortlessly. Only a few seconds of touching his dick and I can feel more of my wetness sliding down my thighs as my body already desperately craves the man I accused of criminal acts against me.

I don't get why I want him so badly. Every cell in my body should run from a man who sees nothing wrong with kidnapping me because he wants me. With climbing through my window. There doesn't even appear to be any reason for his coldness. He just... is.

Something else lurks beneath Tanner's coldness. While his emotions may be reserved and almost impossible to identify, his body is warm. Open. Giving. I can feel his arousal moving in my hand. I remember every moment of him kissing me, even when he hadn't kissed me on the lips. He might be fucked up but I still want more of him.

He kisses me on the forehead.

"You are everything," he whispers. "And if it makes you feel better, I love Avery just as much as I love you. I'm just not a man who speaks his feelings."

As if to prove himself, he grabs my cheeks and kisses me again, refusing to give me a chance to probe and push at those feelings. I let him touch me. Kiss me. If he doesn't want to speak his feelings, I'll let him show me like this. It doesn't take much for us to fall into bed together.

Unlike all the other times, I can move. I can touch him freely. I feel weird. Like I have *permission* to want something dark and depraved that I shouldn't really want at all. His body. His touch. This strange, red-headed man should scare the crap out of me, but I just want all of him. I practically rip Tanner's dick out of his pants and he doesn't stop me.

He is normally the one who lacks patience. Once I wrap my hands around his dick, Tanner makes a strained, desperate groan.

Then he moves his hips without me driving him, the large swollen head of his dick pressing against my tightness. Fuck. He's huge. My chest throbs with the visceral memory of what it felt like to accept the giant stranger inside me the first time.

His body is so large, so fucking impressive, that it shouldn't surprise me Tanner has the dick to match. The sheer size of his dick alone should have told me who pushed my bedroom window open. Maybe he's right. Maybe on some level deep inside... I knew exactly who he was.

Tanner rubs his dick over the length of my lips. His cheeks flush with lust as he gets his dick soaking wet with my juices, but still hesitates just enough that pure agony grips both of us. I need to feel him inside me as badly as he needs to feel my pussy wrapped around his dick. The powerful fire behind our mutual desire for each other makes me moan before he slides inside me.

The soft sound pushes Tanner to move his hips forward and he gives in to his desires, thrusting all the way inside me with one smooth, painful stroke. The knot at the base of my stomach forms immediately and his sheer size forces a moan out of me. He chuckles and nibbles my neck gently as he buries his dick inside me.

Hesitating at first, I press my hand against his back, feeling his warmth and allowing it to spread through me. We are so close to each other and for the first time, face to face. The way Tanner looks at me is strange. A little embarrassing. But oddly pleasant. He has a look on his face like you would when you see a beautiful sunset.

That's the only thing I can compare to because nobody ever looked at me like that for my entire life. It's utterly unfamiliar, but strangely exciting. As my heart races, my fingers sink into the flesh on his back and I pull him close to me. He doesn't share my shame about the desire I have for him. It makes me feel like... it's not so bad to want him.

Even if it makes us both fucked up.

. . .

"I like when you touch me," he whispers. "You're so fucking hot."

He slowly withdraws and thrusts into me, repeating the sweetest words I've ever heard a man say about anyone. It's hard not to feel good as he fucks me. And affirms me. And I don't even care that he bites my neck with pure violence after calling me the most beautiful woman in the world. Tanner just feels good...

When I'm about to cum and digging my nails into his back, he pins my arms over my head and fucks me harder into the bed. It's hot – with nothing but the sound of us moaning together and the headboard slamming against the wall. Our skin makes a loud slapping noise as the heat between the sheets overwhelms the power of the air conditioning.

Sweat builds between us as well as another orgasm. I can feel both of us reaching a peak at the same time. He pins me down tighter. I can feel his entire body tensing as he fucks me. My pussy clenches around his dick and the fullness sends intense rivers of pleasure through me that turn into a climax that hits me at the same time Tanner's climax slams into him.

We cling to each other desperately as we moan and finish simultaneously. He feels so damn good. His cum gushes inside me in thick spurts and the warmth sends powerful tingling through me as he pumps a few more times between my thighs before collapsing.

Tanner is damn heavy, but the weight of his muscular body on mine feels strangely hot. He kisses me once he catches his breath.

"You're everything," he whispers. "Fucking everything."

I don't know why he says all that. But I let him. And I admit to myself that it feels good, even if the idea of returning a man's feelings scares the crap out of me. Tanner rolls off me, the happiest look on his face. My heart flutters again. Maybe I shouldn't, but I feel proud that I can bring him this much pleasure.

That I can bring a smile to my cranky boss's face.

That he can admit he cares about *someone* when he's with me. He grunts and then pulls me in close to his chest. I almost want to run away, but he drags me closer and then he grabs my cheeks again. He's obsessed with my admiration – having me look at him.

I don't mind. He's easy on the eyes, honestly.

"I don't want to let you go," he says. "I know I fucked up... But I care about you and I care about Avery. Don't leave, Quin."

I want to agree to stay with him, but how can I do that *without* Avery here? Tanner might have a different way of expressing his feelings, but my heart is absolutely broken without her here. I miss her. And what does he want from me without Avery?

What about a job? What about a life?

I don't understand what Tanner wants from me.

Or if he hasn't even thought of any of this because he's just a horny biker...

"I don't like that silence," he says. "I want you here, Quin. I'd rather tie you up until you see it my way than beg."

Thirty-Two
Southpaw

Therapy and sobriety have brought the best out of me. Ever since the incident where Anna took off with the kids, I put every last ounce of effort I had into getting my shit together. Therapy until I couldn't take it anymore. Quitting to avoid ever going back to therapy again. Avoiding every Little League baseball diamond within driving distance of our house. And hockey rink. And race track. And dog fighting ring.

It's slow, but I'm making much better progress than before. Realizing how close I came to losing Anna changed me. The way I feel about her is so different from how I felt about other women because she makes me want to change. She holds me accountable. She scares the fuck out of me by making me imagine a world where I don't get to hold her.

I know I have to stop. Avoid every poker table. Every dice game.

. . .

Instead of gambling, I play online chess. Destroying some idiot halfway across the world is the only high that comes close.

And then of course there's Anna. And the kids. Who are much better and much more important than any high. I know I have a problem. I know I'm fucked in the head. But I love my family. I love them enough to try to change. Even if it means waking up at three in the morning with the itch to destroy everything... and instead, calling some guy on *Chess.com* a series of insults Anna would smack me for.

If club business weren't so damn stressful, riding would be an even better distraction. I miss the freedom of the open road. Right now, we have the open road – but no freedom.

Anna and the kids are asleep upstairs so I can have this unofficial meeting in the garage with the boys. This place *used* to be a garage. It's more like a war room now.

Anna says nothing, but I can tell our arsenal of weapons makes her deeply uncomfortable. She understands. She won't leave. But I know Anna has her limits. If I want to protect my family and keep my wife happy – we need to end this quickly.

There's a game on the garage television. I keep sports that I don't feel the temptation to gamble on down here. In this case, cricket. I don't give a shit how popular it is around the world... call me when a cricketer hits a grand slam or slides headfirst into home plate. The so-called sport is boring.

"What the fuck is this shit?" Owen asks, tipping back his third Voodoo Ranger. My brother Ethan sits next to him on his phone.

"It's a sport for fags," Ethan says without looking up. "That's what it is."

Unlike me, he doesn't see any issues with his gambling. He's probably deeply invested in March Madness. Or college games. Something I wish I could get my hands on. Instead, I drink. Can't get too drunk or Anna will make me sleep on the couch again, so even with the whiskey, I need a steady hand. Not easy considering the club shit happening right now.

Hunter's heavy footsteps come pounding down the stairs. Ryder behind him. That's how they always are these days – one twin a few steps behind the other. They used to be about the same size, but Ryder clearly spent all his time in prison trading shit for ramen noodles and lifting weights. He has about thirty, forty pounds of muscle on his brother.

And finally, his hair is growing back. Doesn't make sense to keep it longer than a buzz cut behind bars with the lice outbreaks and the bedbugs. It's easier to tell them apart with Ryder's hair coming in half-gray – like he's seen some shit.

"What the fuck are you watching?" Hunter asks, scowling jealously at the beer before tipping a Mountain Dew down his throat.

"Doesn't Mountain Dew have alcohol in it?" Ethan asks, still barely looking up from his phone.

"No, you fucking idiot," Hunter says. "I've been drinking this shit since I was a baby."

"Let's talk business," I interrupt before this turns into a fist-fight. Tensions have been high as fuck around here after the discovery out in the desert. "We don't have time to argue over liquor."

"Or gambling debts," Owen says suspiciously before leaning against the couch back and finishing off his beer.

"Right..."

Ryder shares my eagerness to get to business. He sits at the basement bar on a metal stool, leaning back in the same position as his brother, who takes the stool next to him.

"Good news and bad news. Ruger has Darlene safely out of the way at Oske's trailer out on the rez. No way a bunch of Nazis ride onto the rez without anyone noticing," Ryder announces to the club, getting started on our business to avoid any discussion of anyone's gambling.

Hearing Oske's name immediately raises my concerns over the bad news. Ryder glances at Owen to fill me in, which only makes me more nervous. My brother looks up at me like he's trying to calm a raging beast. *What the fuck are they keeping from me?*

"I thought we should wait and let her think this through but... she's insistent."

"On what..."

My teeth grind together automatically. Despite my continuous support, Oske remains a pain in my fucking ass. While *occasionally* useful, I find myself wanting to lock her in a damn cage when she isn't doing exactly what she's told.

"Oske wants $1,400 for emotional damages and freedom from her alleged captivity."

"Is that a goddamn joke?"

"I told you we should have just paid her," Ethan grumbles.

"With what goddamn money?" Owen snaps. "Do you have $1,400 in cash lying around because the last time I checked, I'm completely *fucked.*"

"Quiet," I growl.

"If you stopped losing then you'd have the money," Ethan says.

"I said *quiet.*"

Hunter and Ryder exchange glances. I ignore whatever twin-speak they have going on and focus on my idiot brothers.

"Oske can't have $1,400."

"That's what I said," Owen replies smugly, casting a disapproving glance in Ethan's direction. Ethan continues gazing at his phone – a fact beginning to get on my damn nerves – and doesn't notice Owen's smug look.

"She's a crazy bitch," Ethan says. "Small price to pay to get her off our backs."

"Can we focus?" Ryder interrupts, taking the burden of getting my brothers in line away from me for once. If Hunter weren't busy being such a sour puss over the smell of liquor everywhere, he would have been the one to step in. "That isn't even the bad news."

Hunter puts his hand on his brother's shoulder and takes the lead. "Ruger wants to kill Darlene."

"He can't. Not until we get information from her."

"It gets worse," Owen says. "She's pregnant. So he wants to keep her in the trailer until she has the kid, then kill her."

"I don't have time for this," I grumble...

"He doesn't believe in abortion," Ethan says. "Killing babies and shit. It's fucked up."

"Tell Ruger he doesn't have permission to execute his wife. Not until after we have what we need. She's pregnant. She's vulnerable. Instead of torturing her, he should be promising her the world."

"It's Ruger," Owen says. "He's not logical. He nearly killed her on the spot."

"It's a matter of time before he does it," Hunter says. "The Blackwoods are irrational and fucked in the head. We turn our backs too long, that bitch is dead."

Keeping Ruger under control is a full time fucking job. When Doc was alive, he took on the massive project, but Gideon doesn't give a fuck and with the twins gone, Ruger is off his fucking rocker. Some rednecks are built crazier than others. I would think twice before naming my son after a gun. That asshole is just as volatile as a weapon.

"Maybe he won't kill her if she's pregnant," I grumble, barely hopeful that Ruger can manage that much moral fiber. "If he's keeping her alive because of that, remind him of his Christian morals or whatever the fuck he has going on in his dimwitted redneck brain."

"We'll need more than a few of us to get the job done," Hunter says. "No way in hell Juliette lets me go out to the rez without pestering me."

"Ryder can handle it."

"I can't."

He turns red.

"Why not?" I ask, giving him a suspicious look.

"I have my own problems," he says. "Personal business."

"What the fuck does that mean?" Hunter asks, spitting out exactly what's on my mind without me having to ask it.

"It means mind your fucking business."

"It's a woman," Ethan says, barely looking up from his phone.

"Shut the fuck up," Ryder says. "I couldn't get Ruger's crazy ass to listen to me, anyway. He might listen to Gideon. Tanner could put him through a wall."

"I could handle him," Owen says. "But... Not without backup."

"I'll get Tanner on the job," I reply. "He needs to keep his mind busy."

"I heard he has family trouble," Ryder says. "Anything related to Midnight SS?"

"Not sure," I reply, nervous as we get close to the subject of Avery, her identity, and the fact   that the woman Don

Hollingsworth screwed with might very well have a connection to these people...

But fuck if I could even guess what that connection might be.

THIRTY-THREE
CASH

I promise her I'll get Avery back to make her stay.

Quin doesn't know how much more I have hidden. The Midnight SS situation is absolutely fucked up.

Half the fucking Blackwood family dead in the goddamn desert. Doesn't feel right. Next club meeting, we'll have to look at our options from a pool of new recruits and choose which kids to patch in. I used to look forward to those meetings, but now it feels like we're signing up our blood brothers to die.

We need war to end this quickly – I agree with Southpaw there – but that doesn't make it pretty. Unlike my daddy, I never had a dream of running around this country and away from the woman I love. No thanks. I like my women like Quin. Soft. Planted in my bed. Unlikely to have the motivation to run away.

She sleeps heavily on my arm this morning. Her hair smells like the special oil she uses and she snores a little bit – denying it every time I confront her. I know she can't be perfect – that she has a little darkness in her past. But who the fuck am I to judge a little darkness?

She doesn't judge mine...

There's something so fucking beautiful about her sleeping next to me like this... knowing that one day soon, I'll get to make her my old lady. Make her my wife.

Quin stirs when my cell phone blares dramatically. I do let Southpaw call my phone at any goddamn hour of the day. Fuck me, these contraptions are annoying. She groans and paws around in an effort to silence the mysterious noise.

"There you go..." I grunt, moving her over slightly so I can grab my phone and answer it in bed. Quin groans with another complaint as she nestles into my arms while I let Southpaw ruin my morning sleep-in.

"What?"

"What's with the fucking attitude?" Southpaw grunts.

"It's nine in the morning."

"I've been up with my son for the past *seven hours*," he says. "My sleep is *far more fucked up than yours.*"

He sounds like he wants to bite me through the fucking phone. Anger issues. I don't have those with Quin next to me. I kiss her cheek.

"Okay, okay. What?"

"I need you to go out to the rez."

"Are you fucking kidding me?"

"No."

. . .

"Can I bring Quin?"

"You want to bring your nanny to torture a prisoner?"

Wyatt Shaw – master of communication.

"You didn't mention that's what I would be doing."

Normally, he wants me for the business end of things or wrangling a bunch of the chuckle fucks in our club into shape. I don't know why all of a sudden he wants me involved with the Oske situation.

"You know what it's like to have family members you didn't ask for," Southpaw says. "Ruger is beating the shit out of Darlene every damn day out in that trailer and if someone mentally stable doesn't head out there and take control over the situation, we'll lose our chance to get information about the bastards who killed our brothers."

"What do you want me to do?"

"Get him under control. Torture her... but with purpose. And *not physically*. I need information and I'd rather have someone smarter and calmer than Bucky on the job."

"I can't leave Quin here alone."

"Then send her to Juliette," Southpaw says, as if leaving her could ever be that easy for me. "If you get the information we need quickly... I see no reason to keep the bitch alive after she has that kid."

"Got it."

I've lost count of how many bodies we have on our hands. We may not be the ones to start any wars, but when you have a reputation like ours – money, territory, control over hundreds of miles of highway – you're bound to attract a few enemies. I hang up and glance down at Quin, who has her brown eyes fixed on my face.

My heart jumps a little bit at the way she's looking at me.

"How long have you been awake?"

"Are you really leaving?"

"Yes. But it's club business. I'll be back."

"Right," she says with a noticeably tense voice that instantly sends me into a panic. "And you're sending me to Juliette."

"She's your friend. I'm sure she misses you."

She scowls and throws her legs out of bed. "You don't think about anyone but yourself, Tanner."

I swear, women want to wake up angry. I groan and close my eyes as she throws on a robe. I glance at her through one open eyelid to see if she chooses to relax of her own accord. She doesn't. Somehow, before having a cup of coffee, I pissed her off. I'd better get to that coffee.

"Quin, baby. I know you're angry but I think we would feel a lot better if we had a cup of coffee."

She flares her nostrils at me and then storms off. Slamming the door.

Was that a yes on the coffee?

THIRTY-FOUR
QUIN

I should have never believed him when he said bringing Avery home was his "top priority". For 4 days, I have patiently waited for this man and his unending sex drive to leave and return with Avery – the baby girl I fell in love with.

It's not like I don't have feelings for Tanner.

It's just that this detour to Oklahoma makes me feel like... he's not being real with me. He's still the monster who would have thrown Avery to the desert coyotes if given half a chance. I start fussing around the kitchen for the coffee beans and it doesn't take long for me to realize that the arrogant redhead didn't even follow me.

He genuinely thinks my ass is going to bring him coffee in bed?

Hm...

. . .

But just as soon as the stubborn thought comes to me, a better thought comes in. Let him send me to Juliette.

The two of us will get Avery back.

Since when do I need Tanner Hollingsworth to handle my shit?

I'll make his ass some coffee. Pretend that I totally accept my fate. And once I'm in my bestfriend's Santa Fe penthouse... we'll begin creating a master plan.

When I return to the bedroom, I have a smile plastered on my face which Tanner easily matches. Men. They act all tough, but they will do just about anything to avoid conflict. Even matching my fake ass smile.

"Why you smiling, baby?" Tanner asks, reaching his greedy ass hands out for the coffee. He has sexy hands. Don't get me wrong. And sexy everything. He's just an asshole.

"I was just thinking... you're right. I should go to Juliette's. And appreciate how much you protect me."

Tanner sits up and sniffs his black coffee. I can't tell if he's enjoying the smell or checking for poison. Either way, he has no poison to worry about. Not today, at least.

With the cup in one hand, he pats the bed next to him.

"That's right," he says. "I'll do anything. And I promise... I won't be gone long."

"Don't let me rush you," I say, trying not to sound suspicious despite my guilty, racing heart. "You're right. I need to see Juliette."

I *almost* mention missing Avery, but bite my tongue. I don't want to put him on the trail. He tastes the coffee.

"Fuck, that's good," he says. "Remind me to keep you here forever..."

I nod and then whip my phone out. Tanner has his nose buried in the coffee when I shoot off a quick text to Juliette.

Quin: Tanner bringing me over soon. Villain mode.

She's my best friend. She'll know exactly what I mean...

Tanner is overly enthusiastic to get me on the back of his bike for the ride to Santa Fe. I try to convince him that I'm too big for a motorcycle, but he laughs his ass off and tells me that rednecks twice my size ride Harleys... If he didn't laugh like a hyena while trying to make me feel better, maybe it would have worked better.

What really causes me not to beg for him to rent a car is actually trying it. Tanner is annoyingly persuasive. Some might call it mildly threatening. I gear up and cling to him as we hit the highway, heading towards Santa Fe. I still can't believe he's going on some random ass mission while Avery is still in danger, but during the few instances I can put that out of my head... the ride is fun.

Like... it's more fun than anything I've ever done in my life. Even better because I don't have to be in control. Tanner knows exactly how to handle the bike and while I have my moments of pinching his sides like an angry grocery store lobster, I lose myself after a couple hours and just feel... *free.*

I didn't even know I was allowed to feel like this. I want to scream like people do on roller coasters, but with my mouth so close to

Tanner's ear, I don't want to blow his eardrums out. I just grab him tightly and rest my head on his back, appreciating every moment of *this*.

When we get to Juliette's, his face is all red saying goodbye, and not just from the sun.

"I'm not going upstairs," he says. "I have to leave but... promise you're going to be a good girl for me?"

"Duh," I whisper. "I want you to come back so you can get Avery..."

Tanner flashes me a half smile and then he touches my cheek.

"I'm going to miss your ass," he says. "And the rest of you."

He kisses me on the sidewalk and the public display sends a thrill straight through me. Being with Tanner no longer feels totally new, but getting kissed in public is definitely new for me. I don't know how to react, so I freeze at first. He pulls away with a gentle chuckle.

"Come on, baby. Kiss me back."

He sounds so happy. So *into me*. I throw my arms around him and kiss him back. I *like* getting kissed in public. It feels good. Affirming. And his lips are soft. Tanner has always been a great kisser.

When he pulls away, I don't want to say goodbye. But we have to. His eyes get a little misty and then he throws his helmet on. I've never seen this man get misty eyed, so I just stare at him and watch him ride away.

Just when I think he has no feelings... he does *this*.

· · ·

Tanner's sentiment makes it even harder to betray him. I just can't imagine leaving Avery alone any longer. Once I get upstairs, Juliette screams loudly and greets me. She seems so much happier now that she's a mom. Not only does it make me miss Avery even more, it makes me think crazy ass things about Tanner.

Like... having his baby.

It's not crazy as in "impossible". But are we the best people to bring a child into this world? Our relationship is... weird. A strange bond of mutual darkness. We don't need to share our secrets with each other because we share something else.

Juliette gets me her latest sweet treat from the fridge -- strawberry popsicles -- and gives me all her baby updates. Our friendship has only gotten better since we left high school.

"I'm sorry," she says, noticing my sad face. "I know you miss Avery. It's just... I'm obsessed with being a mom. I didn't think I would be."

I appreciate her sympathy. Avery isn't my 'real' daughter though, so maybe I have to pull it together.

I shrug. "You're fine. I just miss her."

"Hunter isn't here," she says. "The club business has gotten out of control. He's hardly here and it gets boring as fuck. I'm tired of going to Target."

"At least he lets you go to Target."

Juliette gives me another meaningful look.

"That's something else we need to talk about."

"What would that be?" I mutter, chewing on the popsicle stick and pretending to be extremely focused on the task.

"Tanner."

"Mr. Hollingsworth?"

"Quin. We're best friends. It's obvious. You have a crush on him. What the hell has been happening over there?"

"Nothing crazy."

· · ·

Everything that has happened has been fucking crazy -- like a fever dream. But with a lot more sex than fever dreams normally have.

"Oh really?" she says. "Nothing crazy?"

"Nope."

"Hunter says Tanner is obsessed with plus-sized women."

"Juliette, ew."

My best friend is also plus-sized. I don't want to think about her husband warning her about Tanner or anything like that.

"That's not what I mean," Juliette says, rolling her eyes but not letting me get away scot-free. "I mean... He snatched you up here in the middle of the night. I don't believe nothing crazy happened after that."

"Why not?"

"Because the idiots in this motorcycle club are crazy. Pure unfiltered all-American crazy."

"Mr. Hollingsworth is just a boring guy who spends all day in his office," I mutter.

I don't even know why I'm suddenly clamming up like this. I guess I've never had a guy to talk about, so I don't know what to say. What types of things can you tell your best friend? I don't want to tell Juliette about my nipples. Or how Tanner's dick feels.

Is that even girl talk?

Juliette laughs. "Right. Hunter has a boring side too."

"Mr. Hollingsworth doesn't pay any attention to me or Avery. Seriously."

"You are such a liar," Juliette says.

"I am not."

"Why are you even lying?" she says. "There's nothing wrong

with fucking your boss. Come on... It's not like he would let you sleep with anyone else."

Juliette has a mischievous glint in her eye that makes me want to shrivel up and die. I used to feel like there were two types of big girls -- cool and funny big girls and then awkward big girls. I was always the awkward one and I still don't get how Juliette can be so... relaxed.

"I didn't sleep with him," I say, doubling down on my lie, even if she's totally going to drag it out of me.

"Oh. My. God. Quin. Stop lying or I swear, I'll beat your ass."

"You can't beat my ass," I tease her. "You're a mom."

Juliette wriggles her eyebrows. "Exactly. My ass whooping genes have finally reached their peak."

"I don't care about Tanner, I just want to get Avery back."

"HA!" Juliette screams.

"What?"

"You called him Tanner."

"That's his name..."

"It's suspicious," she says, circling me like she's planning to salt me and put me on the grill.

I sigh and stick my hand out in an effort to get some personal space.

"You do not have to try to smell the lie on me."

"So you do smell like a lie," Juliette says, standing back and folding her arms.

I can't take it anymore.

"Okay, fine. I slept with Tanner. Happy?!"

"YES!" Juliette says. "YES!"

Okay... She's a little too excited.

. . .

"I told Hunter I would get you to confess. I won a hundred dollars... I won a hundred dollars..." Juliette starts shaking her ass like GloRilla, popping her booty all over me.

"You were betting on my sex life with your husband?"

"I'll give you half," Juliette says, looking back at it with her tongue out and continuing to remorselessly twerk on me.

I give her ass a hard smack which causes her to squeak and dart away from me.

"Sorry! I just knew when he kidnapped you that he was completely smitten."

"Ew, he was not smitten, Juliette..."

"Uh, yes he is. I know he is. Do you like him?"

"You don't even know what you're talking about."

"What? He's like the most responsible one in the entire club. And the richest. Don't tell Hunter I said that but... it's true."

"Who cares if he's rich?" I grumble. But I obviously noticed how luxurious Tanner's place in Arizona was. And that security system he has couldn't have been cheap either. He has several fancy cars at his house too and any time I've seen an invoice or important document in his office, the numbers always have a couple commas.

"You could become his old lady," Juliette says, shrugging. "Then you might care."

"What does that even mean."

"It's a biker thing where they tattoo you and all your problems go away... except all the gang problems."

I stare at Juliette like she has three heads, but she just keeps nodding at me like she's sharing common knowledge. I don't know any healthy relationship that starts with a tattoo and gang problems.

"Juliette, are you crazy?"

"Nope. I'm just realistic. Life could be so damn shitty, Quin. If Tanner wants to tattoo your ass and give you a baby... why not?"

"Because. I don't have Avery. It's not going to be the same without her."

"So you're admitting you slept with him?"

I try to smack her ass again but she squeals and finds herself on the other side of the counter before I can get an effective hit in.

"Okay, okay!" she says. "I'll help you get Avery back like I promised. But if you love Tanner..."

"Who said I love him?"

"Okay. Fine. If you eventually possibly fall in love with him... I support it."

"You have no idea what you're talking about," I grumble. Juliette might not be so positive about Tanner's crazy ass if she knew that he climbed in through my bedroom window to take my virginity in secret.

"He can't be that bad," Juliette says. "He would call Hunter like once a week to brag about how good you were with Avery."

"Seriously?"

"Yeah. I told Hunter that he was totally in love..."

"He's not."

"We'll see," Juliette says. "Now. Where is Avery and how do we get her."

"And what do you do with your kids? And your pregnancy?"

"Right," Juliette says. "Can't leave the kids behind... I'll handle that. Do you know who has Avery? The pregnancy isn't a problem."

Juliette is crazy. Pregnancy might be a problem – especially if something crazy happens and her husband decides we both need to die over it. I know he's crazy protective over her and I can't blame him. Juliette loves trouble. It's why I love her.

"Deborah Shaw. Tanner basically forced her to leave with Avery because his mom is going crazy and wants to do... something."

"Isn't his mom an old white lady? When was the last time an old white lady killed a baby?"

"That feels like something we shouldn't ask the internet in case the FBI is watching," I mutter.

Juliette sighs. "Fine. He's probably overreacting because that's what men do. We'll just go to Deborah Shaw's house."

"You know where that is?"

"Uh, yeah," Juliette says. "But we have to find a car that we can sneak off in and we have kind of a long drive on our hands..."

"Are we going to get caught?"

Juliette shrugs. "Not if I break every law on the way there."

"Okay. What about the kids?"

"I'll call someone," Juliette says. "Do you mind checking on them while I make those calls?"

I nod and then ask her about the car.

"I'll handle the car," she says. "Don't worry. It's been a long time since I've been on an adventure..."

I hope it won't be much of an "adventure" outside of maybe seeing a cool porcupine on the side of the road or something. I just want to get Avery and get back here.

. . .

Tanner would rain hell on me if anything happened to us and my ass isn't ready for that -- at all.

THIRTY-FIVE
CASH

Oske sticks her head out the door of the trailer. Her high, Indian cheekbones are a raw, red color from spending too much time in the sun.

"I'm not letting your white ass in this trailer until you pay up," she says, practically spitting on me over her $1,400.

"Ever considered your girl left your ass because of your attitude."

"MONEY!" Oske yells at me, some of her spit landing on my three day old beard. I glare at her and wipe it off before reaching into my back pocket. Southpaw had better compensate my ass for having to deal with this wolverine of a woman. I've met softer cacti. She snatches it and presses it to her nose, calming down only slightly as she thumbs through hundreds.

"All there," I tell her. Oske looks up at me without the slightest hint of fear.

"Ruger has her locked in my bedroom. He's drunk on the couch."

"Where do you sleep?"

"Outside," she says through gritted teeth. "I'm not falling asleep in the same room as Ruger Blackwood."

There's genuine fear in that last sentence and considering

Oske doesn't give a shit about anything, I notice that fear. I grab her forearm, yanking her out of the trailer and shutting the door. She hits me several times until I let go of her forearm.

"Grab me like that again and you won't have to worry about having more bastards."

"Excuse me?"

"I heard you fucked around and had a baby," she says, getting all puffed up when she notices my slight reaction. "What? I'm allowed to listen to conversations in my own house."

I roll my eyes. Confidently wrong. Typical. I'm not here to set the record straight. I need to find out how quickly I can get this fucking job done so I can get Quin back from Juliette's. I'm sure it won't take more than three days around Juliette for them to get into trouble.

"How has Ruger been?"

"He's worse than Gideon," he says. "He called me a squaw. I should charge Wyatt for that too."

"Ever considered charging us money for actual work?"

"I'm not a whore," she says, wrinkling her nose. "So get that out of your head."

"That's not what I meant," I growl. "Although if you keep pissing me off, I'll charge Ruger fifty bucks to use your disrespectful ass however he wants."

Oske thinks better of pushing me. I'm not like Southpaw. I'll let Ruger on her ass and go have a smoke at the gas station while he does it. Ruger must scare the shit out of her.

"He's a psycho. He spends all day cursing out that pregnant white woman through the door and threatening to kill her. She's pregnant. What does he think is going to happen to the baby?" Oske sounds genuinely upset when she gets to the part about the baby. Her rising emotions remind me of Quin.

Quin would want me to do something... kind.

"You know his wife cheated on him, right?"

"So what?" Oske says. "That doesn't give him a right to hurt her."

"She joined a gang of Neo-nazi bikers after getting out of prison and those bikers murdered our brothers. He can do whatever he wants with her.

Oske looks frustrated rather than angry now.

"White people are so stupid."

"Excuse me?"

"You catch more flies with honey than vinegar," she says, glaring at me. "But whatever. Not my problem. I'm going to go pay my landlord and buy some weed."

She struts past me with a haughty swagger that makes me seriously wonder how Southpaw handles this completely unreasonable woman. I watch her strut towards some shitty ass motorcycle and get on the back – without a helmet.

"HEY!" I yell at her. Oske looks at me, deciding if she's going to listen.

"Bring some of that weed back for me."

"That's going to cost you, white boy!" she shouts back.

I wave her off. Cost me? I'll get her couch back from Ruger. That's about as much as she can expect from me. I walk into Oske's trailer. Either the conversation or the sound of Oske's motorcycle outside woke him up. I can't tell which. I can see why Oske doesn't want to be around him.

"Where's your shirt?"

"Don't know," Ruger says, yawning and nearly allowing his sweatpants to slide down far enough to expose his dick. It's bad enough that I can see a tuft of blond fur sticking out the top.

"You look like a fucking mess."

"Darlene cheated on me," Ruger says, wiping his eyes. "What do you expect me to do?"

I can't hear her, so Darlene must either be quiet in the back on purpose or fast asleep. Ruger has made the rest of the trailer a fucking mess. He has white powder in a heap on a round mirror seated at the edge of Oske's coffee table.

"I expect you to get yourself together."

"Fine," Ruger grunts, sitting up and leaning his muscular form over the table. He starts cutting his line as I take personal note of everything in the room. Guns. A belt. A baseball bat. A pair of black leather gloves. Duct tape. Ruger taps whatever the fuck he's snorting into a thin line with his razor blade.

"Oske's a slut bitch," he grunts as he works on the line.

"What's going on with Darlene?"

"Pregnant."

"It's not yours."

"No, it's not fucking mine," Ruger spits, like I'm the one who knocked the bitch up. He bends his head to the table and inhales enough to knock out an elephant.

"HEY!" I grab him by his neck and yank him back. "ARE YOU FUCKING CRAZY!"

I tilt his head back and Ruger just starts laughing. Probably because he's high out of his fucking mind. A trickle of blood flows from his nose as he laughs louder. His long, blond hair sticks to his neck.

"I don't give a fuck."

"Well you're no good to any of us dead."

I toss him back against the couch. He groans but whatever drug he did must have some type of upper because he sits up and his pupils are so wide that they cover his icy blue irises.

"I don't care…"

"You have to care."

Ruger shakes his head. "She's pregnant with another man's kid. The Nazi guy? He was the guard at her prison. Can you fucking believe it?"

"Does it matter?"

"No," he says. "And I don't need a fucking babysitter."

He wipes the blood away from his nose and onto his pants. He might not need a babysitter, but he definitely needs some goddamn rehab. Or some other way out of his misery.

"I'm not here to babysit you. I'm here to make sure we don't go to prison because of Darlene."

"She's my fucking wife. I can put her in the ground if I want to."

He wipes his nose again and I try to remind myself that he's high before I lose my shit and punch him. Gideon would have tried to maim him just for that line he just hit. Darlene... What Ruger ever saw in that skank, I'll never understand.

"You can put her in the ground once we have what we need."

Ruger grimaces. "I got her to tell me last week."

He leans over the table and starts cutting up another line. I don't know what part to react to first. I let him work on the line, just because he seems more likely to answer my questions if I don't stand between him and his drug.

"Why is she alive then?"

"Because. I want that bitch's baby. I'm gonna get the baby before I kill her."

So it's exactly like Oske said. Worse. How long does he expect to keep this woman captive and torturing her while pregnant? I didn't see myself as the type to care but... it's like a bit of Quin Nash weaseled its way into my head. And my heart.

. . .

"If you torture her, the baby could come out fucked up."

Ruger wrinkles his hose. "How?"

"Brain development."

"That's a load of liberal bullshit," he says. Then he does another line. I sigh. Oske's demands for $1,400 sound more reasonable after a few minutes around Ruger.

I agree, liberals in this country *are* responsible for a lot of bullshit. Couldn't tell you what exactly, but they cause a lot of problems. Doesn't mean you can run around fucking with pregnant women.

"How far along is she?"

"Seven months."

Damn.

Ruger gets up and whirls around towards the bedrooms.

"I should go talk to her again. Get the fucking truth..."

I grab Ruger's shoulder. "You have the truth. And before I let you go in there and lose your head... I need you to tell me."

THIRTY-SIX

QUIN

This was too easy. Juliette borrows a blue Toyota Rav-4 from some club member and we spend two days driving out to Deb's second home in Missouri. Considering how much time I spent locked up in Tanner's house, this road trip is a dream come true. We see everything we can along the old Route 66 highway headed east. It's not like I *forget* Avery, but since I know we're headed to see her and she's safe, I *let go* for a while and it's bliss.

There's almost nothing better than being the passenger princess with my best friend in the front seat. She lets me pick the music, which is a nice change of pace. Tanner doesn't have bad taste, but he doesn't deviate at all from his preference for country music. He would rather listen to the same ten Luke Combs songs while fixing the bike than try one R&B song.

I can finally catch up on Summer Walker's latest releases. Juliette knows all the words already — or at least she's pretty close — so I have to just mumble along and bob my head until I learn the lyrics.

Freedom feels good. We stop at McDonalds and get French

fries and Frosties. It seems so damn simple, but after all that time under Tanner's absolute control, I have a weird craving for fast food.

I nearly lose my mind when I see the price of large French fries. It didn't feel like Tanner had my ass locked up long enough for inflation to take hold.

"Girl, I don't even know what inflation is," Juliette says, when I complain about the French fries. "You think they still have apple pie?"

Of course, they still have apple pie. So we get four.

Our road trip is low-key a food festival, sight-seeing, and jamming out to music. There is nothing like driving through the Southwest like that. Juliette buys us souvenirs everywhere we stop and by the time we make it out east, we have hot pink rhinestone cowboy hats on and matching buckskin vests over our outfits.

The vests are starting to feel more like an impulse buy now that it's been over 80 miles since we stumbled upon a kitschy gas station. Juliette doesn't share any of my hesitation over our yeehaw aesthetic, but I'm wondering if I should have at least showed up looking... normal. Will Avery recognize me in a rhinestone covered cowboy hat?

Juliette parks in front a gigantic ivory house with large pillars and two willow trees a few feet away from the front porch. There are three motorcycles parked beneath the tree, and two cars I don't recognize in the other parking spots. I wouldn't call where Juliette parks a spot exactly but... she didn't hit anything. I can't stop staring at the house. It's huge.

I don't know what I expected Deb Shaw's house to look like but the palatial mansion seems more like something that belongs in New Orleans than Missouri. It just has that old plantation house look to it and it honestly has that spooky, uncomfortable feeling too.

"Can you imagine growing up in that slave house?" Juliette says. "Weird."

"Yeah... it's... old-fashioned."

"It's creepy," Juliette says. "White people are weird."

I wasn't the one who said it. I guess I see her point. Maybe they liked the location. Deb Shaw's house is so tucked away that I can't imagine anyone stumbling upon it. I imagine that it must at least feel safe.

Deb Shaw greets us with a smile. "Avery is upstairs. I'm so glad you're here. I promised Tanner I would help, but my years of raising children are long behind me. I like it that way."

"Is she sleeping?" I ask desperately. "Can I see her?"

Deb agrees and I can't even contain my excitement. I try to act normal and go through all the regular steps of polite human interaction, but I barely want to talk about the road trip. I just want to hold Avery. Smell her baby smell. Kiss her on the head. Promise her that I won't let her go.

Whatever Tanner plans for her in the long term, I want to be there for her. I'll do anything. I'll beg. I'll submit to whatever weird contract he wants as long as he lets me take care of this sweet baby girl. Juliette is that extroverted friend happy to take the lead, so I nod along and drop an insightful comment in here or there, just trying not to seem totally desperate to see Avery.

Deb invites us inside and offers us ice-cream. I almost decline — which is rare for me — until she says, "Once you're settled with the ice-cream, I'll bring Avery downstairs."

So I agree to ice-cream immediately, and so does Juliette. Deb Shaw serves us up giant bowls of Amaretto ice-cream with maraschino cherries and whipped cream on top, leading us into her living room.

"I'll bring Avery down..."

Juliette and I plop down next to each other on the couch. Juliette points to a picture of three skinny boys, each holding a fish as long as their torsos.

"That's Wyatt and his brothers — Ethan and Owen."

"He looks like Owen," I say. "Not Ethan."

Then we both hear the distinct deafening sound of a gunshot upstairs.

It's just one gunshot, but it's enough for both of us to drop our ice-cream on the table and thoughtlessly race upstairs in the direction of the sound. No screams. Nothing. Until Avery begins screaming her head off. *Shit.*

"Do you have a gun?" I ask Juliette, who scampers up the stairs ahead of me.

"No," she says. "We'll work it out!"

I don't even know where I'm following her. We get to the top of the winding staircase and I have to convince myself to stop death-gripping the railing because I nearly slipped on the carpet twice on the way up.

"I think it came from that room," Juliette says, bounding down the hallway towards a white door with a crystal handle left slightly ajar.

"Juliette!" I yell at her as she swings the door open when an armed killer could be in the room.

· · ·

"Stand back!" Deb Shaw yells. I jump back into the doorway and I have to grab Juliette's forearm so she doesn't stumble immediately into the line of fire. Avery is still in her crib, which instantly calms my nerves. The bedroom window is wide open next to the crib.

I wouldn't normally have noticed such an insignificant detail — it's hot in this part of Missouri. But there's a woman standing next to the open window with her hands up and her back pressed against the wall. The sheer white curtains billow around her, highlighting the open window and the woman's likely entry point.

The second I catch sight of her face... I know who we're dealing with. The gunshot hit the exterior wall and it must have gone straight through because there's a tiny hole with light filtering through.

"It's just a .22, but it can put a hole in a bitch's head just as good as a shotgun can," Deb says.

"That's my baby, you bitch," The woman says in a low, desperate voice.

I can't help it, her voice tugs at my heartstrings. The rest of her sends chills down my spine. She looks like Avery. Now that I see her, I see how the baby doesn't look like Tanner at all. She has blue eyes like her mother — exactly the same shape. The woman with her back pressed against the wall doesn't look like she's very young, but the story I heard about Tanner's dad involved a young woman. I guess she looks older than her age.

For her age, she's somewhat tall, not like that makes it any better. She also dresses like it's about ten degrees warmer than it actually is, which shocks me because there's barely any body fat on her. Lots of cuts though – and some of them look self-inflicted. My stomach turns. Anything that even remotely reminds me of the life I left behind makes me feel... sick and detached.

How did this *girl* end up with a bunch of gangsters? She has a busted lip and her hair looks like it hasn't seen a brush in weeks. There are deep round sores at the crease of her elbow. I don't know what those are from but they look weird...

The tattoo on her arm stops me from feeling sorry for how rough she looks. My stomach turns again for an entirely different reason.

I almost don't want to believe what I'm seeing.

What the fuck? She literally has a swastika tattooed on her arm. I barely paid attention in history class, but I've seen enough movies to know that you don't get that symbol tattooed without knowing what it means and without knowing that it means something fucked up beyond belief.

"I don't care if it's your baby," Deb says. "I have another round in the chamber and if you move a muscle, I'll paint her bedroom walls with her mother's brains."

I freeze in terror. I always assumed Southpaw got his terrifying demeanor from his biker dad, but clearly, he got at least a little bit of that heat from his mother. Juliette puts her hand in front of me to hold me back this time. None of us want to move.

"You dumbass," Avery's mother says. "If I know where you live, her daddy knows where she lives."

"Her daddy is dead," Deb says. "But not her family. If you want to live, you will listen to my instructions, little girl. You think you're all tough with those tattoos, but I've been beating up whores like you since I learned how desperate you were for biker dick."

"I'm not a whore," she says. "I'm a respectable white person. I carry myself respectably. I don't let niggers around me or my kids."

She glares at Juliette and I, clearly trying to get a reaction out of us. It works on Juliette who flips Avery's mom the middle finger, but I just purse my lips and try not to laugh. Deb Shaw might not care about this crazy hoe dropping the n-word, but I won't let her get the upper hand by thinking she gets under my skin.

"What did you just say?" Deb says. "Because that doesn't sound like something a respectable lady would say."

"I said," the girl says smugly. "They're niggers."

She screams. Loudly. Because Deb fires at the wall over her head. Two inches above her to be exact. She covers her ears and keeps screaming — clearly not hit, but maybe not aware of it. Juliette and I have our ears covered because we didn't have any warning that Deb was going to actually shoot her. The gunshot nearly blows out my eardrums.

"Calm down," Deb yells. "When I'm ready to put a bullet in your whore ass, I won't leave any room for all that carrying on. Now shut the hell up."

THIRTY-SEVEN
CASH

Southpaw hasn't stopped yelling for the past fifteen minutes. Every minute without Quin has been living hell. Now, she's found some way to add to that mess. Ruger yells an incomprehensible string of insults at Darlene behind the door. She calls him the n-word. I hear the sound of furniture getting knocked around. He better not be whooping her again...

"ARE YOU LISTENING?" Southpaw yells.

He blames me, somehow, for Quin Nash's deviant behavior. If she learned a fucking thing from living with me, she would have never done this.

"Yes, I'm listening," I growl. "I don't have the privilege of losing my fucking cool. I have to convince Ruger not to beat the shit out of a pregnant woman back there and now... this."

I also have to calm Southpaw's ass, which he doesn't realize takes a fair effort, and now I find out that Avery might be in real trouble. Quin is in real trouble. And Deb Shaw has Avery's whore mother captive.

We have too many problems at once and too many problems normally means someone ends up in prison. That's what happened last time. I don't need the club to collect their debt from a Hollingsworth this time. No fucking way.

"We have bigger problems than Ruger and Darlene. The Midnight SS know where my mother lives and she doesn't seem to give a shit. I need you to grab Quin, Juliette, and Avery and *convince my mother to see sense.*"

"She has no more reason to listen to me than to listen to you."

He's quiet for a beat, which means he sees my point.

"Anna says I should recognize when I lack the mental stability to deal with something and leave it to someone with a calmer demeanor."

I can't tell if he's just telling me that to kiss my ass. He does sound uncharacteristically humble, which makes him sound more believable.

"Who says I have a calmer demeanor?"

"She does," He snaps. "Now will you head over there?"

"How fast do you think I can drive?"

"Fast enough to cut Juliette and Quin off on the old Route 66 highway. I don't need them knowing you're on your way."

"Why not?"

"Because... they're stubborn and Juliette could find trouble in a goddamn straitjacket. The fewer people who know they're riding across the country with a baby in tow, the better."

"What about Deb and her prisoner?" I answer. "If they're leaving before I can get there, I don't see how you expect me to handle both."

"Use whatever family you have," Southpaw says. "Use Owen."

Owen is a more mentally stable choice than Ethan, but I would almost rather have a younger Sinclair or a newly patched-in member than a Shaw.

"Are you sure we can leave Ruger here alone?"

"No. I'm not sure. But we have to hope for the best. Hope that his Christian upbringing prevails."

"The last time I brought him to church, he was so drunk he pissed behind the podium," I say, reminding Wyatt of the horrible first Christmas after Ruger's enlistment.

"I'll pray for him," Southpaw says. Like that would be much better...

I don't have much time to argue. Ruger's yelling at Darlene only picks up and maybe if there's any God in this house at all, he's giving me an opportunity to escape this goddamn nightmare. I hang up on Southpaw and hesitantly approach the door. I hear the sound of smacking going on. Then another scream. Here we go.

I throw the door open to find Darlene weeping and crouched in the corner, Ruger standing over her holding a leather belt.

"I told you not to hit her."

"I'm not hitting her. I'm scaring her," he says, relaxing his shoulders and tossing the belt back on the bed. "Big difference."

"She's *pregnant.*"

"That's right," Ruger says, turning to Darlene. "I'm gonna sell her baby to a pack of niggers and see how she likes it."

"I HATE YOU!" Darlene shrieks before descending into violent body-wracking sobs. I would feel more sorry for her if it weren't for the racist tattoos all over her. Or the fact that she betrayed the club. Ruger's information paints an unfavorable picture of his wife. I shouldn't be surprised. Some chicks hang around the club just so they can get shit. Usually drugs, bikes, liquor, or babies. I don't know what the fuck Darlene wanted, but I'm not entirely surprised she wasn't loyal.

"Well, you racist bitch, that's what you deserve," Ruger says. "A bunch of niggers raping your goddamn baby."

Is this Ruger's idea of fighting racism? I put a hand on his shoulder, fighting my urge to use my hand for something a touch more violent.

"Enough talking," I huff. "I need you to promise me you can hold it together until I get back from a short road trip."

"Where the fuck are you going?" he says.

Great. I should have anticipated that question. Answering it will expose exactly how much time I need him to keep it together for and who knows how Ruger will respond to that information...

"Southpaw needs me in Missouri."

"Good. I need privacy with my wife."

"NO!" Darlene shrieks. "You can't leave me with him. He's going to *kill me*."

He very well might. I don't have a problem with him killing Darlene. She's a goddamn psychopath. I remember Ruger working overtime shifts for the club to keep money on her books while she was allegedly behind bars. I questioned how a woman in prison could spend over $4,000 a month, but he never did. That was his girl and while he might be a stupid fucking asshole... that was all he cared about. Loyalty.

"I won't kill her," Ruger says, though he keeps his hunter's eyes trained on Darlene and she looks like little more than lunch to him. I can't tell if he's being honest, and I can't tell if I care. "Plus. Owen is here to look after her."

"Owen doesn't give a shit if I live or die," Darlene says. She whines the sentence, really, but I can't let this woman's tone get to me. It's all a big fucking manipulation with Darlene and I have Hollingsworth problems to deal with now. Not Blackwood problems. They all like crazy bitches. They need to sit their asses up in church and think about *that*.

"Actually," I say, bursting both their bubbles. "I'm taking Owen with me."

"The fuck is going on?" Ruger says, sliding his finger across his throat to intimidate Darlene into another wailing session.

"Can't tell you in front of her. But... it's connected."

"QUIET," Ruger says to Darlene, shutting her up instantly. He doesn't give me much hope that this woman will survive him. I pat him on the shoulder.

"I'd better talk to Owen," I mutter.

"Take Oske with you," Ruger says. "Stupid bitch doesn't even put out."

"She's gay, Ruger."

"So what? I eat pussy too," he says, running his fingers through his hair. "It would be my biggest dream to fuck that colored girl right here in front of Darlene."

It's hard to imagine this man is a result of a deeply religious country upbringing.

"Why don't you head downtown and meet a nice girl at the local bar," I say to Ruger. "You're pent up."

"Get Owen and Oske out of here," he says. "Don't worry about how pent up I am."

"Right."

"I promise I won't kill the bitch until she has the baby."

Owen and Oske are both sitting on the porch drinking and

gambling on a game of Gin Rummy. Shit isn't going well for Owen judging by the smile on the Indian girl's face.

"This game is *not* that hard."

"Remind me to sell you to the first Midnight SS biker I see," Owen grumbles. Oske smacks his forearm and they laugh as if there's something funny about the Midnight SS situation. I never understood people who cope with humor. The only person who has ever helped me cope is somewhere halfway across the country getting her ass in trouble.

"Fun's over," I growl at them. "Southpaw wants us back East."

"Excuse me?" Oske says. "Why do white people think everything is free?"

"Because it is," I snap at her. "I don't think you want us to leave you here with Ruger."

"I don't want Ruger staying in my trailer at all," Oske says, standing up and folding her arms. Owen stands up too, most likely to stop her from recklessly launching herself at me.

"He's staying in the trailer," I tell Oske definitively. "So you can work out another place to stay or get used to it."

"I'm not staying here with him. He's a creep. I'm coming with you."

"Absolutely not. I'm dropping you off at the bus station," I tease her. Oske looks at me glaring until I break into a smile. She punches my arm pretty hard for a girl that small. Wolverine ass woman.

"I need more money," Oske says calmly but firmly. "Call Wyatt and tell him to send me money if he expects me to stick with you assholes."

"We can't keep giving you cash without getting it from somewhere," I explain through gritted teeth. I know Oske only enjoys pissing people off, so I try not to give her the satisfaction. Unfortunately, she observes the slightest twitching in my facial muscles. A smug smile crosses her face.

"I know how expensive it is to get housing out there in the colonizer world. I think you owe me at least $5,000 for using my house to torture some crazy ass white woman."

Owen can't hide his worry. He steps between me and Oske.

"What the hell are you going to do when they start shooting?" he asks her.

"It depends on what you give me," she says. "I can handle a shotgun, rifle. Not so good with a pistol but... I can practice."

Owen raises his eyebrow and looks at me for guidance. I have to run a quick analysis of the situation and determine which choice will bring me the least amount of trouble. Ruger putting his hands on Oske could start an outright civil war at the worst possible time. I might not have $5,000 to give her, but if I stick her on the back of Owen's bike, we can shut her up for the next couple hundred miles.

If we're lucky, I'll get a chance to dump her on the doorstep of some affiliated Shaw and get Oske off my hands. How does she go through money so fucking quickly, anyway?

"She's good with a gun from what I've heard," I answer Owen, registering his obvious surprise. "But I wouldn't trust her with one unless absolutely necessary."

Oske relaxes visibly sensing that she's going to get her way.

"Get a bag packed," I tell her. "Owen will carry you. Before I head back to Santa Fe, I have to intercept my girl and my daughter."

"Since when do you have a daughter?" Oske says, looking me up and down.

Owen steps in so I don't have to. "Get your shit packed, Oske. I don't rid easy."

"I don't need you to go easy on me, white boy."

Owen grins. "Sure you want to play that game?"

She rolls her eyes and struts back into her room to get her stuff. Owen fully expresses his concerns.

"Is this what Wyatt wants?"

"She's your family," I tell him. "I'm doing what makes sense to keep her safe. Ruger is unhinged and I don't know the last time he's been with a woman."

Owen returns my grimace and nods.

"Best keep Oske out of trouble. She has a smart mouth and so does he. Terrible combination."

"She's good with a gun," I tell him. "That much is true. Hope we don't need a woman to save our asses."

"We won't need a woman at all," Owen says. "Mom has that Nazi bitch in her basement somewhere and Avery is with Quin. I heard through the grapevine she treats Avery like her own."

Just the slightest mention of Quin makes me uncomfortable. It's not shame, but this deep desire to protect her and even keep her name away from other men. Even Owen.

"She does," I respond. "She's a good girl."

Owen smirks. "Damn. You are sprung."

"What the fuck does that mean?"

"It means, you're obvious as shit when you like a woman."

I can feel my cheeks betraying me. "Shut the fuck up."

Owen laughs, but luckily, he's smart enough to drop the subject when Oske emerges with a backpack slung around one shoulder.

"I am ready to get the fuck out of here and earn some money," she says. "Let's go."

"Earn?" I grumble.

"Yes," she says stubbornly. "Earn. Now saddle up, white boys. Let's go save a baby."

From kidnapping a baby to saving one... I'm glad Oske is a Shaw problem.

THIRTY-EIGHT
QUIN

Avery sleeps in the back of the Rav-4 in a comfortable car seat. Deb upgraded her seat while she had custody of her in Missouri.

Juliette insists that Mariah Carey is "just as important" to brain development as classical music, so that's what we have playing in the car at a soft, gentle volume. Driving back to Santa Fe with Avery in the back, Mariah Carey playing, and a mission accomplished without either of us dying, we both feel good.

I at least wait until we pass through Kansas to express my doubts.

"Don't you think that was too easy?"

"That's the trauma talking," Juliette replies calmly.

"What are you talking about?" I grumble, wishing I could disappear into my seat. Juliette relishes uncomfortable conversations in a way that I don't.

She excitedly wriggles in her seat as if she's been keeping this conversation topic loaded in the chamber.

"Well," Juliette starts dramatically. "You keep expecting

danger around every corner. You have to train your mind to believe the world is a safe place."

"There's literally a gang of Nazi bikers hunting down members of the club including my boyfriend, and possibly Avery if her mom is connected to them."

Juliette is quiet for a beat.

"Boyfriend?!" Juliette says. "Is that what's going on?"

"Girl, I don't know. It's the closest I've ever come. I think."

"Yes... Finally, you are admitting *real* feelings."

"When did I say that?"

"You are."

"I am *not*," I reply. "And can we focus on the Nazi biker problem?"

"Sure, there may be Nazi bikers," she says. "But we made it this far."

"I'm amazed your relentless optimism hasn't gotten you killed."

"It got me to Santa Fe," Juliette says. "And it got me to go on an awesome road trip with my best friend."

She has a point there.

"Thanks, girl. I love you too."

"See? We're fine. Just relax and don't think about anything."

"We should think about some things," I say.

"Like what?"

"That orange light."

"Oh, we have thirty more miles."

"And we're in the middle of nowhere. Let's stop at the next place for gas."

Juliette is the type of person who "knows her car" and I'm the type of person who never likes driving a car with less than half a tank of gas. She makes me nervous as hell riding around like this. It's not like I don't want to believe in her optimistic world-view. It's just... Avery.

My protective urges surrounding her are stronger than I ever expected when I signed Tanner's contract. At least we have her back. A giant exit sign calms my heightening anxiety as I watch the Rav-4 give more aggressive signals about the dwindling gas tank.

Juliette calmly veers off and coasts us into a spot in front of pump number seven. I swear we must have seven drops of gas left in the tank. She grins at me.

"I told you we would make it!"

"You are the reason I have anxiety."

"Woo!" Juliette says. "I'll pump the gas. You get the snacks. Deal?"

She reaches into her purse and hands me a $50 bill before I can protest. I don't bother protesting since I know her husband gives her a giant allowance and I am hungry as hell. Avery might need some formula and a change too, but I'll get the snacks first and then assess the situation.

The gas station is called Sinclairs. I wonder if the owners have any relation to Hunter Sinclair, Juliette's husband. She seems completely convinced about our safety here, so I assume she must be right. I walk into the gas station, suddenly nervous.

It's just a gas station. A normal one at that. There are those giant machines with flavored ice. Donuts. Several flavors of burned, watered down coffee. Tiles that smell like disinfectant. And one employee at the front. She has dark hair in a single braid that hangs over her right shoulder and hazel eyes that have at least three colors on the irises. Woah. Pretty. But she doesn't look like Juliette's husband. She looks more like Wyatt.

"Hi," she says. "How may I help you?"

I glance down at her name tag. Lacey.

"Uh... I'm just looking around."

"Would you like to try our cold brew?" she asks. "It's a new product we have and nobody out here knows what the hell it is. You look more... urban."

I don't know if I should be offended or not, but I nod and accept Lacey's offer for cold brew. She ducks to the mini-fridge behind her when the gas station's side door opens up, ringing a loud bell, which isn't necessary to announce the newcomer, who yells the second she pushes the door open.

"SOMEONE HELP!" she screams, running into the middle of the gas station floor in a panic. "HELP ME!"

Lacey perks straight up, setting the cold brew on the counter.

"What's going on, ma'am?" Lacey asks, showing enough confusion that I'm guessing this isn't some local flavor accustomed to expressing herself like this. This woman came from the other side of the gas station too, so I can't just look behind me and see where the hell she came from.

"I NEED HELP!" the woman screams, but then she looks straight at me. "COME. YOU CAN HELP ME."

I don't want to go with her -- not without telling Juliette -- but she grabs my arm and starts dragging me towards the door.

"Ma'am!" Lacey yells at both of us, but I don't hear what she says because the crazy white lady who just dragged me outside shuts the door behind us. Now, I really don't feel good.

"I should go..."

There's no one out here. But the white woman's grip on my forearm gets tight. I whip it away from her and while turning my body around, I see that we are very much not alone at all. Shit.

A tall man wearing all black and a helmet gets off a bike, walking towards the gas station door.

The woman blocks the door so I can't get back in, trapping me there for him I assume. I don't give her motives much thought. She's about half my size, so I do something I never thought I was capable of and I suddenly turn into a goddamn NFL player. I grab her ass and haul her out of the way.

She screams, but I scream even louder because the biker shoots at us. Well, he's probably just shooting at me, but he clearly doesn't give a fuck who he hits. The bullet nearly deafens me, but I rip the door open anyway, and since I'm still running, I assume he missed.

I need to keep moving. When I burst into the gas station, I slam straight into Lacey and smack my jaw hard on the shotgun she's holding up. Thankfully, she has the muzzle pointed at the ceiling so we both just scream loudly and shooting pain surges through my jaw from whacking my damn face against the gun.

"GET BEHIND ME!" Lacey says, swinging her black braid over her shoulder and pointing her gun straight into the screaming woman's stomach as she chases after me. Lacey shoves her back, avoiding the trigger as she shoves the woman against the glass.

The biker outside keeps approaching the door and he fires again.

"GET DOWN!" Lacey yells at me. I want to be the type of woman to jump up and senselessly join in a gunfight, but I obey Lacey's command and immediately get down on the ground. I can't just go running into battle when Avery is on the other side of this gas station and for all I know... she's their damn target.

Once I get down on the ground, I abandon loyalty to everyone except Avery and roll around to face the other door so I can army crawl to the second exit and sprint back to Juliette and Avery in the backseat. Juliette must have heard the gunshots, so I know she's in the driver's seat ready for a getaway.

I run towards the other door expecting to see Juliette outside, safely in the car, prepared to drive us both to a second location. Instead when I open the door, I nearly bowl Juliette's wild ass over and get myself shot in the process. She yells at me to be careful and then tells me to duck. I cover my ears and duck, correct about my instincts that her crazy ass fully planned on firing that weapon. She fires and a display explodes.

"He's down by the coffee!" Lacey screams, aware enough to recognize that Juliette is on our side. Maybe she knows her, but I can't tell if that's it. Juliette whips her pistol around, but there are no gunshots for a few more seconds. Then, I hear Lacey scream.

"LET GO OF HER!"

Juliette runs past me and I rise to my feet, still locked on my mission to get to Avery. Unfortunately, the gas station has turned into a war zone. I shove through the door as I hear another two gunshots — from the pistol this time. I hear Juliette screaming one last time as I open the door and run towards the Rav-4.

My first thought is to check for the keys in the car. They're in there. The windows are down, and by some miracle... Avery is safe. I don't know if she's the target or not, but adrenaline pushes me to do everything in my power to escape. Juliette has a gun. Lacey has a gun... they'll be fine.

After checking on Avery through the back window, I rush around to the other side of the car as fast as possible so I can drive. Normal driving wouldn't make me nervous. Driving a Rav-4 faster than a motorcycle scares the crap out of me. I don't want to flip the car. I don't want to hurt Avery.

Glancing back one last time for Juliette, I hop into the driver's seat. I don't want to leave her behind but... if I don't protect Avery, who else will? I can't let anything happen to her. I put my hands on the steering wheel, gripping tightly, frozen in place for just a few seconds longer when I hear the gas station door open and Juliette screaming.

I can't make out her words at first, but she wants me to know something. I move as quickly as I can, leaning over to open the passenger side door. As Juliette gets closer, I can hear what she's saying. Finally. And it's not good.

"THEY GOT LACEY. WE GOTTA GO EAST. WE GOTTA GO EAST."

"East? I thought we were going—

"DRIVE, QUIN. DRIVE THE DAMN CAR."

I start moving before she gets the door shut. But it's Juliette. She screams. She hollers. But she gets the door shut and I skid out of the parking lot back the way we came from. She's my best friend. I trust her. Avery does too, clearly, because she thinks my crazy driving is hilarious and starts laughing, gurgling and clapping her hands in the backseat.

I watch the speedometer climb from 65 to 75 to 85. My hands are white knuckling the steering wheel. At least it's flat out here, but I'm already scared as hell.

"You're gonna have to push that shit to 100," Juliette says. "They have five more guys stationed West that just left another Sinclairs. Lacey will have called Southpaw but... our only chance is heading East."

"Do you think they have people stationed East too?"

"I don't know," Juliette says. "Step on it."

"I can't," I tell her. I don't even want to glance back over my shoulder at Avery, but she's the main reason I can't fuck this car up and push almost 100 miles per hour.

"They're behind us," she says.

"No, they're not."

I don't want to look. I know she has no reason to lie but... I don't want to accept it.

"There's another Sinclairs in 20 miles. If you push this car to 100, we can lose them."

"We can lose our damn lives," I tell Juliette. My heart feels like it's a giant ball of yarn stuck and growing in my throat.

"That man wants to kill us, Quin. I know you're scared but at least if we die... we die together."

"Only your crazy ass would think that's a good thing..." I mutter. But I plant my feet on the gas and push that damn car to 105.

Let's lose those motherfuckers...

THIRTY-NINE
CASH

"Come pick up your girl from Sinclairs," Hawk says in his brief and unbelievably rude voice note to me. No explanation. Quin and the baby are at some Sinclairs in the middle of fucking nowhere. Owen takes Oske back to her people and I get permission from Southpaw to get my girl back from... wherever the hell her ass ended up when I specifically told her to remain somewhere safe.

That woman is impossible to control when it comes to Avery. She has no inherent sense about her and worse, she doesn't seem to see the need for it. I don't know what the hell I'm going to do with Quin once I get her back to make her behave...

It's gonna take me more than a night to get there and I don't want her staying at a damn gas station – even if she has a car somehow – so I ask Hawk to put her up at the nicest place he can find that deep in the middle of nowhere.

Quin makes a fuss about my instructions, but Hawk gets her to agree on a LaQuinta suite with a king-sized bed. I consider getting her room number from him and calling her up but I need time to think about how I'm going to handle Quin Nash... and Avery.

The club still has our hands full with the situation out in the desert and the recent attacks all provoke more answers than questions. Deb Shaw has custody of Avery's mom, but some blond motherfucker and a woman are out there hunting down Avery regardless. We don't know if they're on the same side or if shit really hit the fan with the Midnight SS.

Then there's Ruger's wife... She knows more than she's letting on and the boys in the desert who lost their lives must have learned something intriguing. The folks responsible for all that carrying on now are the Shaws and the Sinclairs. I officially have Southpaw's permission to keep Quin and Avery away from all of this. Truly keep my focus on the family.

I wish I could tell you the drive was something easy on me or even pleasant. The more miles I put on the bike, the further away I get from Ruger beating the shit out of Darlene, the horrible scene of dead brothers, and the potential consequences of an all out war between our biker club and another one.

All of us know what happened when we were young – right before most of us were born and some of us were just toddlers. The Rebel Barbarians had a war with a rival gang over territory along the old Route 66 highway in Texas. The other gang made some effort to intrude upon the land by opening several DVD stores (those were popular at the time), a gas station and then the final straw – a strip club.

Nothing might have happened except they got Lyle Blackwood's eighteen year old sister as one of the strippers right after high school and all hell broke loose. She's dead now. Can't even remember her name but... she died when I was six years old or something. Overdose. Everything about that time brought our fathers into a brooding, negative state. They talked about Iraq more than they talked about that war.

.   .   .

You never want to go to war but you do what you must. And if that's what you have to do so you can save your family, it's what you do.

The LaQuinta sits a few miles off the highway in a compound with an Outback Steakhouse, a Red Lobster, and a closed down Panera bread with a sprinter van parked out front. It's not a Four Seasons, but at least it's safer than sleeping in that damned Rav-4...

Finding Quin's Rav-4 in the parking lot brings me some peace of mind. I pull the bike up next to it and stick the keys in my cut pocket. I'll get a couple of my cousins to come out here and get the bike. Bring it to the next club meeting. That shouldn't be too long from now... and I have another bike.

More important for me to get to Quin and Avery. I walk into the LaQuinta and meet immediate disapproval from the woman at the front desk until I get all the way into the place. Then she smiles and greets me with a very sonorous Texan drawl.

"You must be Tanner Hollingsworth."

"Yes, ma'am."

She glances down at a sheet of paper and then back at me.

"I'll let Miss Nash know you're on your way to see her," she says. "It's room 444."

Her friendliness goes beyond Southern politeness, so I suspect Hawk greased her palm a bit for this extra customer service. I'm just glad he took my *strong recommendation* to keep Quin Nash safe seriously. Once the good woman at the front desk picks up the phone, I follow the signs to the elevators without much ceremony.

My ass hurts from so many hours on the bike without any

real rest and without a few cigarettes, a cup of coffee, and a handful of Quin Nash's ass cheeks... I doubt I'll feel anything but tense all the way from my calves to my neck. The elevator seems to crawl and I damn near want to pry the doors open when it slows to a halt.

On the fourth floor, I have to stop myself from sprinting to the room at the end of the hall. When I get to the door, I knock and then impatiently grab the handle without thinking.

"It's me," I say. "Quin? Open the door."

I sound unusually desperate. My cheeks heat up. She has this effect on me and I don't know what the hell I'm meant to do about it. She takes longer than thirty seconds to get to the door, so I bang on it again. Quin opens the door halfway through my third knock.

Holding Avery. Who looks fast asleep. Quin presses her finger to her lips.

"Avery is sleeping," she whispers.

My heart and my dick move at the same time. Avery looks so peaceful and cute nestled on Quin's shoulders and as for Quin... By some goddamn miracle, that crazy ass woman is *safe*. That's all I can hope for, right? Her safety. I look at her and Avery with all the love I feel.

"Can I come in?" I ask, suddenly bashful.

"Yes," Quin says, her protective expression melting into the prettiest smile. From the first damn time I saw this woman, I had this intense attraction towards her and the longer I know her, the more I watch her raise this child she doesn't *need* to love, the more I feel for her.

I walk inside Quin's hotel room, marveling at how she

somehow manages to make *every* space she inhabits feel different and more feminine. She just has that special touch to her that goes beyond her looks and attitude. I swear the damn room smells like one of those patchouli scented candles my mom was obsessed with burning in the living room.

When I shut the door behind us, I finally feel better. We're alone. Together. It's been so fucking long since I've seen this woman that I don't know if I can muster any type of self control. She has a blankie spread over the bed, but I don't want her to set Avery down.

"Wait," I tell her. "Don't set her down. I want to say hello."

Quin turns back to face me, unable to hide her surprise.

"Are you sure?"

"She might cry a little but... I can handle it. I miss her."

Quin holds her out to me and in her sleepy state, Avery doesn't react. At first. She feels no bigger than a burrito to me. Tiny. Innocent. So goddamn cute. I hold her against my chest and something *strange* happens. This overwhelming sensation pulses through my chest. My limbs. It's like I never want to let this little baby go. It's like I don't even want to set her down and give her a chance to grow up.

Hugging Avery like she's about to escape me wakes her tiny butt up even more and she starts squirming and questioning everything... smacking me with her little fists and making gurgling noises that sound a little like protest. Quin giggles.

"Being a baby must be crazy," Quin says. "You fall asleep on a bed somewhere and then bam, you wake up in the arms of red-headed giant."

We exchange a glance that feels like it should stop the damn world from spinning. I can't handle it. Not without doing something. I kiss the top of Avery's head and pull her closer to me. Her gurgling picks up and I kiss the top of her head again.

"DA!!!" Avery says.

Quin laughs. "She's never done that before."

I make eye contact with her. Avery, not Quin. I have to be honest, there's a part of me that always avoided looking too deeply at Avery's face. What if that baby had been mine, huh? The guilt would have torn me up in a way it never seemed to bother my father. I guess it's because he wasn't home to watch how all his bastards broke our mother's heart.

Hurting anyone like that, especially someone I love would destroy me. I definitely couldn't imagine doing that to Quin.

"She's beautiful," I whisper.

"I know," Quin says.

"DA! DA!" Avery says. Then she laughs and points at me.

Quin gasps.

"Oh my God."

"What?"

"I think she's talking."

"She is not talking..."

"DA!!!" Avery says again, pointing at me and casting some doubt on my self-assured claims.

"She's pointing at you," Quin says. "Let's see if she does it again..."

"DA!DA!" Avery says, giggling again.

"She's calling you *dada*."

. . .

"But I'm not…"

I trail off. After a few arguments with Quin, I know when to keep my 'stupid' opinions to myself.

"Of course you're her dad," Quin says. "Who else would be her dad?"

I hold her close. *Mine.* Just like Quin.

"Come here, sugar plum," I whisper, gesturing for Quin to join my embrace. "You're right. Who else could it be?"

I put my arm around Quin's waist and hold her soft body as close to mine as possible. I kiss the top of her head and vow never to let either of these women go…

FORTY
QUIN

I don't know why Tanner seems so different. He falls asleep on the couch seconds after we get home. I put Avery to bed and return to my room, not bothering to wake him up. He has his tongue hanging out and some beastly snoring going on, which is the most vulnerable I have ever seen Tanner look. I throw a blanket over him before I disappear to my room.

It's not that he seems different. He seems more... *gentle.* He barely kissed me before we left, but Avery demanded both our attention, so there wasn't exactly time for romance. At least we're back here. Back home... *for now.*

I know Tanner and I doubt we're going to stick around much longer but for now, this bed and this place feels safe. Soft footsteps against the cool stone floors in the hallway wake me up in the middle of the night. My eyes snap open. After everything I've been through, I can't sleep through even gentle and soft footsteps.

My body rolls out of bed instinctively and I reach for my phone – which isn't really a weapon, but I'm tired and operating on instinct here.

"It's me."

. . .

Who else could it be?

"Hey," I mutter groggily. My body relaxes as Tanner joins me, sitting at the edge of my bed. His presence brings me a lot of comfort after our long road trip and the gas station incident. He puts his arm over my shoulder and pulls me close so he can kiss my cheek. His lips are soft but his beard is all prickly and ticklish. I squirm a little, only making him kiss me again. And harder this time.

"You can't leave, sugar plum," he whispers. "I don't want you to leave."

"Who said I was going to leave?"

"I mean..." Tanner says. "I want you to be my girlfriend... then we have an engagement... then you become my wife..."

"Your wife?"

"Yeah," Tanner whispers. "Then I put a pretty little tattoo on the back of your neck... *Property of Cash...*"

Okay. That started off good but quickly became... scary. Tanner laughs when he sees the look on my face.

"I know you're not tatted yet but... it won't hurt."

"You think that's what I'm worried about?"

I might be worried about the pain too, but there are far more pressing issues than the tattoo needle that is currently nowhere physically near me.

"What are you worried about?" he whispers. "The 'L' word?"

"The fact that you can't even say it should be a red flag to you."

We face each other and just... *look.*

"Come on," Tanner says. "It's obvious."

He takes a breath and my heart is about to sink with disappointment. No matter what he feels... it's not really the same if he can't say it out loud.

"I love you," Tanner finishes. "I love you more than I have ever loved a woman. And I want you to stay here with me... forever."

"Tanner–

He interrupts. "Not here. We're moving. But... wherever I am, I want you with me."

My eyes start watering before an answer comes out. He doesn't understand how much it means to me to have someone who would do anything to protect me. But I still have a secret I've kept from Tanner. One he might want to accept.

"I'm a murderer."

He laughs.

"Okay."

"That's it?"

"Sounds like you already got away with it," Tanner says. "I'm more concerned about... the other thing."

"What other thing?"

"That you haven't said 'I love you' back..."

He grabs my cheeks and kisses me, defeating the point a little bit. But not by much. Kissing him feels better than talking. Better than fighting. Better than anything I have experienced in a long time. When we finally pull away, my heart is jumping in my chest like crazy and the words are ready to leap out of my mouth.

"I love you too," I say.

"Good," Tanner responds gruffly. "I love you too."

"Good," I answer back.

Our eyes meet again. Fire. Chemistry. Something brilliant, explosive, and worth waiting my whole life for. I don't stop myself from jumping on him. Tanner grunts in surprise a little but quickly adjusts, pulling my body over his thighs so I straddle him with my legs spread as wide as they can go. I might be full-figured, but I don't have much height, so it's easy for me to lose my balance in this position. At least it would be if Tanner didn't grip my ass cheeks and keep me positioned safely on top of him.

"When are we going to get married?" I ask.

Tanner laughs.

"What the hell is so funny?"

"I knew you were excited."

"Of course I'm excited. I told you... I love you."

"True," he says. "But I disappoint you sometimes. Like with Avery."

"You love her too," I whisper. "And you will do anything to protect her. That's all that matters."

. . .

The more caring Tanner acts, the harder it becomes for me to resist him. His hands are on my butt, which doesn't make resisting him any easier. He plays with my butt cheeks like he's trying to juggle them and follows up his extremely horny action with a question that threatens to lowkey kill the mood.

"Did you really kill someone?"

His pale, strawberry blond eyebrows pinch together seriously. We never talked about this before and talking about *it* scares the crap out of me. Even if I'm pressed against Tanner and I feel something much more immediately terrifying than my past pressed up against my thigh.

"Yes."

"Who?"

"That's the most important question?"

"No," he says. "But it's the question I have."

"My step-brother."

"I see," Tanner says, his grip on my ass getting tighter. This isn't the reaction I thought he would have. He gazes all over my face, but his emotions don't seem to change.

"So the club handled it?" He asks, his hands moving from my ass to my lower back.

"I asked Juliette for help."

"Perfect," he says. "Mind telling me what state you committed that felony in? I'll pick the furthest one away."

"So Hawaii or Alaska?"

Tanner wrinkles his nose. "Maybe I'm not so good with geography. Somewhere else... where I can ride to the clubhouse."

"You could technically ride from Alaska."

"It ain't in the middle of Russia or something?"

I make a private mental note to remain in control of Avery's education — and our future children. I might have to trick Tanner into sitting in on some of the classes too.

"We could move to California."

"No fucking way," he says. "After this, I need a break from club business. I want it to be just us... and Avery... and... any future kids we might have."

Just mentioning future kids makes his dick jump. I can feel the giant thing moving in his pants. His dick jumping at the word "kids" feels threatening, but Tanner hasn't hidden his intentions for a second. He wants to get me pregnant. Tanner has never hidden his bizarre motivations. He leans forward, pressing his nose into my neck and sending a ticklish jolt of pleasure straight through me.

He sticks his tongue out and presses it along the side of my neck.

"I could tattoo you right there," he growls. The spot of spit on my neck tingles from the cool air conditioning when he pulls away. The gush between my thighs completely defies the words that spill out of my mouth.

"I'm not letting you tattoo that crazy shit on my neck."

"Fine," he says, wrinkling his eyebrows. "I'll have an artist get it done."

He touches the wet spot and makes a big circle with his fingers. I'm guessing Tanner's delusional ass thinks that's where he's going to tattoo me? This man has lost his damn mind. I try to wriggle my neck away from him, but Tanner reacts with lightning speed. His hand fits firmly around my neck like a necklace. He doesn't squeeze, just holds me in place firmly.

He could squeeze. And he definitely wants me to know that. But for now, he's just holding me in place and demonstrating his power and control over me. Power and control that I give to him freely despite knowing he's a crazy ass redhead with a strong lust for plus-sized women and knocking them up. At least knocking *me* up...

One hand on my ass, the other hand on my neck. The dominant position gets Tanner rock hard.

"Are you going to fight me, sugar plum?"

I can't move my head, but I can still move my eyebrows. I can give Tanner the defiance he pretends to hate so damn much... I make the most disapproving facial expression I can.

"Yes."

"Okay," he says. "Give me something and I'll let you pick the spot."

"Is that your idea of compromise?" I ask him, fully skeptical that Tanner has any sanity left. Now that he has me in his clutches, he really thinks I'm going to go along with this tattoo. I still have Juliette on speed dial and her husband is letting her take flight lessons – on a simulator while she's pregnant.

"Yes," Tanner says, nodding mischievously. "No way in hell I'm letting my woman around those dogs without a tattoo."

"I'm a homebody. I'll gladly stay home."

Tanner smacks my ass with his free hand. Hard. I scream loudly and then his hand tightens around my throat just enough to turn the scream into a squeak. He relaxes his hand when I wriggle my butt desperately in an effort to escape his cruel combination of spanking me and squeezing my throat.

"What is wrong with you?"

"Showing you what could happen if you hang around a bunch of bikers without a mark."

"I already said I won't be around any bikers."

Wrong answer again. Are we going to be here all night?

"You're okay with another man touching your ass?" Tanner accuses, his grip on my ass tightening to the point of violence. At least his grasp on my throat remains tame... for now.

"When did I say that?"

A flicker of worry crosses his face. "I don't want you away from me for too long and if I have you close, I need you safe."

"This is not about my safety. This is about some hypermasculine bullshit."

"I'm not hyper," Tanner says. "I'm thinking this shit through."

His hand moves from my neck and he touches my collarbone. "What about right there?"

"That's as close to my neck as you could possibly be."

"If you wear *modest* clothing, you could cover it up."

I roll my eyes. First of all, what type of backwards comment is that? Second, Tanner has seen my tits and ass. It would take a California King Bed top sheet with a hole cut out of the top to hide my figure and even then, I can't be sure that would work. I've never tried it.

"I don't have tattoos Tanner..."

"Damn it woman... I will either spank you or spoil you until you listen to me..."

"What woman in her right mind would pick a spanking."

Tanner laughs again.

"If you were in your right mind, you wouldn't be here," he says. "Let's both be honest."

Our lips press together again. My pussy gushes with desire. I want him so badly. All of him. The house. The baby... the *future.*

Maybe I can handle a little tattoo.

"What if it's *small*," I tell Tanner. "I'll let you put it on my collar bone then."

His dick jumps again.

"Where do you want to get married?"

It's my turn to laugh at his goofy ass.

"That's all it takes?"

"Yes," he says. "I'll take you anywhere."

"Disney World. Orlando," I tell him. "That's where I want to get married."

"See? I knew you were crazy."

"What's crazy about Disney?"

"Not enough bikers."

"Shut up," I whisper, smacking his chest playfully before leaning over to kiss him. I'll never get tired of this man's lips.

"Fine," he whispers once I pull away reluctantly. "Disney. Whatever you want. I'll give you *whatever* you want as long as you take those clothes off baby..."

He's so hard that there's a spot of heat where his dick sits along the length of my thigh. I can feel the magical energy between us even before we take our clothes off. Tanner doesn't wait for me to get started on my clothes. He helps strip me naked and I pull away his shirt myself while he gets his pants and underwear off.

We both want each other so badly it hurts. Our bodies shudder with desire and everything between us is urgent and clumsy. It feels good to cling to Tanner's strong body after the hell I went through. I know it's not over for the club... but our love story feels like it's at that *happily ever after* point.

It doesn't mean your story is over.

"I love you forever, sugar plum," he whispers as he guides his dick to my entrance. "Forever..."

There's so much more to learn about the bodies in the desert, the Midnight SS biker gang, what Tanner left out in that Oklahoma trailer, Avery's mother, and the secrets we both have in our past.

. . .

But right now, it's just us in this bedroom making love and we're so in love that the rest of the world gets quiet. It's just the two of us — Tanner and Quin — joined forever.

FORTY-ONE
STEEL

The night Steel discovers the Midnight SS clubhouse...

I have to keep this scrawny ass brat Joslin out of trouble –
away from Nazis, away from my family. Away from everyone. I don't know what the fuck provokes me to save her life
when the smartest thing to have done would be put two bullets
in her head and toss her ass in the grave with the rest of them. But
that's not what I do.

Instead, I toss her ass in the truck and drive out of there while
she gives me this terrified look like she doesn't know if I plan on
killing her or sending her ass to prison with me.

She doesn't know that I've been to prison. And I don't plan on
going back. No fucking way.

I paid my debts for Gideon. We grew up like brothers and I
couldn't let him go down for murder. But that was it. I saw shit
that no sane man ought to see. I can't go back there. Doesn't
matter what happens.

Joslin sits with her arms folded and her knees clutched to her stomach. I don't know how a grown ass woman can be as small as she is, but she is definitely a grown woman. She has a fully developed figure despite being petite. Fully-developed. And fully embedded in a world of criminal bikers.

How the fuck else did she get out here?

"We'll be out of the danger zone soon," I try to tell her reassuringly as we hit the main road. I don't need the GPS anymore once we get to the highway. I know exactly where we are and how to avoid detection. No one will guess a rival biker would be driving around in a truck. I suppose they had a point about that.

She gives me a withering look.

"I need to know what you were doing out there," I ask her. She shakes her head.

"Don't be a brat," I respond gruffly. "I saved your life and I just had to see half my fucking club headless in the desert. I need to know what you saw."

Her lower lip quivers and she ducks her head, a mass of black hair covering her face so I can't read her expression. Women. They always want to make a big deal of things at the worst times

"Okay," I tell her. "Don't talk."

I don't know how I'm going to survive this drive back to Oklahoma from the middle of the desert in Arizona with a woman sitting in absolute fucking silence. I reach over and open the glove compartment, ignoring her as she dramatically gasps and tucks her legs in closer. Touching this woman is the last thing on my fucking mind.

My fingers close around a metal flask. Fuck yes... I don't even know what's in it, but I can tell from the way the liquid sounds inside that it's damn good liquor. Or at least liquor. All liquor tastes damn good when the craving you have is strong enough. I pry it open, swerving a little bit, and pour as much as I can down my throat.

The flask jerks on its own and I cuss loud as liquor sprays everywhere. What the fuck? Joslin uses my moment of distraction to finish her extraction. She takes the flask, presses down the window and without a word – she throws away my liquor.

This crazy fucking woman throws away my liquor...

"HEY!" I scream. "WHAT THE FUCK!"

I grip the steering wheel tight with both hands, resisting the urge to smack the shit out of this woman.

"You shouldn't drink and drive."

"Is that right?" I grumble.

She doesn't answer. Heat rushes to my cheeks. To my ears. Everything hits me at once without the liquor to at least smooth some of the shit over. Bodies in the desert. Some gang of Nazi freaks. This woman... pretty enough to be a high-earning whore and she sure as fuck has a whore's attitude.

"I can't sit here in silence."

. . .

She doesn't look at me. Or speak. I look over at her. I guess she must be mixed race. Mostly black, though. Her skin is pretty dark. Not my type but... strangely pretty. I prefer women with curves most of the time but I don't know. Joslin has enough tits to fill my hands I guess...

Glaring at me, she covers her chest. Guess she doesn't like me looking over and speculating.

"If you had any sense of self-preservation, you would do something to keep me entertained," I grumble.

She turns on the radio. Static blasts through the car. We're in the middle of fucking nowhere. Ain't no goddamn radio. After a few seconds, she realizes the situation and shuts it off. Guess she has no problem with silence. I give her another stiff look.

"You know what I mean."

She glares at me. "Animal."

What the hell did this damn woman just say to me?

"I'm an animal for saving your fucking life now?"

"I'm..." she scowls. "It's not like you care."

"What?"

"I'm married. Well. I might be."

"What do you mean you might be?"

"I think I killed him."

I scoff in disbelief.

"You? I don't think so. Trying to scare me won't work, princess. We have a long drive ahead of us and the shit you put me through has me tense."

She shoots me another glare.

"I'm not lying."

Like fuck she isn't. I know women. They'll say just about anything to get out of sucking dick. My body tenses up at her obvious disrespect, demonstrated by that damned lie.

"Where's your wedding ring then?"

"I told you. I killed him. I obviously didn't keep the ring."

There's a little bite in that sentence. I grip the steering wheel tighter, incapable of pushing out the darkness rushing into my head and the need for immediate relief. If I have to stop myself from doing what I know I shouldn't, I have to keep her talking. Fuck, I have to keep myself talking.

"If you killed him, where is he then, huh? How the fuck did you end up in the middle of the desert like this?"

She looks at me through the dark eyes that identify her ethnicity as something other than fully black, despite that thick head of coiled and textured hair. Sunk beneath thick lids, they make her pretty facial features quite a bit softer. I run my tongue over my lower lip, failing to suppress the urges that come with looking at this woman's face.

"It's a long story."

"We got nothing but time, princess. So you better start talking or start sucking dick."

She wrinkles her nose. "I won't be doing either."

"Hm. We'll see about that."

Steel & Joslin's book releases on October 4th 2024. Click here to order the book:
bit.ly/barbarians5

Click here to get a text message when the next book drops:
bit.ly/textjamila

THE END

Character Glossary

The Four Families

The Sinclairs
The Shaws
The Blackwoods
The Hollingsworths

The Hollingsworth Family

The Hollingsworth family extends across all of Route 66 but the Hollingsworth family home sits in Lubbock, TX. Due to extensive real estate dealings, several members of the Hollingsworth family own property at the end of the old Route 66 highway in Santa Monica, California.

Don Hollingsworth, died in the Amarillo clubhouse fire – Tanner's father died in the Amarillo clubhouse fire. He was the Hollingsworth family patriarch and left behind an enormous trust which various family members and other individuals stake claims to throughout the series.

Annabel Hollingsworth, b. – Don's wife and 'old lady' Annabel is proud of her Southern heritage, including all the dark and dirty parts of her family's past. After her husband's death, she avoids most dealings with the Rebel Barbarians and focuses instead on her family and ensuring healthy marriages amongst the young Hollingsworths.

Tanner Hollingsworth, CASH, b. 1991 - The eldest son of Don & Annabel, Tanner runs the majority of the family businesses in Texas & California. While the Hollingsworth family is known for their distillery and liquor production, they have diverse investments across the Southwestern United States. Tanner alone owns over 800 acres of land across the Southwestern United States.

Deacon Hollingsworth, RAGE, b. 1993 - Tanner's younger brother. He manages three of the distillery businesses and has multiple "side hustles" of varying profitability.

Cody Hollingsworth, INDIAN, b. 1999 - Tanner's younger brother. He owns two gigantic dude ranches out in Oklahoma.

Lacey Hollingsworth Blackwood, b. 2005 - married to Jairus Blackwood at the end of this story in a marriage arranged by Reaper Blackwood and Deacon Hollingsworth.

June Hollingsworth Blackwood, b. 2000 - married to Ruger. Ruger discovers June's cheating ways and runs her out of his house back to Texas where she is currently hiding out with her brother Deacon.

Kylie Hollingsworth, b. 1999 - Tanner's younger sister. She manages the distillery in Southern Missouri and is currently unmarried.

Don Hollingsworth's Children From Extramarital Affairs

These are the confirmed biological children of Don Hollingsworth from his extra-marital affairs.

Grayson Hollingsworth, b. 2004 - He has not yet patched into the Rebel Barbarians MC, but maintains strong ties to the club because of his father. Grayson's mother was a seventeen-year-old girl that Don thought was eighteen (allegedly). She hung out with bikers in Oklahoma when one night her boyfriend passed her around the gang of bikers and she ended up pregnant with Don Hollingsworth's baby, confirmed by paternity test.

Beau Hollingsworth b. 2002 - Don met Beau's mother while out for a ride near the Hopi reservation. He swears he "didn't know she was Indian" when they had a baby and denied Beau's existence for the majority of his life. When Beau was 20 years old, he patched into the Rebel Barbarians and manages a branch of the family business out in Santa Monica, California. He maintains ties to his mother's family on the Hopi reservation.

Savannah Hollingsworth b. 2010 - Don met Savannah's mother, a stripper named *Dixie Dazzle* at a club meeting in Amarillo Texas shortly before the clubhouse burned down. Savannah ran away from her mother and stepfather's house and currently lives with her half-sister.

Unknown Hollingsworth Family Members

Avery Hollingsworth b. 2021-2022 - Tanner Hollingsworth finds a baby on his doorstep named "Avery" by his aunt Deb, Wyatt's mother. He cares for Avery while he searches for the identity of her parents and why she's on his doorstep.

Andrew "Andy" Hollingsworth , b. - Not a patched in club member. Don and Debbie Hollingsworth's brother. He is involved in several crooked businesses and isn't a part of the MC because he doesn't like motorcycles and prefers boats. He was the 'black sheep' in a family obsessed with bikes.

Bethany Hollingsworth, b. — Andy's wife. While Andy may be a crooked business man, unlike his brother, he has always been faithful in love. He remains completely devoted to Bethany from the first day they met. Bethany doesn't have direct involvement in the club, but because of her sons, she occasionally assists with club business.

Their children

Mason Hollingsworth, GAS, b. 1996 - member of the Rebel Barbarians MC.

Gage Hollingsworth, CORNBREAD, b. 1998 - member of the Rebel Barbarians MC

Reed Hollingsworth, HOG, b. 2000 - member of the Rebel Barbarians MC

Georgia Hollingsworth Blackwood b. 2003 - in an arranged marriage with Tobias Blackwood who is currently serving time in federal prison.

THE SHAW FAMILY

Harlan Shaw, HARLEY, Club President – married to Renée, who he had two daughters with until Renée died in 1994. Harlan's daughters from his first marriage are Kelsey and Tylee.

Harlan remarried Deborah Hollingsworth, who became his old lady and they had four children together: Ethan, Wyatt, Stacy, & Owen.

Renée Shaw, Harley's first old lady – Tylee & Kelsey's mother who died in 1994.

Deborah Hollingsworth Shaw, Harley's Old Lady – married to Harlan Shaw. She had two children with Harley while he was married to Renée Shaw (Ethan and Wyatt). After Renée's passing, Deborah and Harley married.

Tylee Shaw Sinclair, b. 1990 – Harlan and Renée's daughter. Works for the family, fell in love with Isaac Sinclair.

Kelsey Shaw, b. 1993 – Harlan and Renée's daughter. She works for the club and lives on her own in a small trailer ten miles off Route 66 in a small Missouri town.

Ethan Shaw, BEAR, b. 1989, Officer – Harley's eldest son. The angry one.

Wyatt Shaw, SOUTHPAW, b. 1991, Jr. Officer – Harley's second son, the main character of the book *Biker's Surrogate.* His old lady, Anna Shaw, recently married him and they have a beautiful baby together.

Anna Shaw, Southpaw's old lady b. 1993 – Anna, a former nurse, encountered the Rebel Barbarians during an escape from a creepy suitor and fell into Southpaw's clutches. Their initial meeting was filled with confusing emotions, but eventually, Anna chose Southpaw.

Owen Shaw, SCRAP, b. 1996, Officer – Harley's youngest son. The patient one.

Stacy Shaw, b. 2000 – The youngest of the Shaw daughters, she still lives with Deborah Hollingsworth.

Claude Shaw, ROTTIE, *club member* – Harley's brother.

Michael Shaw, KEY, *club member* – Harley's brother.

Christian Shaw, SPADE, *club member* – Wyatt's second cousin, Claude Shaw's son.

THE SINCLAIR FAMILY

Randall Sinclair, RANDY, Club Vice President, b. 1956 – Club Vice President and patriarch of the Sinclair family. He is Harley's best friend who served in Afghanistan in 1991. He had twin boys, Ryder and Hunter after his service in the first Gulf War. He served along with Lyle Blackwood.

Karen H. Sinclair, b. 1979 – Karen Hollingsworth married Randy when they were very young and she had twin boys after his service in the first Gulf War. Karen had a past as a biker chick, defying her father's wishes to ride with the various club members.

The twins...

Ryder Sinclair, STEEL, Officer, b. 1992 – Hawk's twin brother is currently serving time in *Lansing Correctional Facility* in Kansas.

Hunter Sinclair, HAWK, Jr. Officer, b. 1992 – main character of *Biker's Servant*, Wyatt's best friend from high school and his right hand man. He possibly has a problem with alcohol.

Juliette Sinclair – Hunter's wife, the main character of Biker's Servant. She is Mackenzie Sinclair's mother and a talented painter/visual artist. She escaped abuse in the Midwest before she met Hunter on the run.

Barrett Sinclair, BENCH, Officer, b. 1967 – Randall's brother and fellow club member. He has one divorce under his belt from Selma Sinclair, but remains in a contentious marriage with his second wife, Caitlin Sinclair.

Selma Sinclair, b. 1969 – divorced from Barrett Sinclair. Isaac Sinclair's mother. Tylee's mother-in-law (who hates Tylee's red hair). She was Barrett's high school sweetheart and remains bitter about their divorce. She hates Caitlin for stealing her man.

Isaac Sinclair, GHOST, b. 1986 – married to Tylee Shaw Sinclair.

Caitlin Sinclair, Barrett's old lady, b. 1975 – Magnum's mother and Barrett's old lady and current wife. He marries Caitlin after divorcing Selma when Isaac was 10-years-old.

Magnum Sinclair, CONDOM, Officer, b. 1992 – Caitlin and Barrett's son. Hawk's cousin. He owns an apartment building in Santa Fe.

Coleton Sinclair, SINNER, *club member* - Hunter's first cousin. His mother, a single mother, was Randy Sinclair's sister. Coleton never knew his father. His mother tried to keep him away from the club, but failed.

THE BLACKWOOD FAMILY

Lyle Blackwood, DOC, Enforcer, b. 1958-2023 – Religious Gulf War veteran who distrusts Wyatt Shaw.

Brexlynn Shaw Blackwood, Doc's old lady, b. 1968 – Claude Shaw's sister, Harley's cousin. She is bitter and doesn't like Harley very much. Religious. She is currently in prison for conspiracy to commit murder.

The twins

Jairus Blackwood, BISHOP, Officer b. 1992 – Gideon's older brothers live in Montana on a ranch and only come down to Texas for the quarterly meetings and club business in the summer.

Jotham Blackwood, PINS, Officer b. 1992 – Gideon's older brothers live in Montana on a ranch and only come down to Texas for the quarterly meetings and club business in the summer.

The other siblings

Gideon Blackwood, REAPER, Jr. Officer, b. 1994 – Religious and violent contender for the throne of the Rebel Barbarians motorcycle club. Ex army ranger.

Tobias Blackwood, PRIEST, Officer b. 2000 – currently in prison for aggravated assault. Runs the prison's weekly worship session. Sells weed. Called Priest because he didn't have sex until he was 22 years old, the week before he got initiated and went to federal prison.

Ruth Blackwood, b. 2006 - Lyle's precious youngest daughter. She is the family's biggest rebel, currently attempting to enlist in the Air Force.

Doc's nephew... adopted into the family

Ruger Blackwood, BUCKY, new member, b. 2004 – Lyle's nephew. Loyal to Lyle. Collects hunting knives. Socially awkward.

Darlene Song – Ruger's wife. She spent some time in prison. She should still be there.

AFTERWORD

Thank you for reading Quin & Cash's Story...

The good girl goes bad story I wanted to write from the very beginning has been a wild ride for me. Quin has been through hell and I wasn't sure what dynamic she would have with Cash, but I knew I wanted a plus-sized female lead with Cash from Day one.

Did you make it to the end? Thank you so much if you did. I truly appreciate it. This was a wild story with a character that most would consider to be completely irredeemable.

I love their "secretly matching my freak" dynamic and the way Quin brought out the softness in him. The next book in this series will be... NOTHING like this one.

You got a taste of Ryder's personality in this book and there is SO much more coming in the next few books, including future updates on characters from ALL four books...

Get ready for this action packed, smut-filled adventure where the Rebel Barbarians question everything and have to face the Midnight SS and their little Neo-nazi problem head on.

Fans of all the previous characters will want to stay tuned for their favorite characters reappearing in Book #5 and future books.

If you enjoyed books like Mafia Playmate, I think you will *really* like Joslin/Ryder's book...

There will be **at least seven books** in this series. Book #6 will be about one of Wyatt's brothers and Book #7 will be Ruger Blackwood's love story.

After this book, this will hopefully raise some eyebrows. My patrons are brainstorming what kind of woman could possibly end up with Ruger Blackwood and we are cooking the next story together.

I started a tradition in the afterword of sharing some recommendations with you and hopefully I can do that today...

If you enjoyed the dynamic between Quin/Cash, I have a few books with a similar dynamic.

Mafia Surrogate is a dark nanny/boss mafia romance with a plus-sized female lead and a male lead with a gigantic pierced dick. Yummy.

My book *Purchased For Pleasure* is a little "out there" but also has a similar dynamic.

My *third* recommendation is *Purchased For Seduction* — this one is a Greek mafia romance book that I recently updated.

The next book in the Rebel Barbarians MC Series will have even more family, even more biker lore, and honestly, I can see myself writing *so* many books in the series, that I would *love* to keep going with that continued support from you...

I have books planned for most of the current members and lots of possible members we can bring to life as the series continues.

What do you think? Are you enjoying the series so far? If you *are* enjoying the series and made it through this personal letter — thank you!

I would truly appreciate if you left a review on this book and put a 🍪 emoji in the review so I know you read the afterword... It will be our little secret. 😊

My final word on the upcoming book?

There will be plenty of dark romance themes and more about our previous couples.

The next chapters will be live on Patreon first.

Click here to learn more about my behind the scenes community: www.patreon.com/jamilajasper

I cannot thank you enough for being there on my journey.

If you made it to the end of this author's note especially, double thank you.

I hope the wait for the next book doesn't drive you insane.

Forever grateful,

Jamila

About Jamila Jasper

The hotter and darker the romance, the better.

That's the Jamila Jasper promise.

If you enjoy sizzling multicultural romance stories that dare to
go there you'll enjoy any Jamila Jasper title you pick up.

Open-minded readers who appreciate **shamelessly sexy
romance novels** featuring black women of all shapes and sizes
paired with smokin' hot white men are welcome.

Sign up for her e-mail list here to receive one of these FREE hot
stories, exclusive offers and an update of Jamila's publication
schedule:
bit.ly/jamilajasperromance

Get text message updates on new books:
https://slkt.io/gxzM

Extremely
Important Links

ALL BOOKS BY JAMILA JASPER
https://linktr.ee/JamilaJasper
SIGN UP FOR EMAIL UPDATES
Bit.ly/jamilajasperromance
SOCIAL MEDIA LINKS
https://www.jamilajasperromance.com/
GET MERCH
https://www.redbubble.com/people/jamilajasper/shop
GET FREEBIE (VIA TEXT)
https://slkt.io/qMk8
READ SERIAL (NEW CHAPTERS WEEKLY)
www.patreon.com/jamilajasper

JAMILA JASPER

Diverse Romance For Black Women

More Jamila Jasper Romance

Pick your poison...

Delicious interracial romance novels for all tastes. Long novels, short stories, audiobooks and more.

Hit the link to experience my full catalog.

FULL CATALOG BY JAMILA JASPER:
https://linktr.ee/JamilaJasper

Mafia Playmate
(PREVIEW)

https://bit.ly/bostonirishmafia1

BOSTON IRISH MAFIA ROMANCE SERIES

Click here for the complete collection:

www.jamilajasperromance.com/catalog

Content Awareness

Read this passage if you require content warnings for sensitive material. I do not give detailed content warnings that will spoil the plot, but be aware of this note.

This is a mafia romance story with dark themes including potentially triggering content of **all** varieties, violence, frank discussions and language surrounding bedroom scenes and race.
All characters in this story are 18+
Sensitive readers, be cautioned about some of the detailed romantic material in this dark but *extremely hot romance novel.*

DESCRIPTION

A large pink box arrives on Aiden's doorstep with a woman inside.
His mail-order bride arrives in her birthday suit and tied up in knots with a pretty pink silk ribbon.

Aiden never requested a dark-skinned beauty...
His family would never approve of such an impure connection.

Who is this woman? What does she want?
A note in the box reveals the truth...
The woman in the box - *Valentina* - is a gift from an anonymous sender who wants something dark and twisted in return.

ONE

AIDEN

You have one job in the Murray family. You grow up, you get your marks, you listen to Pa, you marry a nice Irish girl, preferably a blond or a redhead with lighter features.
You do what Padraig Murray asks.
You pray everyday and you keep your rosary wrapped in your pocket. You stay loyal. You keep our bloodline strong.

P a demands a meeting with me now that I'm back in the city. He claims it's important, but it can't be that important if he wants to meet me during the Red Sox game. It feels good to be home. There's something special about Boston, but maybe that's just it – paradise is wherever our family is.

After Pa, I'll go home and see Roscoe, my Rottweiler. Then get my shit together and call my younger brother Darragh to check in on his training and find out if Rian's around. Over the weekend, I'll head to Leominster to visit Callum and then Sunday after church, stop by to see Ma and Odhran. I brought a gift home with me for Tegan, Rian's daughter, and I can't wait to see my niece's face light up when I give it to her.

If there's one thing I don't miss about being home, it's a never ending list of shit to do.

I meet my father at our usual casual meeting spot, Mulligan's, a place where we aren't afraid to celebrate Irish pride. A place where you can catch the Red Sox game and no one can catch your conversation. *It's as much home as anywhere else.*

I spot my father hunched over the bar from the street, his face illuminated by a warm orange bulb as he watches the pre-game announcer talk. I prefer football to baseball, but Pa bets on all their games, so he likes to keep his eye on the Red Sox each season.

When Pa calls, you answer, and he's desperate to know about the affair with the Italians – what the fuck happened, have I found the renegade cousins who pissed off the Italians, and whether I've killed them yet. *I haven't.*

It's all bad news and my ass is on the line if I don't find a way to sort out all the shit that happened in Long Island. At least we're guaranteed peace with the vicious Italians. *Those greaseballs aren't any better than the blacks. 'Trust 'em as far as you can throw them', Pa told me. But for now, we have peace and that's what matters. At least to me.*

I enter Mulligan's and the conversations fall to a hush. *Aiden Murray's back.* I clear my throat and the conversations continue. But there are more phones pulled out than before and two guys sitting in the back leave. I don't hate the reputation I have. Most of the bar fights I earned this cutthroat reputation in were Darragh's fault, but that doesn't change what people say about me.

Darragh, my younger brother, can still throw his weight around in the ring, but he got his practice here, in this fucking place. Our last fight here was over a girl. Darragh kicked some Puerto Rican's ass and a few of our boys jumped him outside... I don't know what happened to the guy after.

My father slides a twenty-dollar bill across the bar to the bartender, Finnegan O'Malley, a one-eared ex-hitman, who in turn fills up two glass pints of amber Sam Adams. Pa's already several drinks ahead of me. *Great. The news can't be that bad then.*

I pull out a bar stool next to my father, who barely acknowledges me, although he must've caught me entering the bar through the reflection on the glass behind the bartender. He shoves one of the pints across the bar towards me. He knows I prefer Guinness, but I don't mind starting with this. I can see my dad's reflection in the glass. He looks older than I remember. He's pushing 70, so I shouldn't be surprised by the large streaks of gray through his slick hair which was once blond, but changed color throughout his life, settling on a dark chocolate brown, like Rian's.

I glance at the television to check the score, but the game hasn't even started yet. I can smell the alcohol coming off of him already.

"You can have a Guinness after you drink this," he says. "I heard you did good work with the Italians."

He sounds raspy, but calm. My tension dissipates. This is just a normal, father-son meeting. Nothing to worry about.

"I didn't find Eoin or Robert. Haven't heard fuck since they all screwed with Vicari," I say as I take a sip of my beer.

"Maybe the Italians killed them," he says. "They're a violent, vicious group of people."

"Yeah."

Like we're ones to talk. Pa's done with his Sam Adams already and waits patiently for me to catch up, as if I could catch up to a man who's been drinking for an hour. At forty, it's not so easy for me to keep up with long nights of drinking. I don't know how he does it.

He waits for me to have a few more sips, his eyes glued to the television. Chris Sale throws the first pitch. It doesn't go so well. My father glances down at his glass and sighs. "It's going to be a long night."

"That bad this season?" I grunt, glancing up at the Detroit batter sliding into second.

I've been too busy to keep up with baseball. My father grunts. Yeah, it has been that bad.

"Any other news?" I ask him, finishing off the Sam Adams. Dad grunts and snaps his fingers for the bartender, Finnegan. The buff, tattooed bartender hustles over as dad orders two Guinnesses without opening his mouth. Bad news if he's drinking Guinness.

"Cops got Rian last week. They're charging him with manslaughter."

Manslaughter?

"What did he do?"

"What the fuck do you think he did?" Dad responds calmly. "He killed somebody, they caught him. That boy's not careful enough and I have to pay to get his ass out of trouble. Maybe some prison time would do him good."

"That's what you said the first three times," I grunt. Sale throws a good pitch and my father's face visibly brightens.

"If it weren't for Tegan, I'd let him spend a few extra years behind bars," Dad confesses. "Your mother won't let me do that to his daughter."

"What's going to happen to her?"

"I don't know," my father says. "No one has seen the kid in a week."

"What?" I growl, sipping at my beer and hoping this is my father's idea of a joke since he sounds dangerously unconcerned.

"What do you mean no one's seen her? Is she with her ma?"

My father shrugs.

Rian's notoriously bad taste in women landed him with a child he should have never brought into the world. She's a sweet girl, but doomed by a mobster father and a whore mother.

Her ma doesn't live in Boston anymore. She wants nothing to do with Rian.

"Where does he say she is?"

"Last time he saw her was the night he got arrested," Pa says before taking a sip of his beer.

"What about the cops? Did they give her to his lawyer or something?"

I don't have a single paternal instinct in my body, but my mind courses with worry over Tegan, despite my father's calmness.

"She'll turn up," he says, pouring more alcohol down his throat.

Fuck, Rian. My brother must be an even worse parent than our father. His daughter's missing and he's behind bars and there's no one else to look for her except...

"I can find out where she is. Once I get Roscoe and take care of–

"It would serve him right if something happened to her," my father says coldly. "Her mother isn't Irish. He keeps fucking up. I'm tired of cleaning up his messes. Now *drink*. This is not why I asked you here."

I bristle at his comment, but it's just Padraig Murray. This is who he's always been and my brother should have had the good sense to keep his dick in his pants. I made it to forty without fathering bastards all over Boston. Rian should have been more careful. I drink a few more sips, but I can't let this go. *Who else will worry about the fucking kid if not me?*

"How the hell did Rian let this happen? Can I talk to him?"

"Best that none of us talk to him. The cops listen to everything. I can get messages into the prison and messages out, but I don't want you talking to him."

"Fine," I grunt, finishing off my first round of Guinness and ordering us another. I try to pay, but my father stops me and then finally answers my other question.

"Your idiot brother trusted a woman," he says. "He wants a mother for that little girl so badly, that he's willing to do anything. He's willing to kill for a woman who doesn't deserve him."

"I didn't know he had a woman," I grumble.

"*Had* is correct," Pa says. "She's dead."

I wish I could tell you a chill ran through me, or I had some other human response to my father's announcement. I don't need a university degree to understand what he's implying. Rian had a woman, she got him locked up, so my father had her killed.

"Will that affect his case?"

"No," Pa says. "It was very clean."

"Who?"

"None of your business, Aiden. You worry about your shit, I'll worry about your brother."

I want to feel sorry for Rian, but he deserves it for crossing our father. This is what happens when he pisses off Padraig Murray. More problems for all of us.

"How much time is he facing?"

"Three years since he's been in jail before. I tried to get that stupid motherfucker to get his life together, but your brother just wants to be a fuck up."

"Who's the lawyer?"

"Someone from Nigel & Bancroft."

At least he isn't cheaping out like he did for Rian's first case. I don't want to push my father's buttons, and despite his outward calm, he must be furious at Rian for drawing more attention to us, but Rian has his uses.

"It's Rian," I remind him. "Crazy fucking Rian. We need him out soon. There are some jobs only Rian has the balls to handle."

Padraig snorts. "He takes after my father. Too proud and too violent for his own good."

We created the monster Rian Murray is. He's our responsibility.

"He needs another woman."

"He needs a woman who isn't a fucking spic," my father spits. "At least the child looks white."

"What about this previous woman? What'd she look like?"

"It doesn't matter," he grunts. "She's dead. Now drink. We have more important things to talk about than your idiot brother and his shitty taste in women."

I drink because Pa commands it. I do everything he commands and have since I was a child. I have the burns and scars to remind me of what happens when you disobey my father. At first, I hated him for what he did to me, but to keep an organization like ours together, you need to inspire fear.

You have to be cruel to survive – that's just how the world works. I can't let Tegan go. The second I see Darragh, I'll ask about her and track her down.

I drink so I don't lose my temper. He doesn't give a fuck about Tegan. No one does. Maybe he's wrong and one of my sisters took her in. But who would do that? Evie's saddled with her drunkard husband and two unruly kids of her own – Katie and Patrick. Kiara's off at university and Maeve's sixteen, too young to have any involvement.

"I need to tell you something important," my father says somberly, as if there could be something more important than my missing niece right now. I'm burning with desire to leave, but if I get up without my father's dismissal, he'll hurt me. Or someone I care about. Not like there are many of those people yet. It's foolish to get close to people in this life.

"Then tell me."

If he notices my tightening tone, my father doesn't acknowledge it.

"There's a plot against my life. I don't know who. I don't know why but... there's someone out there trying to kill me," my father says, the faded tattoos on his knuckles even more wrinkled than I last remember. He's getting older, but aside from his physical appearance, he shows no signs of slowing down. If anything, he's desperate to prove himself more. If he wasn't ordering more killings than necessary, maybe Rian wouldn't be locked up.

I don't want to dismiss his concerns as paranoid, but he's the leader of our family. There's always a plot against his life. It comes with the territory. My father doesn't have to worry because he has us. *Family.*

"Fuck that," I grunt. "No one would be stupid enough to try to kill you. April 2013, four days after the bombing. An entire decade ago. That's the last time anyone tried."

I was thirty back then, old enough to be the one who ended that war before it started. Back then, we only killed when necessary. I got five tattoos that year, one for each kill. Each a painful release, each representing a necessary act to keep my family safe.

My father smirks and keeps drinking. He shrugs. "That's what I thought. But I'm serious. This time is different. This time the bastards might just get me. I'm getting old, Aiden. Most guys in our line of work don't make it this far."

"What happened?" I grunt, urging my increasingly drunken father to get to the point. His cheeks blaze tomato red with alcohol and his blue eyes swim with tears, again brought on by drinking rather than any emotion. He grunts and knocks his biggest gold ring against the bar's surface contemplatively.

If anyone tried to kill him, surely Darragh would have mentioned it. He's responsible for keeping our father alive.

"I feel it in my bones," Pa replies. "Someone wants to destroy our family."

"Yes," I grumble. "Our cousins. But they're gone and if they were anywhere near this city, we would have heard about it."

"I don't know. Something big is coming for us. I feel it."

"We can make decisions based on feelings now?"

"Cut the shit, kid. You know my instincts are good because you're like me. You can smell shit before it hits the toilet bowl."

"I'm home. If anyone tries to kill you, they'll have to get through me, Darragh, and Callum."

My father smirks. "My boys. I'm proud of all of you. Except Rian. He's a piece of shit."

Ah, Padraig. Honest as fuck, especially when he's drunk.

He might not be proud of Rian, but he still loves my brother enough to spring for decent lawyers and to make sure Tegan goes to the best day school in Boston. Once she's old enough, she'll go to Milton or Dana Hall, or another nice private school where she can meet someone to untarnish her sullied blood, that is as long as I can find her. If Rian's behind bars, she could be anywhere. Hopefully not with her mom's people.

She belongs with us, even if Rian made mistakes. She looks like us and that's good enough to cover up his shameful behavior. I don't know what Rian was thinking with that Puerto Rican chick. Tegan's mother was low class.

Let's hope my brother's behavior doesn't come back to haunt all of us. Let's hope his daughter is safe, sound asleep somewhere and protected.

"Thanks, Pa," I mutter, uncomfortable with even this much emotional closeness between us. I love my father, but trusting him too much is dangerous. Rian found out the hard way that it isn't worth it to defy our family beliefs, and it definitely isn't fucking worth it to screw around with the wrong women.

"And Aiden? I need you to hurry the fuck up and find a wife. I'm getting old and I want to retire, but I need a family man to lead this family. You're the oldest. Why the fuck can't you keep a woman? Do I have to send you back to Galway?"

He wants a real answer.

"Not interested in chasing after girls, dad. All they want to do is take your money and ask where the fuck you're going. I've had enough."

"That old dog won't take care of you when you get old."

"Neither will some Boston snob who could take my ass to the cleaners in a divorce."

He laughs, which is the best reaction I can hope for. He quickly moves along to talking about the game and his plans for the business, and then asks me questions about Long Island. They're a mess out there, but doing better under John Vicari's leadership. We're developing a few buildings together and are prepared to make a lot of money in the real estate game. John does cleaner business than his father. Too bad the old man died of a heart attack... that's the word anyway.

"I need you to find a nice girl," my father reminds me once he's almost blackout drunk. He can barely keep his head up. *Great.* I'm not dragging his ass outta here tonight. If he wants to get so wasted he can't sit up straight, I'll leave him for Finnegan.

"We have this conversation every time we talk."

"This time, I'm serious. I want to retire. I don't want you bringing home no spics either like the Duffy boys."

"Fuck's sake, Pa. You can't talk like that around here anymore."

"I can say whatever the fuck I want. I want Irish children. Irish fucking children and I need you to have a wife so I can retire."

"Retire any old fucking day you want," I growl. "It'll be good for you to stop worrying about who I fuck or marry or the fate of the fucking family."

"The fate of the family matters," he says, taking another sip of his newest glass of beer before rubbing condensation off the sides with his napkin.

"I'm too old to have kids," I growl. "I'm too old to get tied down. You and mom were lucky you even found each other."

That's bullshit and we both know it. They stay together because they're Catholic, because back in the eighties, my dad killed someone for her father and won my mother like a prize. He also put a baby in her quickly and then kept her pregnant. There's nothing romantic about their love story or marriage in the Murray family.

"If you can't find a girl, I'll find one."

"The last girl you found me was a crazy fucking redhead who wanted to bring Roscoe Jr. into the bedroom. No thanks."

My father shrugs. "She was white. Do you know how hard it is to find a white girl around here who hasn't been fucking ruined by some fucking Puerto Rican or black guy?"

"What do you want from me, Pa?"

I know what I want. I want an end to this conversation, and I want my father to give me a fucking break about women and dating. All the Irish and Catholic women in Boston know to stay away from us, and the ones who don't learn their lesson pretty fucking quickly.

"Find a nice white girl with big tits and blond hair and get her pregnant so I know you're fucking serious about family. That's what I want."

"Give me time."

He continues, getting to what I suspect was the original point he wanted to make before the liquor got to him. "And get your ass to the site in Back Bay tomorrow bright and early."

"Why?"

This is the first I'm hearing about something wrong at the Back Bay construction site. I know something's wrong because my father doesn't do anything bright and early unless there's a problem to solve.

"You'll find out tomorrow. You just got back. Go home. Pet the dog. Your mom's tired of walking that big fuck. He nearly knocked her over near Harvard Square."

"How is mom?"

"Pissed off."

"Why?"

"Eh. Upset about another woman. It's nothing."

It's nothing. Dad just got his second mistress pregnant and even if we all know about it, we're all supposed to pretend it's no big deal that our elderly father knocked up a Irish teenager who he supposedly hired to clean the construction company office.

I hate how he treats our mother. What's the point of having a family or a woman if you hurt her? There's no getting through to him, but I have to try for my mother's sake.

"You treat her better, pa. Seriously. She needs you."

He grunts. "Get your ass home kid and get a white girl pregnant."

"Thanks, dad."

"If you can't find one, I'll find a good Irish girl who needs a green card and bring her over to you!"

My father is the last person I want picking my romantic partners. I mutter something to him about cutting back on liquor, then I pat my father on the back and leave the bar. This is the closest we've felt in years, but there's still a wall between us and there always will be. I felt closer to him when I was younger, when it was easier for me to justify the life I led. I know I'm a screw up, I know I don't belong anywhere near a woman or a family or any of the fucking things my father wants from me.

He knows it's wrong to bring a kid into this life, but he did it anyway. He knows that we're villains, but he doesn't care. Fuck, I don't care either, I suppose. I'd just rather not ruin a perfectly good woman.

I drive out of the city listening to rock classics on the radio. Just as I turn down my street – I live at the end of a cul-de-sac – I notice the large box on my front step. There are only five large houses at the end of this cul-de-sac, all of us with wide open well-maintained lawns around traditional New England colonial houses.

The box on my front step is fucking enormous – and I don't remember ordering anything for delivery. My hand moves swiftly to the pistol under my seat. I feel no fear as I reach for the gun and slip a mag out of my pocket. I feel ready.

Leaving the city for any amount of time always carries a risk, especially since I didn't exactly leave the place with a house sitter. The last time my teen brother Odhran house-sat, he trashed the place and had a threesome in my bed. I hop out of my black GMC Sierra with the gun under my coat and approach the box slowly, glancing furtively over my shoulder for anyone who might have eyes on me.

The box has holes in it. It's large. Pink. Wrapped in a bow. I reach for the bottom of the box and try to lift it. *Fuck.* It's heavy. I drop the box and I swear I hear a sound coming from inside it. *Is that possible?* I try to peek through the holes but it's too fucking dark and something's telling me opening this box will be a shit-show. It has to weigh about a hundred pounds. Maybe more. I'm no weakling, but it still takes a measure of back strength to lift a box that fucking heavy.

I open my front door and greet Roscoe Jr., my rottweiler, as he bounds towards the door to greet me. His coat looks shiny, the nub of his docked tail wags back and forth. Pa's choice, not mine. He runs up to the box and sniffs at it a bit.

There's definitely something in there and it gets his attention because Roscoe utters a low bark.

"Roscoe, go lie down."

Once he heads off to his bed, I throw my doors open wider and eye the giant box to decide how to carry the fuckin' thing. I would call Rian if his stupid ass wasn't in jail. I could call Callum, but he's still hung up on some fucking girl and won't answer my calls because I won't sugarcoat my opinion of him. Then there's Darragh... He's probably twice as drunk as Padraig. Not a good option either.

I'll have to carry the box myself. I stretch a little and then grab the edges of the box and grunt as I carry it a few feet inside my doorway. I set the box down more gently. *Is there something alive in there?* If it were an animal, I suspect Roscoe would be barking from his spot in the house, but he's laying down as I commanded, gazing at me curiously and wagging his tail.

He's probably wondering why I'm not taking him for a walk since I'm back. *At least he didn't bite the sitter this time.* I close my front doors and then search for an opening on the giant pink box. Finding none, I start with the ribbon and peel it away. The box comes up to my waist. It's *enormous.*

If it didn't weigh a hundred fucking pounds, I would assume it's a novelty gift or something extra special from one of my brothers. Which of my piece of shit brothers would get me a welcome home gift? It's not like either of them are here with a six pack of Guinness right now...

I peel the top of the box open and there's another box inside it, also pink. I open the second box and stumble backwards as I expose the contents. I don't mean to act like a fucking idiot, but I nearly fall over, because this is the last thing I expected to find on my doorstep. I just got back to Boston... How long has that box been out there?

Holy fuck, why isn't she screaming?

I gain control of myself and approach the box again, heart pounding because my second assumption is that the human female in the box might be dead and that's the reason she hasn't made a sound. The sick thought twists my stomach into an unyielding knot.

I slowly approach the box again, ignoring my heavy breathing, focusing instead on taking in as much information as possible about the situation. I move the flaps of the box open and stare at the woman's face.. Suddenly, her eyes snap open before swiveling around and looking me directly in the eye..

Holy fuck, this woman is alive.

"What the fuck is this?" I grunt to myself. Not to myself. I'm not alone. I dry swallow and run my fingers through my hair. She's black. Someone tied up a black woman in a pink ribbon, wrapped her up like a gift and put her in a box on my doorstep. This has to be a sick joke.

I'm almost too scared to reach into the box and touch her, but I have to touch her to get her out of the fucking box. Whoever this woman is, she ran into the wrong fucking people and ended up in the wrong living room.

I have tattoos and vows of loyalty to prove how I feel about people like her. "Don't worry. I'll get you out of there."

I don't know why I'm bothering with comfort. I reach into the box and grab her at the base of her spine before hoisting her out of the box and gently setting her on the ground. My stomach lurches. This is some sick, twisted shit. Whoever did this to her stripped this woman naked, bared every inch of her dark skin, the color of Arabica coffee, and wrapped her in a pink ribbon, contorting her limbs and running the ribbon over her bare breasts, between her thighs and in loops around her body so she's wrapped up like a chocolate present.

My body has an unconscious, primal reaction. I could unwrap her like the present she's been wrapped up to be, but I need answers quickly.

She has a gag in her mouth, a round white ball that keeps her lips spread open and hooks at the back. Her eyes roam around the room in terror as I reach into my pocket for my knife. I've killed people with this knife and now I'm using it to save someone.

Her skin prickles with goosebumps as I touch her. I apologize, but I need to brace myself against her to get her free. I press the serrated edge to the ribbon and make the first cut.

I cut her legs free. She groans as her legs fall in a curled heap. She cries out and tries to jerk them again, but however long she's been in that position was far too long for her to have full control of her legs and hips.

"Don't move," I remind her. I touch her skin again and my stomach lurches. Fuck, her skin is so dark. I look pale as fuck touching her and even putting my hands on her drives guilt through me. She's black. She's the wrong kind of person. I run my tongue piercing over my lower lip as I focus on all the parts of the ribbon I have to cut free.

When I have her limbs mostly free, she rolls onto her side, groaning in pain as her arms and legs curl in an awkward and splayed mess next to her. Even her wrists bend at an unnatural angle. I know she's alive, but the woman still looks dead.

I swallow slowly. What the absolute fuck is this?

"I'll take the gag out, but you can't spit or bite or do anything of that nature. Do you understand?"

She stares at me, but she can't say anything. I approach her mouth slowly and reach around her to find the clasp of her ball gag. I unhook it and take it out of her mouth. She groans again and winces in visible pain as she attempts to close her jaw. She slowly moves her hand to her face and rubs her cheek, groaning.

I crouch next to her, staring at her in awe, knowing that I shouldn't but am completely incapable of taking my eyes off the naked woman in front of me. If her nudity makes her uncomfortable, that hasn't sunk in yet. My cock stiffens inappropriately in my pants and I clasp my hands in front of my dick, refusing to take my eyes off her.

Her breasts are small, but they protrude forward in tiny, dark orbs with nipples that are even darker than her extremely dark skin. Holy fuck, I didn't know nipples came that dark. My eyes widen inappropriately and I pray she doesn't notice my leering. Who sent this woman to me and what exactly did they send her for?

Christ, Aiden. Get a grip. You're staring at her crotch now and it's obvious.

She's waxed completely and my gaze snaps to the bare, dark brown lips. I wonder what this strange woman conceals between those lower lips and what color her flesh is between those thin, toned legs. I clear my throat.

"Who are you?"

"Read the card with the gift," she manages to say, with a raspy voice and an accent I can't place.

"I asked you a question."

"Read the card with the gift," she repeats.

I raise an eyebrow and walk towards the box. There's a large card at the bottom, about 8 x 10 inches, printed on thick paper. I pull it out of the box and read the note, muttering it out loud to myself. *What the fuck is this?*

Dear Mr. Murray,

We hope you enjoy your object. Your task is simple.

Use the object wisely. Have unprotected sex with the object and film a 4K quality video.

Compress the video file and send it to the email address below.

The object may be initially unwilling but both of you will face strong motivation to comply. The object understands that documentation of her existence belongs to us and if she fails to comply enthusiastically, we will destroy her identity.

If we do not receive the video within one week of today's date, you will both lose what's most important to you.

Tegan Murray counts on you to succeed. We have possession of the girl and you would be wise to listen to our orders if you or your family want to see her safe.

Do not call Padraig Murray. Do not call anyone else, or you will both suffer.

It takes less than a second to fire a bullet.

You must comply. When you're finished with said object, it is yours to keep.

Sincerely,

Your Benefactors

OA

. . .

"What is this sick shit?" I growl, throwing the card back into the box, causing the woman still kneeling on the ground to flinch. My heart thuds.

These people have Tegan and this woman might know where she is and who they are. I won't be a part of this sick fucking game.

TWO

VALENTINA

"You have to do what they say," I say to him. "*Please.*"

It's not what I want to say, but these were my instructions if I wanted to survive. I never saw the people who put me in the box, but I heard their instructions and their threats clearly.

My throat burns raw as I attempt to plead with the man in front of me, hoping that he'll spare me. *He's involved with the people who took you. He's dangerous.*

The more I talk, the quicker he'll piece the truth about me together. I don't want this man to know *anything* about me. My voice. It's bad enough that he's seeing me naked. It's bad enough that he's about to take a part of me that I never wanted to give to strangers, that I always wanted to *mean* something.

I want to keep a piece of myself to myself. I've never had that privilege before. I won't have it tonight. He's an utter stranger to me and a terrifying one at that.

The gigantic blond man glowers at me, his blue eyes enough to melt me in place. He's 6'4", his hair looks slightly unkempt. Black ink swirls around his pale skin in a variety of Celtic knots, cursive Bible verses and symbols that I don't understand. *Lots of tattoos. He must be a gangster. Something like that.*

I hate that I'm naked, but I'm glad that I'm free. There was nothing but pain in that box. The drugs helped at first, but they didn't last thirty-six hours. That's how long it took to get here from Idaho. Technically, the drive takes twenty-five hours, but I tried to measure time – I have a good sense of it because of the piano – and I know they took thirty six.

There's no getting out of this. Maybe this one won't be as wicked as the first.

"Who are you?" the man growls at me. "Who did this and what the fuck do you have to do with this?"

His anger sends a surge of terror through me as his face reddens with frustration. He has absolute control over this situation and he knows it. I can't afford to freeze and make it worse by proving to him what he already knows – I'm vulnerable, weak and utterly at his mercy.

I position myself to cover my breasts as much as possible as well as my *other* parts, but he's already seen every bit of me. Modesty is entirely pointless.

"My name is Valentina," I rasp out, my voice getting stronger as I tell him my name.

"Is that your real name?" he growls, stepping forward and towering over me.

I'll never know if I had another name. I've been called Valentina since I was a little girl. Sometimes Val, but never anything else. I must've had a life before, but I don't remember any of it. All I remember is Pulsifer. He was my father, my abuser, my everything. I wouldn't call this freedom, but there's still a weight lifted because this is the closest I've ever come to leaving the governor's mansion.

The blond man is even taller than I thought he was. I'm more vulnerable naked and despite wanting to stand up for myself, I shrink back from him.

"Yes," I say as firmly as I can manage.

"Who sent you? Because I'll be damned if I screw around with a n–"

He stops himself, but my skin feels a flush of outrage and humiliation as his lips hover over the n-word. I want to hit him, but I don't know what type of man my new master is yet. A racist. That part I understand. He's not the first racist I've had to deal with. He might be the richest though. *He lives in a mansion.*

"Who sent you?" He roars. His face reddens as he screams and his creepy blue eyes look bloodshot. I shouldn't cross him, but I stopped giving a fuck about what happens to me a long time ago. I've already experienced the worst.

"I don't know. All I know is they want you to do what's on that note."

I don't want that. I have to go through with it, but I definitely don't start off wanting that monster anywhere near me.

"No," he growls, his jaw tightening. "I... This is fucking ridiculous. Tell me who sent you, woman."

His anger mounts and my fear intensifies. I'm no stranger to racism, but for the word to nearly fly off the tip of his tongue like that. *How can someone who looks like that be so ugly inside?*

He reaches into his jacket and I know he's reaching for a gun before he pulls it out. The men who sent me here weren't any better than the man who received me as a gift. My throat tightens and I try not to lose control of my bladder as he pulls the pistol out of his jacket and points it straight at me.

Men are all the same and they're all violent disgusting pigs who will put a bullet in an innocent woman's head if she gets in their way. They'll use us up and spit us out and there isn't a man alive capable of real love...

"If you shoot me, you'll die," I state plainly, trying to sound like I have control of the situation. I'm not lying, but I'm also not stupid enough to mean that as a threat either. "And whoever you love enough for them to threaten will die too."

"I don't give a fuck," he snarls. "Who sent you?"

I don't believe that he doesn't care. I sense a crack in this man beneath his outrage. His anger cloaks his genuine concern. If he wanted to kill me, he would have done it already.

"Do I look like I was in control of the situation? You have their instructions. Are you going to do it or not?" I say to him sharply. Talking to him like this could be dangerous, but he doesn't react to my strengthening voice or sharp tone.

"Am I going to rape you?" He growls, lowering the gun. "Is that what you're fucking asking me?"

He has a thick accent which I can finally place. *Boston.* I'm in Boston, or close enough to Boston that men sound like Matt Damon in *Good Will Hunting.* I don't know anyone in Boston, but maybe that's for the best since I don't know any good people. Never have.

I don't respond to him. He reads the card to himself again and mutters a long string of curse words. I'm already naked and despite his apparent hesitation, the man hasn't offered me clothes. He doesn't know if he's going to do it yet, but I do.

He's going to have sex with me.

"You have to follow the instructions," I say to the terrifying blond man pleadingly. He still hasn't told me his name and I don't know if he will. He might worry I'll go to the police. "At least according to them." Hopefully he thinks of another solution since he's clearly some type of gangster.

I've been through enough shit to know that the police don't care about women like me. The police have *never* cared.

"This is a crock of shit," he hisses, spittle flying from his mouth as his face reddens with pure vitriol. "I have *never...*"

He glares at me like I'm responsible for this. Every inch of my body aches and I have little patience for this bastard acting like I'm the fucking problem.

"Never what?"

He glowers. "I've never been with... I don't... I don't fuck black women."

His voice drips with disgust, but I don't mind because I find this man's racism equally repulsive. He's more bothered by my race than the fact that I arrived on his doorstep naked, wrapped in ribbons, and sent to him in a box.

"You have to follow their instructions. I don't know what happens to you if you don't, but I know what happens to me."

I'll be lost to my past forever.

"Who fucking sent you?"

"I don't know."

I should have expected his next actions. He's a sicko, because the people who sent me only send gifts to sickos. My boss... My *old* boss was probably worse than this man. He was certainly much uglier, but all cruel men are the same.

He quickly racks a bullet in the chamber before re-leveling the gun to my face so I am forced to stare directly down the barrel.

"Kneel," he commands without wavering. I can see in his eyes that he's capable of shooting me. He runs his long pink tongue over his lips. He has a piercing through his tongue, a giant gold knob with a Celtic knot in the center. *What the fuck?*

My knees ache and I can't stop myself from groaning as I obey him. I have no choice but to listen to him despite the pain shooting through me. My stomach turns and if I'd eaten anything in the past 48 hours, it would've come up on this rich white man's hardwood floor.

My head lolls forward and I struggle not to cry out as more pain surges through my legs.

"Who sent you?"

"I don't know," I answer truthfully. If I had those answers, I would disappear in the middle of the night and find some way to get my real identity from the people who own me, or I suppose owned me before him.

"You must've come from somewhere," he says, his finger hovering near the trigger. It never occurred to me that he could do worse than hurt me, that he could kill me. *But he might. The men who did this to me never considered that.*

"My master sold me."

"What the fuck?" he snarls. "What the fuck does that mean?"

"I grew up... I grew up in a house with an older man. He sold me when I turned twenty-five."

"Sold you to who?"

"I never saw. I just know... I know what kind of company he keeps."

"Who was your master?"

"Governor of Idaho. Ezekiel Pulsipher," I respond as calmly as possible, even if just saying his name brings back flashes of horrific memories that still torment me every night. Who needs sleep, right?

"I don't know who the fuck that is," he spits. My chest swells with odd satisfaction that there's a corner of the universe not entirely ruled by Ezekiel.

In any other situation, his confusion would have been confusing. Old Zeke was a king in his universe and I wasn't the only girl in his harem. *He owned me since I was six years old. I don't want to tell this criminal about that, but I wouldn't feel sorry if this psychopath turned on my old master. I wouldn't feel sorry if these modern slave owners met this monster.*

I glare at him. I'm not here to give him an explanation. He's not the victim here, I am, and judging by his accent and other cues slowly coming into view, I'm on the other side of the country with no identification, no proof of who I am...Nobody knows I'm here.

It doesn't matter that I'm alone, I have to survive. I don't know what life will be like on this side of the country, but this is the best chance I've had to escape my entire life. *I can fool this white man. I know I can.*

"Why would someone do this?" He snarls.

"Maybe you're a criminal. Maybe they want revenge," I offer, perhaps pushing him too much with my attitude. His body tenses when I say the word *criminal.* Men. They think they're so careful with their emotions, but they get careless when they're underestimating you. Men get careless when they think they have the upper hand.

"I can't do what they want," he says, keeping the gun fixed at my head. This does little to warm me to him. "I can't screw... If my father found out... he would paint the sidewalk with your brains."

Charming. Now I have a definitive answer about the extent of this man's criminality.

He sets the gun on the table behind him and re-reads the card for the third time. His face turns several shades of red.

"This is sick," he spits, glowering at me with familiar, racially motivated revulsion. In most situations, I can't actually know if a man is racist. I have proof about this man.

"You have to. Whoever sent me paid a lot of money. You messed with powerful people," I tell him. "And they have someone you love and if you don't do this–

"I haven't messed with anyone," the man growls, interrupting me. "Get up."

I thought the pain shooting through me would knock me unconscious, but I had too much pride to ask him for relief. I slowly rise, my limbs barely cooperating. I look and feel ashy. I hate that I missed my routine. Spend a any amount of time in a box and you will miss the most damning prison you had before. My body still aches.

He looks me in the eye and I'm too scared not to meet this man's gaze. He's a predator and showing a predator fear gives them permission to pounce.

"My name is Aiden."

Aiden. I shouldn't care what his name is, but hearing it makes me consider him differently. The name sounds forceful and as rooted in his heritage as his Celtic tattoos.

"Great," I reply softly, unclear about what to do with the information.

He clears his throat and speaks again, "I thought you should know before we..."

"So you changed your mind?"

I shake before my body knows I'm shaking. This has happened before. Men have *taken* my body several times. Ezekiel *owned* me and believe me, he made good use of his property. Aiden. The name sounds Irish, but the man standing in front of me is All-American. He's 6'4" tall with *very* pale blond hair, but a thick crop of it. It's nice to see a man who isn't bald and who clearly works out. He's very muscular and the gun is out of the way, which sets me at ease.

"I don't know who sent you, woman. But I intend to find out. Seems like the best fuckin' way to do that is follow their instructions."

I knew it.

Aiden reaches for me and I fight my gut reaction to flinch. I don't want him to know how much I fear him. I want him to worry that I'll stab him in his sleep. I want him to feel like he's risking his life every time he rapes me.

Aiden puts his hand on my shoulder. I expected his touch to be rough, but it's very soft.

"Do they have anyone you love?"

I don't want to tell him, but his blue eyes harden and I sense that I'd better tell the truth if I want him to get this over with. His hand cups my shoulder too gently for me to describe. After the sharp angles and the pain of having my body squeezed into a box, his softness is surreal.

"I... I don't know."

"I don't want to hurt you. I won't rape you."

"If you don't have—

"I know," he growls. "But I won't hurt you. You have to consent. I..."

"I belong to you," I tell him, refusing to look away from him. I want him to gaze into my eyes and see a human being. A part of me desperately wants to shame him. It's hard to stare into those eyes and not feel something. He has intense and expressive eyes.

"No," he whispers. "You belong to yourself and once this is over, I'll have to let you go."

I fight back laughter. He won't let me go. I know men like Aiden better than he can even understand. I've lived my entire life in a world of pain and depravity.

"They'll hurt you if you don't do it. Surely my life isn't as important as yours."

"You're right," he growls. "But I've never fucked one of your kind and I don't intend to rape you either. That's not *my* thing."

He says it with the implication that he knows someone who prefers rape. And there he goes with the race talk again. *One of my kind...*

"You have to do it."

"Then agree to my terms."

"Terms."

I don't phrase it as a question and I don't want to sound too eager either.

"I'll give you money."

"So I won't be a slave, I'll be a prostitute."

His face reddens. "I'll send you away. You said they have someone you love. So you have a family?"

"No. I don't."

His hand drops from my shoulder and I glance down at his crotch. Despite Aiden's assurances that going through with this is the furthest thing from his mind, his dick bulges from his jeans. The bulge sends a deep surge of discomfort through me and my head swims.

There's no escape. All my smart-mouthed comments and my internal pleas that I might be able to survive this... I have to go through with it.

"What do you want, then?"

"A place to rest my head for a few nights. Time to get on my feet."

"Done."

He clears his throat. "I'll film it on my phone. I just... I've never..."

Aiden suddenly leans forward and kisses me. His lips surprise me with how soft they are when they first make contact. I want to scream, but it's a good kiss that draws me into Aiden's world instantly. His smell consumes me. His fingers claw at my cheeks as he holds me suddenly and keeps me still so he can kiss me.

Before Aiden, kisses felt like... cottage cheese. I want to push him away but the kiss is too fucking good for me to break away from it. I don't want to upset him, anyway. When he breaks away, his cheeks are red.

"I'm fucking dirty," he says and the revulsion in his voice tells me that he means it.

He doesn't look like he hated the kiss despite the words coming out of his mouth. He leans forward again and kisses me. This time, he spreads my lips apart and slides his tongue into my mouth. The piercing teases my tongue, sending a shiver straight through me. It's better than the first kiss and I kiss him back. He's the first man I've ever kissed back, the first man who has kissed me well enough for me to even try.

Men have done so many horrible things to me in my life and not one of them has kissed me properly. Aiden pulls away again and he pushes hair out of my face.

"We'll do this in my bedroom. Go upstairs. Third door on the left. Shower first."

Shower first. I don't like his tone, but I can't exactly blame him for it. I've been trapped in a box for several hours in a row and I probably smell exactly like it. At least he isn't pointing a gun at me anymore, and doesn't kiss me like a gross, perverted old man. He kisses me like... he would be a good lover.

That's another experience I've never had, another sad truth about my life that I never want to dwell on.

It hurts to walk up the stairs, but my body revels in the most freedom I've had in days. I almost want to race up the stairs to get to the bathroom quicker, but I walk patiently to the top and follow Aiden's instructions to find his bedroom. I can hear Aiden talking to his dog, telling him to stay on his bed for the next little while while he's busy. His house smells new, even if it's an old colonial that has probably been around since Boston's founding.

The bedroom is *extremely* neat. The floor smells clean and as my bare feet touch it, I feel like Aiden's right to wrinkle his nose at me. I'm the dirty one. *But he's sexually aggressive, and a racist one at that.* I can hear him following me up the stairs. He walks slowly, but he has a heavy gait. That may come in handy later if he tries to sneak into bed with me when I want to sleep. If I need to fight him off. That type of thing.

I had to fight off Pulsifer sometimes. That got easier as I got older. Aiden's a lot bigger than some decrepit governor of Idaho.

I find the bathroom door open and I walk inside. He has a clawfoot tub that could hold seven people. Judging by the perverts Pulsifer normally deals with, Aiden probably has had seven people in this tub at once. It sickens me to think what other secrets he could have. I flinch as he appears behind me. For a man with a heavy gait, he can apparently walk quietly when necessary.

"Get into the shower. Take your time. I'll set up the camera."

He sounds nervous, which makes me nervous. I imagine him being completely cruel. A monster would be crude and quick. Monsters *really* want you to cry. Aiden doesn't have any of those traits. He glances at my breasts, his cheeks redden and he swears under his breath.

"I can handle the shower," I say to him. He stares at me for a few seconds before leaving the doorway. I relish this alone time. I'm too grateful for my survival to think about escape. I wish I could tell you otherwise, but this is the truth. I grew up being passed around America's dirty underworld. Escape stopped being a real consideration when I turned eighteen and realized this was my destiny – permanent sexual slavery.

I clean myself as best as I can and try to ignore the numb feeling spreading over my body as I anticipate Aiden's actions.

Most men are very rough. You can close your eyes and do your best to block out the pain, but nothing stops the dirty feeling of being powerless and having another person use you like an object.

Once I'm clean and have spent as much time in the shower as I think I can get away with, I step out and grab one of the insanely fluffy white towels hanging from the rack. As soon as I put it on my skin, the luxurious warmth spreads through me and the towel is so soft that I get a momentary feeling of safety.

I've carved out a life for myself despite my circumstances. I don't want anyone to feel sorry for me. I've learned how to play the piano. All the men who owned me had books that I enjoyed reading. I write poetry too, though none of it is good enough to share. Who would read my poems, anyway? Certainly not this blond hunk of muscle. His brain is probably the size of a pea.

He returns to the doorway and scowls as he watches me dry myself, reminding me that he's oversized and perpetually disgusted by me. I'm not shy about him seeing my body. He's seen it all anyway and he's going to have sex with me on camera, so there isn't a point in pretense.

"I took a vow that I would never touch a woman of another color," Aiden growls, sounding angry with me, like it's my fault that I'm black and he's racist.

I don't respond to him.

"I don't know if I can get hard," he says. "You might have to work to get me off."

I purse my lips. I have to ignore his suggestion that I'm too ugly to arouse him. White men. I try not to generalize them, but it doesn't help that all the men who have hurt me have had brilliant blue eyes, just like Aiden's. He has more of a pretty boy look, but he still has those cruel blue eyes.

"Have you done this before?"

"Yes."

I'll respond to his direct questions, but other than that, I have nothing to say. It's not like he cares.

"I'm sorry."

I give him a curious look, but I don't say anything. It's smarter not to say anything.

"If it helps, I'll make it good for you," he says in a gruff and gravely voice.

Don't bother. I want to say something cutting, but I don't want to anger him. Violence and sex are intertwined in the male brain, especially men like Aiden, a giant clearly used to getting what he wants.

This time, not responding to him provokes cheek redness. White men are always turning red when their feelings are about to take over. I brace myself for another racist comment.

"Whoever sent you must know my family. They must know about our beliefs and I want you to be clear about mine. I know my history and my heritage. I believe firmly in the superiority of my people over all others. This will not change because I stuck my cock in you," Aiden says, his voice trembling with rage as he stares at me.

I drop the towel. I'd rather him finish this than continue listening to his racist tirades.

I don't flinch, even if I want to. His words cut me deep, but Aiden, for all his complaints, still reacts like a man. His gaze drops decisively to my breasts and his teeth instinctively sink into his lower lip. His supposedly difficult to rouse cock bulges forward in his pants. *It doesn't look like he's struggling to get hard at all.*

He's even redder than before and his left hand clenches into an angry fist. I hope he's not the hitting sort. Those are always harder to deal with.

"Get on your knees," he commands, asserting power over me as my naked body renders him powerless to continue his racist little speech. I don't defy him. Despite my complete disgust with Aiden, pleasing him represents my best chance at survival, so I consent to his commands.

Any position on my knees still hurts. If Aiden cares, he doesn't show it. He walks towards me and crudely thrusts his hips into my face. His trousers smell like cigarettes and beer. His pants pockets bulge with car keys and a few other objects I can't identify. A simple, brown belt cinches over his dark blue denim.

His thighs are thick and muscular, barely held back by his pants. My heart quickens as he shifts his stance to his left side, cocking his hip. I glance down at his shoes. Brown boots. The tips are probably steel, so I don't want to do or say anything that could provoke him to kick me. I'm in enough pain as it is.

"The camera's over there," he says. "We'll have to move. I just wanted to see if you would obey me."

He leans forward and kisses the top of my head. *He's fucked up. It aches down here on my knees and I'll have to get up again.*

Aiden commands me to my feet and I follow him back out into his bedroom. He shows me where he has his cellphone set up on a bookshelf right in front of Sun Tzu's *The Art of War* and an extremely tattered copy of *The Holy Bible.*

"Kneel there," he commands, pointing to a spot in front of the lens. "It's already recording."

I obey him and quietly kneel before Aiden, facing away from the camera. He walks into the frame and commands me again, "Look up at me. I want to see your face."

When I gaze at him, he frowns with that mixture of revulsion and disapproval I already recognize as his gut reaction to me. Despite his cruel facial expression, he's still hard. I can still see the bulge in his jeans and it's terrifyingly huge the closer he gets to me.

"I don't cum from getting head," he says. "But I doubt you can arouse me without it. Take my dick out."

He's so full of shit. This man has the biggest erection I've ever seen. *He doubts I can arouse him? Something is making him unbelievably stiff and there's no one else in the room but me.*

Taking my time to remove his cock from his jeans is the only way I can postpone it. I've seen dicks before, and most of them are completely unpleasant to look at. Many of the ones I've seen are shorter than my pinky finger. The governor called some of the world's most depraved men his friends.

Aiden remains resolutely planted in place, glowering down at me as I unbuckle his belt and then slip the jean button through the loop before unzipping his pants. Because of his muscular butt, I can't rely on his jeans to fall off on their own. I hook my fingers through the back, making contact with Aiden's ass as I pull the jeans down. As I ease his jeans over his ass, I can't help but notice how deliciously round and muscular his ass feels. My hands fight the urge to cup his firm glutes and focus on the required task - getting his dick out of his jeans.

His breath catches as the jeans slide down, revealing an equally toned and muscular pair of thighs. He has tattoos everywhere, but the thigh tattoos are the most alarming. *Choose death.* He has a skull, several Celtic knots, Bible verses, and intricate designs woven together in a tapestry of a criminal's life.

A pair of crisp white boxer briefs cling to Aiden's thighs. More details of his bulging cock become apparent to me. The monster curves slightly in his briefs, the thick head oozing fluid that creates a wet spot where the tip touches the fabric.

The elastic waistband of his boxer briefs sticks to his hips and as I remove his underwear, I expose more tattoos and worse. He has scars and partially healed wounds all over his body, not to mention more muscles. He's the most muscular man I've ever seen this close and it feels wrong to notice.

All the men who fucked me were ugly and cruel with bodies and tongues that failed to arouse me. This man might be a sick motherfucker but at least he's handsome. It's a small comfort, but I've never touched a man with such well-defined muscles, and the least I can do is appreciate it.

His cock springs free and juts forward with all the arousal Aiden claims he doesn't feel. His body doesn't lie. I haven't even touched him yet, but his cock already protrudes with pure enthusiasm. Once I get the briefs over his ass, they remain taut and stretched around his thighs.

I can't help but stare at Aiden's dick. I've never seen one as big as this. His dick is nearly the length of my forearm and it's thick, with a dusky pink color. The tip reddens immensely, like he's sore from how hard he is. *His dick is so red.* Tufts of trimmed dirty blond hair cover the base of his cock and his shaft is so heavy, his erection leans to one side.

Clear fluid oozes from the tip.

"Don't just stare at it. The camera's rolling."

He probably doesn't mean to be insensitive. He's nervous about this too. It's not like he wants me in this position. I grasp the base of Aiden's cock to hold it up and he makes an uncomfortable grunting sound. He pulses with heat and saliva pools in the corners of my mouth against my will.

He's huge. I run my tongue over my lips so I can get them wet enough to stretch around Aiden. I lean forward and he grunts, nearly jerking back.

"I can't..."

I grasp his shaft tighter. It's too late to back out of this. Before Aiden can pull away from me and deny both of us a chance at survival and escape, I run my tongue over the head of his cock and lick up every drop of the clear fluid emerging from the tip. Aiden's next groan sounds more like an uncontrollable moan of pleasure.

Pleasing him is good. Pleasing him will bring this to a quicker end and I'll have a much greater chance at survival if I please him. The thought occurred to me that once my use has run out, he'll kill me, but I can't dwell on that. If pleasuring this man ensures my survival, it's what I'll do.

I tighten my lips around the smooth, bulging head of Aiden's big cock. He makes an ungodly pleasurable groan as I get his dick head wet with my spit and prepare myself to take the length of that enormous thing down my throat. If I gag, he could hurt me. I have to make him like it. We're being filmed, aren't we?

I tighten my lips more and get Aiden's dick even wetter. His next groan is even louder than the first and he touches the top of my head instinctively before remembering himself and jerking his hand away from me.

Men enjoy having lips around their cocks, but this man really likes it judging by the moans coming out of his mouth. I flatten my tongue along the underside of Aiden's shaft and then slide the full length of his dick into my mouth.

Tears prickle in the corners of my eyes as I stuff every inch of Aiden's dick in my mouth. He groans with pleasure again and I tighten my lips around the base of his cock as I feel the tip tickling the back of my throat, threatening my gag reflex to erupt. I squeeze my eyes shut and focus on breathing slowly through my nose.

As the tip of Aiden's cock touches the back of my throat, he moves his hips slowly with one thrust, and then he erupts. His climax happens so quickly that we're both equally surprised. The tears threatening to pierce the corners of my lids fall freely down my cheeks. I make a gagging sound as Aiden pumps thick ropes of cum into my throat.

The first warm gush fills my mouth and as Aiden tries to remove his cock from the sticky deposit of fluid between my lips, even more spills from the tip and he leaves my lips, face and mouth a mess of cum as he stumbles away and gains his composure after a few steps, making the conscious choice to put as much space between us as possible. There's surprise evident on his face, especially his eyes. *They're terrifying.*

I cough once and try to swallow the cum in my mouth, but that does nothing to remove the thick ropes coating my face and lips.

"Fuck," he says. "I've never..."

"I'm fine..." I whisper, leaning forward, trying to wipe the cum off my face and not wanting to look Aiden in the eye out of pure humiliation. I look ridiculous, I'm crying and there's cum all over me. I worry he won't go through with the instructions on the card. Then what? I'd rather stay here, thousands of miles away from the governor than to *ever* return. If Aiden doesn't finish this, I don't know who might come looking for him.

Aiden crosses the room, standing straight in front of me with his cock hanging limp. My body tenses with uncertainty. I can't predict how he'll react. He crouches in front of me, forcing me to gaze at him with concern. *Is he going to hit me?*

We're face to face and Aiden takes his finger, places it beneath my chin and turns my face so I'm staring him right in the eye. We're still on camera, but it doesn't feel like it. This moment is just for the two of us.

"That was the best head of my life," he whispers. "Once we make this fuck tape, I'll pay you back for that with my tongue. I owe you."

The touch of his finger and the intense blue gaze feel romantic, but Aiden's words emerge with a business tone. There's no romance here. I nod slowly and he rises to his feet.

"Get up," Aiden commands. "Get on the bed and face the camera."

He won't look at me as he commands me this time. I don't want him to look too closely. He's seen more than I would show a stranger, if I ever had control of my life enough to make the choice not to. I avoid gazing into the camera lens directly, but I obey Aiden and position myself in all fours on the bed.

I feel lewd on display like this. I tilt my head downward so my hair falls down over my shoulders to cover my breasts from the camera's view. It's not exactly modesty, but it's the closest I can manage given the circumstances.

I glance over at Aiden through my peripheral vision. He's hard again, with barely any time between this and his previous orgasm. The way he spoke about his ability to cum, I expected a man with some type of sexual dysfunction, not a seconds-long refractory period.

My throat tightens as I imagine my body stretching to accommodate that thing. I nearly choked on Aiden's dick in my mouth. That enormous thing could make me bleed if he isn't careful.

"Arch your back," Aiden whispers. "I want to see your ass."

It might be my imagination, but I swear his voice shakes like he believes the words emerging from his mouth represent the worst taboo. He approaches the bed slowly with that gigantic cock jutting from his hips.

"I've never filmed something like this," he murmurs as he draws closer. Aiden presses his large hand to my lower back tentatively. His hand is so fucking warm. His warmth spreads through me and I squeeze my thighs together to avoid any biological reactions to his touch.

I can't control my response to him. Aiden moves his hand down my lower back over my ass cheeks, his palm curving around my soft cheek. He makes a low growling sound in the back of his throat as he touches the inside of my thigh and discovers my wetness.

"That will make it much easier," he murmurs in response to my wetness. I think that'll be it, but Aiden slides his finger through my juices, swirling his index finger in slow circles through the juices on one thigh before moving to another. "But this is the only time. I don't fuck around with black women. Understood?"

I don't answer him. I just nod. If I'm going to have sex with this racist, I want to get it over with quickly. Judging from what happened before, maybe this won't last long. That's my best hope.

Click here to order Mafia Playmate:
https://bit.ly/bostonirishmafia1

Patreon

13 SEASONS OF SERIAL CHAPTERS

NEW preview chapters published WEEKLY on my Patreon.

Read all 6 seasons of *Unfuckable* (Ben & Libby's story)...

Unfuckable

For a small monthly fee, you get exclusive access to over 375 chapters of my first completed bwwm dark and spicy serial romance, as well as the spin-off serial...

DESPICABLE

The second serial, despicable has 300 chapters available for all Patreon subscribers to access instantly and... we officially have a **third completed spin-off bwwm romance series.**

And yes you get access to all of this at the $5/month tier with more benefits at more pricey tiers.

The third serial is about Clover + Thomas. Thomas has a shocking connection to a character in the second serial and Clover is an all-new African American female lead.

POWERLESS

This series has three *very long* "seasons" of chapters, the length of five full-length novels all-together.

You will probably have over three months of binge-reading before catching up to current content, making this one of the most 'bang for your buck' author Patreon subscriptions out there.

Don't take my word for it.
Check the post history:
www.patreon.com/jamilajasper

PATREON HAS MORE THAN THE ONGOING
SERIAL...

⚡ **INSTANT ACCESS** ⚡

- NEW merchandise tiers with **t-shirts, totes, mugs,** stickers and MORE!
- **FREE paperback** with all new tiers
- **FREE short story audiobooks** and audiobook samples when they're ready

- #FirstDraftLeaks of Prologues and first chapters **weeks** before I hit publish
- Behind the scenes notes
- Polls and story contribution
- Comments & LIVELY community discussion with likeminded interracial romance readers.

LEARN MORE ABOUT SUPPORTING A DIVERSE ROMANCE AUTHOR

www.patreon.com/jamilajasper

Thank You Kindly

Thank you to all my readers, new and old for your support with this new year.

I look forward to making 2023 an INCREDIBLE year for interracial romance novels. I want to thank you all for joining along on the journey.

www.patreon.com/jamilajasper

Thank you to my most supportive readers — my Patreon subscribers!:

Queen Ke
Jamie C
KimW
Warrior_pprincess
SavageSam
Roslyn H.
Katrina
LMSYT
Lainey R.
Naomi
GrumpyMillenial
Jay
Asia A.
Angela D.

Danyelle C.

WakeupMakeup Slay

Jocelyn F.

Nikki O.

Cdublu

Carla

Jonathan

Kelly

Jessica

Jasmine

DARSHELL

Dawn

Tiabuena3

Leigh

Yvonne

Ashlee

Crystal

Marshybabyyy

Shout

Quaniquequia

TK

Kayla

Shronda C.

Ma-Eyongerie

Kayla

Chantell

Kheiara

ophelia

Vickie

Cass

Kamil

Kaela

Love

Miryam

Charlene

Summer

Lola

Eryn

DD Davis

Symone

Deborah

Beatrice

Valescha

Khadija

makhalaab

Kaya

Glitter Garden

SavageSam

sybil arroyo

Ncsportsfan79

Jessica G.

Danielle

Yola

Joslin

Alexciz

Stacia

Ayanna

Asia

Hailey

Kaya

Nikki

Naomi O.

Jessica J

Chakiya

Noelle

kourtnee

Martha

Nikki Valentina

xjkpop

Valeria

BlkBae

SweetS

Msteeq

Rhonda

Darrah

Killa

Shavon

Misty

India

Kassandra

Imani

Nala

Chantell

Benvinda

Roger

Lexi B

Zapphire

Vbrooks

Tasha G

Kiera

Valencia

Stacy

YANITZA

Texansgurl76

Emma

Tinette

Jenny

Mariah

Nale

Tanisha

Trenita

Shelle

dulcemaria413

Shanice

Letarsha

Tania

Neeka

Julia

Linda

Lisa

Jiannie

Jillian

Tameka

Asia

Scarlette

Olwyn

R W

Fayefaefee

Brianna

Tiffany

Katie

Diamond

Kera

Tia

Love Reading

Dominique

Sheria

Jennifer

Georgette

Monique

Wendolyn

King Turtle22

Jessica

Nic M.

JustChill

DJC

Atira

TheeLastHokage

Yvonne

Chrissy

Janelle

Rian

LaRonda

LaRonda

Deanna

dlawson382

Jasmine

Haley

Belinda

Sercee

Yvonne

Jadelock

Farah

Tamiya

Quin

J.Payton

Geek Girl

Ashley

Rubi

Pilar

Sandra

Jurnee

Anni

Shannet

Joneesa

GlitzyHydra

Amanda

Barbara

Brianna

Jamica

Lyons

MARY ANN

Marketia

SarahD

LoverofHawaiiHearts

ceblue
Yolanda
MonaGirl Lewis
Dianna
Mary
amna
Nysha
fayola
Ty
Abria
Shyra
Andi-Mariee
Jamila
Naee's World
KEISHA
Jennett
Fredericka
Candece
Chante
Pholuv
Lydia A
Sabrina
JM
Jackie
Mo
Natrilly83
Ashaunte
Tolu
Margaret
Wendolyn
Lori
Dionne
ZLB
Kristina
Nicol

ELBERT
A. Harris
Jesi
Brenda
Desiree
Angela
Frances
LaShan
Only1ToniD
Debbie T.
Tiffanie
April L
shawnte
Kay
Lisema
Yvonne F
Natasha
Colleen
Julia
Amy
Jacklyn
Shyan R
Kiana B
Pearl
Javonda
Sheron
Maxine
Dash
Alicia
margaret
Love2Read
Juliette
Monica
Sandhya
MaryC

Trinity
Brittany
June
Ashleigh
Nene
Nene
Deborah
Nikki M
Dee
TyKira
Kimmey
Laytoya
Shel W
Arlene
Judith
Mary
Shanida
Rachel
Damzel
Ahnjala
Kenya
momo
BJ
Akeshia
Melissa
Tiffany
sherbear
Nini J
Curtresa
REGGIE A.
Ashley
Mia
Tink138110
Phia
Sharon

Charlotte

Assiatu C

Regina

Romanda

Catherine

Gaynor

BF

Perpetua

Tasha G

Henri Ann

sara

skkent

Rosalyn

Danielle

Deborah J

Kirsten

ANA

Taylor R.

Charlene

Louanna

Michelle

Tamika

Lauren

RoHyde

Natasha

Shekynah

Cassie

AnnaBooms

Keitheena

Nick R

Gennifer M

Rayna

Anton

Jaleda

Kimvodkna

JaTonn
Jazmine
Anoushka
Raynischa
Audrey
Valeria
Courtney
Donna
Patrisha
Jenetha
LaKisha J.
Ayana
Taylor
Christy
Monica
FreyaJo
GRACE
Kisha
Christine
Alexandra
Amber
Natasha
Stephanie
LaKisha
kristylove7
Cynthea
DENICE
Latoya
monifacd .
Doneishia
Mariah
Gerry
Yolanda T
Yolanda P
Susan D

Phyllis H
Alisa K
Daveena K
Desiree S
Kimberly B
Robin B
Gary S
Stephanie MG
Georgette A
Kathy
Marty
JanetDaniels
Megan
Shelle
Delores
Janet
Lydia
Phyllis
Freda
Charlott R

Join the Patreon Community.

Made in the USA
Middletown, DE
04 December 2024